Between Two Enemies

A series of sudden, sharp slaps, like trees breaking under winter ice, sounded from the hill behind them, and Peshtak began to fall. They turned, wavered, then advanced again, hoping to gain the Pelbar canoes. A sharp fight ensued on the shore, first with bows, then short-swords, but always punctuated by the sharp slaps from the hillside behind. Finally, with a yell, the Peshtak rushed toward the boats in a tight body.

"Let them through," the Pelbar guardcaptain shouted. The Pelbar ran aside, putting arrows into the hostiles when they could get a clear shot, then closed in behind. Grim Peshtak formed a half ring, backing slowly, loosing their remaining arrows silently as boats filled with men and shoved off . . .

THE PELBAR CYCLE
by Paul O. Williams
Published by Ballantine Books:

The Fall of the Shell

Paul O. Williams

A Del Rey Book

BALLANTINE BOOKS • NEW YORK

**For Sherwood, Megan,
Gwyneth, and Caitlin**

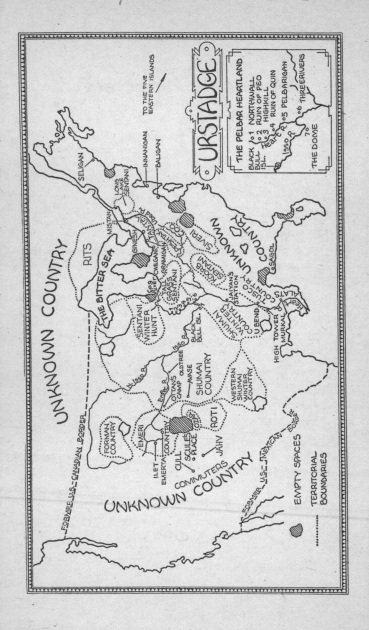

Principal Characters

Udge: Protector of Threerivers

Bival: the Southcounsel of Threerivers

Warret: Bival's husband

Gamwyn and Brudoer: twin boys, age fourteen, of Threerivers, sons of Rotag and Pion

Sagan: Protector of Pelbarigan

Ahroe: a guardcaptain of Pelbarigan

Jaiyan: a giant Sentani trader who lived at the north edge of Tusco country

Misque: a Peshtak girl, age fifteen

Artess and Reo: twin sister and brother, Tantal by birth, growing up at Murkal

A complete glossary of characters and places may be found at the end of the book.

1

High in the curve of the Broad Tower of Threerivers, the southernmost of the three Pelbar cities on the Heart River, Bival stood with her hands behind her, looking out across the water. She scanned the hills and trees for the first fall eagles but saw only the last of the vultures that haunted the river in summer. Behind Bival, Udge, the Protector, sat silently playing cross squares with Dardan, her closest crony, while three others sat watching and drinking hot tea.

Bival thought she caught a glint of light from the westbank trees a half-ayas or more downriver from the city, but, squinting, she saw no more. Then, shifting her eyes farther downstream, she saw a small boat coming upriver. It still lay too far off to see in any detail. She shaded her eyes. "I wish we had accepted that device, that telescope the Pelbarigan Academy offered us," she mused. "A boat is coming."

Udge raised her eyebrows. "Patience. You will see it soon enough. We need none of their innovations. Now. This is a game best played without distractions. Dardan, I am going to put your Protector in check." Udge moved her white minister diagonally across the board.

Dardan grunted and continued to study the board, then blocked the move with one of her males.

Meanwhile, on the west bank, three Peshtak scouts gazed through the fall foliage at the city. Steelet, the eldest, a smooth-faced, slightly stocky man, said, "The early scouts were right. A strange swine-bellied-looking place. High curved walls with terraces. One large guard tower. Three other strange-shaped towers—almost like land snails. But even stranger. Look at those walls. Swinish diamond patterns. How many egg-sucking Pelbar in there?"

"Who can tell? We think not many. Maybe not five hundred. I don't like it, though. Remember what happened to the Tantal at Northwall."

Steelet spat. Just then a fourth man came running quietly through the woods, waving his arms for silence. He scooped dirt and sand onto the tiny fire—and the fish propped by it with sticks.

"A boat," he hissed. "One man." He still knelt, smoothing and heaping the dirt, as Durc, whispering curses, tried to extricate his catfish from the mess. A word from Steelet and they all crouched, still. A fabric-covered canoe, with a light load, approached, near the bank to escape the channel currents. One thin old man paddled it. Durc and Gnau silently strung their bows and moved toward the shore bushes.

As the canoe neared their hiding place, the mournful recognition horn sounded, long and ringing, from the watch at Threerivers, and the man in the canoe took up his short bull's horn and returned the call. Steelet placed a hand on the back of each bowman, and the Peshtak crouched to watch the man draw near and pass upriver, with long, slow strokes. He was a Sentani, almost toothless, but sturdy and knotty-armed. Steelet cursed under his breath.

Finally he whispered, "I told you not to light that fire."

"Even a mere underling has to eat sometimes," Durc said. He again scraped at his catfish. "He didn't smell the fire. It was small and all dry sassafras."

"I don't know. He seemed to pause in one stroke. Maybe not. To be sure, we'll move upstream after sunset. Bullguts. This makes no sense, anyhow. Even if we took this city, how long could we hold it?"

"We could make a treaty."

"This is not a good idea. We should try south, down the Heart."

"Tell it to Annon. See how he likes that idea. With all those leather-backed Tusco."

"Shut your erupted face before I fill it with that gritty fish," Steelet said, glancing around. But the other three had fallen silent, watching the boatman dip and stroke toward the strange city rising into the hazy light. Steelet quieted too, focusing on the haunting bulk of Threerivers as if he could commit it to memory.

When the old Sentani had finally paddled to the city, four guardsmen met him at the stone landing. They were dressed in maroon tunics and narrow-legged pants tied below the knee with banded fabric belts. They wore short-swords loosely hung on their left sides. "Ravell," said one. "It's been a long time. What do you have? A light canoe. Aren't you trading then?"

"Trading? Yes," said the old man, stretching. "I've got something for Bival. It ought to be worth my trip." The youngest guardsman turned and trotted to the city's small entrance to inform the council member, who had finally recognized the old trader from her high window and begun the long descent to the river to meet him. They were old acquaintances. In the past she had often asked him to bring her objects of strange design. He had, only faintly understanding why, and she had explained to him the curious likenesses she saw in unlike objects—in snake scales and pine cones, vine tendrils and snail shells. But always there remained a certain reticence, a distance between them.

The people of Threerivers were secretive. Traditionally, during the centuries of hostilities with the outside tribes, the Pelbar had stayed behind the great walls of the city, except for truceweeks. Unlike the other Pelbar cities, Pelbarigan and Northwall, they at Threerivers had not broken their long habit of shutting out others even in the sixteen years since peace came to the Heart River following the great battle at Northwall.

Nonetheless, the city had imaginative people in it, and one of them was Bival, who questioned the traders in detail when she could. She had even been to Pelbarigan, but regarded it as an overgrown, squarish, boorish, bustling place of industry, without sufficient aesthetic refinement.

Ravell was a lone trader, who plied the Heart River all the way to Tusco country in the south, meeting the Tusco and trading in the neutral zone far below the mouth of the Oh River, bringing cotton, rice, and southern teas. But this time, meeting him, Bival saw he had none of those things, but only a small bark box which he held out to her.

She took it, puzzled, and looked up at him. "Ravell. How long has it been? Three years. Come in to the Room of Visitors and eat. What is this? Is this all?"

"It is for you. It will be worth my trip, I think, when you see it," said the old man, puffing his sibilants through slack lips. "It was hard enough for me to get it," he added. "It will be costly. I am asking seven winter tunics."

Bival raised her eyebrows. But later, inside, as he sucked at his sweetened tea, Bival lifted the lid of the box and moved aside the rabbit-skin linings, and saw a strange shell. Taking it out, she gasped. It was obviously an exact model of the Protector's Broad Tower, a symmetrical spiral shell that topped the center of the city, above the terraces. The shell was bound with blue ribbons. Bival could see that it had been split with great care, and that the ribbons held it together. She gently untied them and took the shell apart, again drawing in her breath as she saw the interior partitions of the beautiful unfolding spiral, each exactly placed, each gently curved. Now she understood the reason for the room divisions in the Broad Tower. Craydor, the designer of Threerivers over three hundred years ago, had simply used a model like this. Amazing.

She looked up at Ravell, who sat silently regarding her. "It came from the southern sea, the bitter water beyond the mouth of the Heart," he said.

"You? Were you there?"

"No. I got it from the Tusco of U Bend. I ventured beyond the neutral zone, without really knowing, and they took me and enslaved me. I spent three years there. But Jaiyan heard of it upriver, and he warned the Tusco traders to let me go or hear from the Sentani of Koorb."

"So they gave you the shell?"

"I stole it from their white tower. I judged they owed me that much. It was one of their curios, but when I saw it, I knew you would want it."

"Seven tunics?"

"Seven."

"You shall have them. Come back in the morning for them."

The Sentani demurred, holding up his hands. "I must stay inside tonight."

"Inside? It is never done here. You know that."

"Not far south I smelled a faint fire. Just before the horn sounded I caught a glimpse of men in the bushes, armed, watching me. I was glad for that horn."

"Men? What kind of men?"

Ravell shrugged, holding out his hands. "All I know is they were men who didn't want to be seen. I saw one bow, small and recurved."

The guardsman nearby overheard and said, "I see no reason why he couldn't stay inside, Southcounsel. If you permit, I shall ask the guardcaptain."

She inclined her head, and the man departed. Then she returned the shell to the old man, and he carefully replaced it in the box. "Until morning, then?" She held out her palms, and they touched agreement and good-bye. Then she turned and left.

Later, in the small, stone-walled room she shared with her husband, Bival rummaged in a wicker box as she asked, "Where are the chits we have been saving?"

"Not in that box. Look on the enclosed shelf. Why do you ask?"

"I need them."

"You? Need them? They are almost all from my after-duty work. What do we need?"

"We? This is too important to quibble about, Warret. The most amazing thing has happened. The Sentani trader, Ravell, has brought a marvelous shell—the model for the Broad Tower. I had suspected Craydor had a real model. It's like her. For years I have been trying to understand Craydor's designs. This is a key."

"But I had been saving the chits for a pellute. For three years. I had nearly enough. My afterduty work."

Bival stood up straight and sighed. "Warret, I am simply not going to argue. It's too demeaning. You'll benefit from this. You'll just have to trust my judgment. That's an end to it."

Warret stared. "An end? Just like that? Yes, it is an end." He began gathering his clothing off his shelves.

Bival frowned. "What is this now? More opposition? Will you never learn your place?"

Warret didn't reply, but continued wrapping his clothing in a bundle.

"You took an oath of marriage. A Pelbar oath. Just tossing it aside? You agreed to obey. No one ever said it would always be easy."

"I am exercising my oath from a greater distance." He turned toward the door. She stood in his way. He simply stopped, passively.

"Now you are going to put those things back on the shelves."

He turned and set the bundle down, cramming it onto a shelf.

"Don't be a child. Fold them as they should be."

"I like them that way."

"I will see you put on water-lifting." Warret didn't reply, but simply stood in one spot. She finally tired of staring at him and returned to her hunt for the chits. He never moved. With an exasperated sigh, she counted them over, returned two to the wicker basket she found them in, and left to exchange the remainder for seven tunics.

Later, when she returned, carrying the heavy clothing, Warret was not there, nor was his bundle of clothes. Bival slumped on her bed in thought, smoothing the tunics with her hands. Her husband would come to agree. She saw a gain in power through the shell. He would benefit in spite of himself.

Meanwhile, across the river, a squad of guardsmen following Ravell's directions found the dead fire of the Peshtak scouts. By torchlight they searched the area, finding only a few stray tracks that told them nothing.

As they left, the Peshtak leader, Steelet, remarked from a thicket several hundred arms away, "I was right. The old man did see something. Bullguts on him. On you, too, Durc. We'll watch tomorrow, then return to the Oh. This city may be our answer, but I doubt it. All this pigrooting land is too flat and open. Give me mountains to hide in."

In the morning, when Bival awoke, her husband still had not returned. She made a mental note to request that he be returned to water-lifting, for Threerivers still raised all its water from underground springs to the spiral tower high over the city. From there it flowed down to all the bathing rooms and kitchens, as well as to the curved terrace gardens that arced in tiers around the southern half of the city roof, stepping downward in graceful sweeps, thickly planted all growing season.

Below, Ravell awaited Bival anxiously. Because of the strangers, he wanted to put a whole day and a night of steady paddling between him and Threerivers. "I'm going back to Koorb," he told the Southcounsel when she arrived. "I think I've had enough trading for a while, maybe for always." He smiled toothlessly, handing her the box. She was so eager for it that she scarcely said a proper goodbye.

Letting Ravell out, the guardsman grinned. "I think she's pleased," he remarked, giving the trader a gift of a small ceramic jar of honey, encased in wicker for travel. They palmed good-bye and the guardsman helped the old man shove his canoe out into the current. They gave each other one last glance, smiling. Then Ravell swept the west bank with his eyes and began to dig his paddle into the water in deep, strong strokes, driving out into the channel.

Bival could hardly contain her excitement. Finally, high up the spiral stairs to the Broad Tower, she paused on a landing. She would give the shell one close, private examination before showing it to the Protector. She put the box on a broad window ledge, where the rising sun could stream in on it. Undoing the bindings, she set the shell out, its two halves spread, and soon stood lost in a contemplation of its form.

She didn't hear the twins, Gamwyn and Brudoer, bumping down the stairs above her with bags of trash and laundry collected from the Protector's quarters and the council common room. The boys were fourteen, bored, energetic, and busy shoving each other, giggling and pretending anger. As they rounded the curve to the landing, Brudoer swung his bag, and Gamwyn, avoiding it, jumped back, into Bival. She lurched. With a gasp she saw the two halves of the shell, like wings with no bird, caught in the autumn breeze, falling, spinning, gliding, catching on the last terrace wall, shattering, then falling again, in white flakes diminishing over the edge of the high city wall. She whirled.

The boys stood in stunned silence. With an incoherent yell she struck out at Gamwyn with her heavy, ringed hand, laying open his right cheek. She continued to pound on him as he shrieked and staggered, holding his blood-spattered face with crimson hands.

After a shocked moment, Brudoer shucked off his belt, and swung its heavy buckle at Bival, in quick, furious arcs, unmindful of the horror of what he, a mere boy, was doing to a city leader.

She spun at Brudoer, holding her hands up and grabbing at the belt. Gamwyn sank to the stone floor, holding his face. Bival finally caught the belt and jerked it, sending Brudoer sprawling as two guardsmen ran breathlessly up the spiral stairs. One seized Brudoer, who still struggled, screeching, "Let go, fish face. Look at my brother. I'll kill her. Let—" The guardsman covered his mouth with a forearm.

"Southcounsel," he began.

She struck at Brudoer again, but the guardsman turned, shielding the boy with his body. Bival's head and hands were bleeding. "Confine them," she said, curtly. "They attacked me. And you, Brudoer, after all I have done for you, with your poor, slow head. Garbage. What a fool! Teaching mathematics to an assassin. Now, guardsman, confine them. Do it now. I must go to the infirmary." Without another word she descended the stairs, leaving the two nonplussed guardsmen with the boys.

"What happened?" one asked.

"I don't know. I don't know. I bumped her," Gamwyn murmured, holding his bleeding cheek. "I'm sorry. Good Aven, Brud, what have you done?"

Brudoer couldn't answer. The other guardsman still held an arm across his face. When the boy tried to bite him, he strengthened his grip cruelly until Brudoer stopped struggling. More guardsmen arrived and Brudoer was taken downstairs. Two men knelt over Gamwyn, saying, "Take your hand away. We won't hurt you. Come on, now. Take away your hand." When he finally did, blood welled up behind it, and the guardsman gasped slightly. "Can you walk?" he asked.

UDGE rubbed her chin meditatively and stared at Bival, who stood respectfully in front of her, her head bandaged where Brudoer's belt buckle had sliced it. It was high sun. The other three quadrant counsels sat at ease, but silently. Bival had recounted her version of the incident.

Udge sighed. "There is no need to tell you this is not good. But it merely signifies a further need for discipline. With the outside world more restive, with the changes at Pelbarigan and Northwall, naturally the males will want more freedom. And you, Bival, by taking this boy as a student—"

"Ah. But he seemed so apt, so discerning, Protector."

"—by taking this boy as a student, have by the misfortune of your liberalism, led him to the very outrage he has committed against you. The males shall not have more freedom. They . . ."

Outside, the watch guardsman had fitted his mouthpiece into the signal horn, a spiraling stone built into the tower, and sounded a long call of farewell.

"What is that?" Udge asked. She rang for a guardsman and asked again. The woman disappeared and soon returned.

"Protector, the Ursana has sent the boy, Gamwyn, to Pelbarigan by boat for treatment of his wound by the new physician, the one from the ancient dome."

Udge suddenly stood, smashing her teacup on the floor. "Guardsman, get the guardchief. Have that boat recalled. Bring the Ursana here to me. Go." She paced to the window, squinting out. Already the boat was far upriver. It seemed some time before the guardhorn blew for its return. As Udge watched, the guardhorn blew repeatedly, but the boat did not turn. True, there was a breeze. But it was not that strong. They should have heard. She watched as an arrowboat set out in pursuit then turned from the window. Bival had not moved. The guardchief stood silently by the door, awaiting the Protector's attention.

Udge looked hard at her. "Was not the boy a prisoner? Why was he allowed to leave without notice? Do you realize what you have done?"

"A prisoner? I was not told. What did he do, Protector, other than to bump into the Southcounsel?"

"That is enough. Were you not told? Was that not clear?"

"Bival said so, yes, Protector. But she was angry. There was no legal ruling. She herself so bestially wounded the boy that—"

"Silence. You are not a judge. You are a functionary. I order the arrest of the boy. You are to carry it out. Have Wim brought to me. Now go."

As the guardchief turned to leave, she nearly ran into the Ursana, a rather short old woman, heavyset, who wore her hair piled in two tiers, tightly bound. The Protector glared at her.

The old physician was panting. "You sent for me, Protector?" she asked mildly.

"I wish an explanation of why you exceeded your authority by sending the boy to Pelbarigan. Why did you not inquire for permission?"

"Permission, Protector?"

"Well, answer."

The old woman sighed. "Protector, will you give me the opportunity to answer completely?"

"If I wish."

"Then, Protector, you will get no answer at all. I am not a male to be herded. My family will stand behind me. So will the laws of Craydor. It is you who exceed your authority. I am willing to answer to the entire council, which you so seldom call."

Udge looked around for the teacup she had smashed on the floor. She raised her arms, then dropped them. "Very well. But make it short."

"The boy is horribly hurt. Look at it as a physician would. I am supposed to heal. I could sew the wound, try to keep it from growing angry, try to keep down the boy's fever, perhaps even aid his healing—with a broad scar on his face. It's a young face, Protector, still as smooth as a girl's. Or was. Now it is swelled and destroyed. There is a chance, too, that he may die. We know the skill of this old physician, Royal, is far beyond mine. I thought—"

"Paaaah," said Udge.

The Ursana simply raised her hand. "Please take another view, Protector. A political view. What if he were to die? The males are already disaffected. The boy's act was only slightly wrong, though it had a bad consequence for Bival. If the males and their sympathizers felt that we withheld proper aid from the boy, and he did die, it would cause us more trouble than it is worth. If he returns healed, and the scar is slight, as I expect, we will have drawn strength from the opposition, because we will have proved ourselves wise and just rulers, as Craydor advised—and as Pell herself held proper."

"Are you through?"

"Yes, Protector."

"I believe it would be helpful if you retire. I will allow you to recommend a replacement for my review."

"A replacement? At last. Yes, Protector. I will prepare a roll on the matter. I may go to Pelbarigan myself, then, to see this Royal." The Ursana turned to go.

"Did I dismiss you?"

"Only from office, Protector, thank Aven. I am going. This is not a formal meeting. I know the protocol." She turned away again, then paused, turned back, and added,

"You of all people, Bival, should recall Craydor's statement, 'A shell is a design for life. Beyond that, though beautiful, it has no beautiful function. This is true in all the ways you can look at it.'"

Bival glared. "Stick to your bandages. I know more about design than any other five people in this city. Go and grind some of your useless medicine."

The Ursana raised her eyebrows. "What you did this morning certainly didn't arise from a stupendous knowledge of design." She left, then leaned back in the door and added, "Or what you did to Warret."

Bival screamed and started for the door, but the North-counsel jumped up and stopped her. "Easy, Bival. One casualty a day is enough. We have plenty of problems. Let her talk. It makes no difference. Your temper makes us all vulnerable."

Udge was at the window, looking upriver. She could see nothing.

Brudoer had been shut into a prison room in the lowest part of the city, where the walls were thick, and all the rooms divided by heavy arches and broad pillars. That section of the city was given over to ice-storage rooms, general storage, mushroom culture, and the large prison rooms. These stood in a row of six, dim and tall, with high, narrow windows. They were quite plain but beautifully made. It had been Craydor's view that people in need of imprisonment should be able to contemplate order and beauty, however abstract.

Fitted into one wall of Brudoer's cell was a bed-bench surmounted by an arch in which one word, "Mercy," was neatly chiseled. In several bands around the room, letters were also chiseled, but they made no sense or words. The diamond pattern of stone from the outside walls was repeated in miniature on these walls. Against the inside wall a stone bench lay.

But Brudoer saw none of these things. He was still seething with fury and worry. Sometimes his rage seemed to rise like a red rain, drenching the room. Whenever he began to calm, the image of Gamwyn's bleeding face as Bival struck him would surge up in his memory, and the wave of anger would again rise. He would beat his fists against the wall, then suck his bleeding knuckles, hunching, watching the drops of blood and tears spatter the smooth stone. He would never rest until he had some revenge. He vowed it. Never.

It was the second quadrant after high sun before the arrowboat, with its guardcaptain and one other guardsman, came within hailing distance of the larger boat with Gamwyn. The lead boat never turned. Though tired, the men in it dipped and stroked, steadily, and the pursuing arrowboat still had a long chase before coming alongside and then ahead.

The guardsman in the bow raised a shortbow. "Halt. Protector's orders. Halt and bring the boy back."

The paddlers stopped, their backs slumping. They were all guardsmen, too. All males. The man in the stern called, "Come close. Look at him. He may be dying. Come and look."

"Never mind that. It is a clear order."

"Come anyway."

Reluctantly, the arrowboat steered alongside. Gamwyn lay amidships, breathing fitfully, his bandaged face greatly swelled, his eyes glazed.

"Nonetheless," the guardcaptain in the arrowboat began, as the guardsman in the stern of Gamwyn's boat deftly flipped the narrow craft over, dumping the two in the river. They flailed and struggled.

"All right, men, paddle," the man in the stern called. Wearily, but with a gleeful shout, they took up the rhythm and moved upriver away from the arrowboat. "Wait," said the guardsman in the stern. He turned and looked at the two in the water. "All right. They can swim. Now, let's go. We can take it easier now, but we have a quarter sun to make today still. They have lost their weapons." He laughed and dug his paddle into the water, pulling and chuckling. Then he looked again at Gamwyn and fell silent.

"Don't worry, Gam," he finally said. "We'll get you there. You just hang on." He thought the boy nodded weakly.

When the boat had not returned by sunset, the Protector became uneasy. She had already replaced the guardchief with Wim, a family member with some guard experience. She had also replaced Suth, the Ursana, as chief physician. As she waited impatiently, a minister, Newall, came with a request from the workmen of the north quadrant for a special prayer service, for the harmonization of the present situation.

"They want to sing hymns in the chapel is all," Newall said. "They are upset. May they? I think it will calm them."

Udge mused. "They may if the women sing with them."

"The women do not wish to, Protector."

"Always the males. Born to make trouble. My condition remains."

"Protector . . ."

"No. They may sing all night if they sing as whole families. Now that seems plain."

Newall paused, then left. Udge turned to Bival and said, "You really did something this time, Bival. I wish you could explain it all to me. A shell? It doesn't seem worth it—though it may be just the occasion we need to enforce order once and for all."

"It wasn't just a shell, Protector. It was the model for this very tower we are in. It came all the way from the sea to the south. Craydor must have had one. This leads me to believe that the other towers also came from real models, not from Craydor's own creations or modifications of familiar shells. This would accord with her theory of architecture—the use of natural forms as much as possible. Even with the short time I had the shell, I could see how she had used it. I could see its strengths, and how she modified the partitions within it to fit our needs here. This whole structure, in spite of its modifications, is essentially separate from the rest of the city, riding on it. I am sure of it. It is like a little fortress in itself. How she managed to curve and fit the stone, though, is beyond me. If we could understand that, how much we could do."

"There is no need. The city is built. It is holding up well enough."

"But Craydor left instructions for additions if that ever became desirable. She herself built and added enough times."

"That was Craydor. We have to run the city our way now."

A guardsman rang the small bell outside the door. Udge admitted her. "Protector, the arrowboat is back."

"And the boy."

"They would not return. The Ursana picked her own guardsmen, it would seem. They overturned the arrowboat, dumping the guardcaptain and her crewman."

Udge struck her hand on the wide arm of her chair, then rubbed her smarting knuckles. "We will send a message bird ahead of them," she said.

"Yes, Protector. At first light it shall be done."

"Now."

"They will not fly at night, Protector. If we had accepted the new message sender Pelbarigan offered us, perhaps then—"

"Silence! Everything will fall apart if we take all their innovations on. Message birds have always worked well enough."

"Yes, Protector."

"I will prepare the message. You may return for it in a few sunwidths."

· The guardsman bowed and left. Bival followed. Udge was alone. She went to the window, running her hands over the walls. She couldn't understand what Bival was talking about. Designed like a particular shell? Well, perhaps she was right. But the old politician couldn't see any importance in the fact. From below she could hear, faintly, massed voices singing, all male voices. She rang for the guardsman and said, "That singing. Was there a prayer service, then, against my order?"

"No, Protector. It's only some workmen singing down in the ice caves. They often do that for their amusement."

Udge listened. "It's more than a few workmen. Have the guard tell them to desist. They are a disturbance."

The guardsman hesitated just a moment, then bowed out, saying, "Yes, Protector."

So Brudoer, who leaned, exhausted, against the wall of his cell, listening to the rich harmonies echoing mellowly among the heavy stone archways, heard hurrying footsteps, and shouting, then angry voices. The singing stopped. Again the face of Gamwyn swam up in his thoughts, but he was too weary to respond. He lay on the stone bench, staring at a single dim star he could see through the tall slit of a window. It seemed to tremble and melt, but as he calmed, it too seemed more steady, a hard point of blue-white light.

III

It was not until nearly high sun on the third day that the message bird came back from Pelbarigan. Udge had been waiting impatiently all that time, calling her guardsmen several times each day quadrant to inquire.

Win, the new guardchief, spread the message before the Protector:

> Yr. mess. received. Cannot return boy Gamwyn now. Too hurt. Think he may live with care. Will send when all well. Yr. Grdsmn. gone to Northw. on grnds of persecutn. We wil wk tht out with you & Northw. in time. Gd. wheat harv. at Northw. Our apples prime. If you take radio, we can conver. abt such matt. as ths. No delay. Do you need help? Bless of Aven. Sagan, Prot.

Udge snatched the message and read it through again. She flashed a look at the waiting guardsman and said, "Call the four quadrant counsels." Waiting, she tapped her fingers, crumpled the small sheet, then had to smooth it out again.

When they arrived, she handed the message to Bival and asked her to read it aloud. Afterward, she said, "See? She mocks me. Your *mess* received. Bless of Aven. Again she advises we take that contraption, that *radio* from those Avenless wretches from the dome. To talk about wheat and apples."

"Perhaps it would have helped, Protector," said Cilia, the Westcounsel.

"No. It would effectively bring us under their control. Craydor built this city because she had a superior way, both architecturally and socially. It is our duty to maintain that."

"What about the guardsmen, Protector?"

"They are lost. It would be of no use for us to attempt legal action, despite their disobedience."

"Perhaps not. We should try, Protector."

"No. It would bring further embarrassment. Look at the tone of the letter. Sagan sees only an injured child, ferociously hurt by an irresponsible official, all because of a frippery. She could have prevented the guardsmen from going to Northwall. We will never get their return, or any discipline, now, from that pack of mongrels and Shumai lovers at Pelbarigan. Our silence on the matter may act as a reproach. We will have to control our own society and seek to maintain order that way. The whole Pelbar way is threatened. Well, they promise to return the child—if he lives. Of course he will live. We will see then what will happen."

"What of the guardsmen's families, Protector? Will they not urge them to return?"

"No. All six are young and unmarried. All come from impeccable families. But none of those families is really for me."

"Well, then . . ."

"Don't you see? Is it so difficult. They could not have planned it so fast. They had been thinking about defecting beforehand. They weren't only saving the boy. They were escaping Threerivers and their responsibilities."

"We'll have to select guardsmen with more care, especially the males."

"I've looked into that, Lamber. Two are from your quadrant. All have exemplary credentials. We could not have known. They kept their traitorous thoughts to themselves."

"Perhaps we will have to set up a system of informers, Protector."

"Perhaps. Perhaps."

The guardchief rang the small bell at the entrance. When she was admitted, she stood at attention and announced, "Protector, the boy Brudoer refuses to eat."

"No matter," said the Protector. "He'll grow hungry. He is doing our work for us."

"Our work, Protector?" the Eastcounsel asked.

"Punishment, Suwor. Punishment. He needs discipline. His stomach will betray him sooner or later. Be sure the food is savory."

"He throws it at the wall, Protector."

Udge stood and clenched her hands. "Then make him clean it."

"We have, Protector. He simply cleans it without protest, and without a word."

"Then he must be manacled."

"Protector. It is against the law of Craydor."

"Ah. For punishment, yes. But he is clearly mentally unbalanced. It is for his own protection."

Wim stood silently for a long moment. "This is very hard, Protector," she said at last. "I believe that to be a lie."

"Do you like your new position? I will not force you, Wim. I will give you a day to think it over."

"There is one thing, Protector. The water-lifters know that Brudoer is not eating. They are restive."

Udge paused, then said, "That is your concern, Wim. Control them. Now go."

The guardchief bowed and left.

"Protector, perhaps we need to make concessions sometimes," Cilia said.

"Concessions? Once you show weakness, it is exploited. Is this not the most ordered Pelbar city? Look at Northwall now—an anarchy. We will keep ourselves the way we are, Westcounsel. Now, leave me please. I must think this out."

Afterward, in the growing dark, Udge, sipping tea, gazed out the west windows at the thin clipping of the new moon. By shifting her head she saw that the curve of the window fit the curve of the moon if one sat in the exact center of the room. No doubt Craydor planned that, too. Udge was getting a little sick of Craydor, meeting her at every turn. She could scarcely afford to offend Wim much. She could not easily find a more faithful guardchief. But perhaps she would have to. Who could have known Wim would have such scruples? Clearly, it would all take time.

She saw Brudoer's weakness—anger—and would exploit it. No one could attack a counsel, no matter what the provocation. From somewhere outside, Udge heard a Pelbar hymn being played on a flute. She heard another one take up the harmony from far away. Males again. She felt a small burst of anger. They were telling her that she could end their singing of hymns, but they would make their music anyhow. Yes. She would indeed have to build a system of informers. Again she saw devotion to Craydor standing in her way. Damn Craydor. How could she keep the city to its founder's ideals when the founder's own ideas blocked her?

* * *

Bival returned to her room, but without Warret she could hardly make herself stay there. She felt his reproach keenly. She could not be angry with him forever. After all, he had worked hard for those chits, and she had simply taken them. But the shell was so valuable. . . . She knew that there were more secrets to Craydor's designs than ever were evident. She kept making new discoveries. Even the device, now not used, to employ falling water from the spring in the underbasement of Threerivers to raise water the first ten arms of its upward journey to the spiral tower was the work of a genius. Bival would work to restore the system, saving the water-lifters that much.

The Ursana had quoted Craydor in a new way for Bival. Though she felt anger at the time, she had begun to think. The old physician saw design largely in human terms, not as architecture or legal code. Bival began to forgive her treachery. Obviously the Ursana had seen Gamwyn's face as a design, now horribly violated. Bival shuddered. Then she felt the loss of her shell again, and anger once more flashed through her. What would she do? She too looked out the window at the setting new moon, an eyelash of beauty in a quiet fall sky—two curves meeting, like the successive arcs of the terraces. Why had Craydor made them that way instead of rounding the terraces as bands— arcs of different radius from the same center? She tried to think that out, but her troubles bubbled up into her musings like swamp gas. Finally she lay down and stared at the dark curve of the ceiling. There was the moon again, in shadow. Bival closed her eyes.

Far below her, Brudoer lay in hunger, hating himself for bumping Gamwyn, hating Bival and the Protector, crying again and again, yearning to lick some of the stew off the wall where he had thrown it again. No, he would not.

From outside the prison row, back toward the ice caves, he heard a single flute playing, gently, he thought. It was the hymn of reconciliation:

> Like two birds circling high in air,
> each free, each tied to forces there,
> so let us—

Brudoer clamped his hands over his ears, pressing his bruised palms against them.

Several levels above him, in their small family rooms, Brudoer's parents sat in the darkness. They talked quietly, worriedly.

"What did the men say at work?" Rotag asked.

"Nothing. They studiously avoid it."

"Are you being frank with me? I know they are concerned. I know they have been singing at night so Brudoer can hear. Pion, I'm not a spy for the inner council."

"I feel their worry and anger. They don't blame Brud. These tensions have been around for a long time."

"You always increased them with your tales of Jestak and the Shumai heroes."

"Oh, bird sweat. What am I supposed to do, discuss the writings of Craydor?"

"It might have been better, judging from the results. But I'm really worried. Brud isn't eating. There is talk now of invoking physical punishment."

"Isn't it that already? And what about Gamwyn? Hasn't he been physically punished?"

"They mean a public beating, Pion. There hasn't been one for years."

"To beat a boy? Even Udge has more sense than that."

"I fear not. She seems more determined all the time, if I can judge by what I hear. You have to get Brud to submit and apologize."

Pion let out a low growl, startling his wife. "Submit," he said. "Submit."

"We must. It's the way things are. You aren't a Shumai primitive, to go wandering around in the wilds. This is our only home."

"The guardsmen got to Northwall."

"By a ruse. That's no way." Rotag began to sob softly in the darkness. Pion sat by her and embraced her. "I don't know. I don't know," she said.

That evening, Sagan, the Protector of Pelbarigan, stopped in to see Gamwyn. Royal, the dome physician, had knitted the boy's face together and stopped the swelling. The Haframa, Pelbarigan's native physician, sat with him. She was reading from the scriptures of Aven, even though she saw Gamwyn wasn't listening. When the Protector arrived, the Haframa moved and set the chair for her.

"He can't talk well yet, Protector," she said.

"Thank you. I will not stay long. So you are Gamwyn

the Terrible, destroyer of the snail shell. Are you feeling better?"

Gamwyn blinked and swallowed. "A little," he said. "May I stay?"

"Until you are well, small one. Then you must return. That is Pelbar law." Gamwyn shuddered, and the Protector put her hands on his arm. "Do you trust me?" she asked.

"Trust?"

"I see no very easy way for you, but perhaps a hard one. Can you do hard things if they are good ones?"

Gamwyn considered. "I don't know."

"Well, you decide. I will come back and ask you again in a few days. Meanwhile, be quiet and get better." She leaned over and kissed his forehead. The amazed boy smelled roses faintly.

In the doorway, Sagan turned. "Have you met my grandson? Garet?"

"No," said the Haframa. "He hasn't been here."

"He isn't much older than Gamwyn. I'll see that he comes. Good night." She left, her guardsmen following. The Haframa gave the boy a slight, mysterious smile.

A half-month passed. At Pelbarigan, Gamwyn mended slowly. At Threerivers, Brudoer grew weaker, until finally someone pitched through the door grating a large pebble with a note attached. The guardsman at the end of the prison row lounged, studiously inattentive. Brudoer smoothed out the paper and read in the dim light:

> Eat. You will need to be strong. Gam is getting better, we hear. He will return in ten or fifteen days. Whatever they do, you will need to be strong. I know little. Mother is very worried. Try not to hate so much. Leave that to me. All the city is upset. I will stand by you—if I can. I think that pigeon dropping Udge is intent on a public lashing. You will need to be strong. I can sense that. Pray. The man are praying for you. Get rid of this note. Father.

High in the Broad Tower, the Protector asked again to have Craydor's law of imprisonment read to her. Bival read:

> A prisoner is to be put in the first of the cells if it is open. In each case that shall be called his cell upon

incarceration. In thirty days, the situation should be resolved and the prisoner should be again united with the community or excluded from it. In no case may the prisoner be returned to his cell at the end of thirty days. In serious cases, he may be returned to his cell, that is, the first cell, after 120 days out of it.

"Now, do you hear what Craydor has said?" Udge asked.

"Just what we always knew. In a matter of perhaps eight days now, Brudoer will have to be let go—at least for 120 days—or else excluded. It is all so strange. We have never used the six cells in my lifetime that I can recall. No one even goes there. The guardsmen found them thick with the dust of years. Wim told me. They didn't even know what they looked like."

"Stick to the point. Look at the wording. Craydor said the prisoner may not be returned to his cell, that is, the first cell. Look at it. She left a way out. He can be put into the next cell for thirty days. We can entice him to anger if he won't submit. She must have foreseen a time like this, when the cells would come into general use."

"But why keep him in the cells? Why not put it all behind us?" Cilia asked. "Look at the trouble it has caused, Protector. Why keep it up?"

Udge glared at her. "I am amazed that you don't see what is happening. He has become a symbol of the weakening of authority. Our whole government is at stake. You can feel the stirring. We have to win this one, even if he is only a wretched boy. We have to stifle this general sedition, and it is here we will do it." She slammed her right fist into her open palm.

Bival felt herself very uneasy. The Protector's plan seemed untrue to the spirit of Craydor somehow. Yet she had caused the incident, and Udge was protecting her. She could scarcely object.

The new guardchief rang the bell. "What is it, Rawl?" Udge asked.

"The boy is eating again, Protector."

"Aaaaaggggh," Udge said. "Too bad. Well, we have won that much over his willfulness. What have you been feeding him?"

"Rich stew as you suggested, Protector."

"Change it. Give him plain food. Potatoes. Give the order."

The guardchief paused a moment, then bowed and left.

Late that evening, Bival descended to the damp under-basement of the city. Warret had been living in the outer room at the entrance to the ice caves. She had finally recovered enough from her anger at him to seek a reconciliation. Balancing a lamp, she pulled the door by its curved iron latch. Warret was asleep on a stone bench, on which he had spread old fiber bags. He had covered himself with a woven rag spread. The room dripped with damp chill, but he had arranged a small vase of dried weeds on a shelf, and stacked his clothing neatly beside it. Two books of Aven and one mathematics text newly printed at Pelbarigan lay by them, creating a slight sense of domesticity.

Bival sank into the one wooden chair and regarded him. He seemed deep in slumber. She reached out a hand to him and shook him gently. He stirred and turned, then blinked his eyes open. "It's too early," he said, then, seeing Bival, shrank back, murmuring, "Oh, you."

"Come upstairs with me."

"I have seen that the room has been kept clean. You cannot fault me on that."

"I haven't come to fault you. Come up with me. Somehow I will make good your chits. This is embarrassing and demeaning. Look at you in this filth. I am now commanding you."

Warret sat up and glared at her. She could see he was thinner and worn from the water-lifting. "Never. I can't. You're oppressing those poor boys. How could I look at any of the men? With him over there in prison because of you, you rancid wretch?"

In spite of her intentions, Bival felt the instant flash of an interior explosion. She threw the lamp at her husband. He ducked. It smashed on the wall, showering oil that burst into flame on the rag spread. Warret rolled upright and blotted it out, singeing his hands, wincing, grunting in pain, but persisting until all the flames winked out. Darkness flowed up, drowning the room. Bival stood in its center, fists clenched, trembling, feeling an egg of fear crack open in her. She could see nothing. Warret kept perfectly still. It had all gone wrong. What would he do? Bival turned and groped for the door. Pushing it open, she saw the guard's light, and reoriented herself. She turned and paused, mouth tight, then fled upstairs once again.

* * *

At Pelbarigan, Gamwyn grew stronger. He was often visited by Garet, the Protector's grandson, and eventually ushered around the bustling city, even to the academy with its mixture of peoples. He was dizzy with new impressions, but they meant little to him. One warm afternoon, the boys sat among fallen leaves on the bluff top.

"Garet."

"Yes."

"It was all my fault, you know. I want to get another shell for Bival. Then it would all be right."

"Another shell? You can't. They come from the sea all the way down the Heart, I hear."

"I've thought about it. I can't return to Threerivers. I will go. All the way. I can do it."

"You're only a boy. And untraveled. There are the Tusco and Alats, not to mention all the dangers of the wild country. You've never been anywhere."

"Maybe. But I am going to go. You have to promise not to tell."

"I'll keep the secret. But you will be taken to Threerivers under guard."

"There has to be a way. Do you think it can be done?"

Garet mused. "I doubt it. And it would be an embarrassment to our guardsmen if you escaped."

"What would Ahroe say?"

"Mother would be bound to prevent you. My father would laugh. She might, too, privately. But escape's out of the question. It's too wild an idea."

"But you won't tell."

"I won't." Garet eyed the younger boy. What a crazy notion. Him? Alone on a trip like that? "There may be Peshtak, too. I hear they are raiding westward again. They've killed some of the Tall Grass Sentani again. Look. The idea's too crazy. It's only a shell. A little piece of crumbly white stuff. Here, though. Do you know the way to the Koorb Sentani country? If you do run off, you could say you were going to get a shell and go to Koorb. They would take care of you."

"Who wants to be taken care of? I want to make this right."

Garet looked closely at him again. Now that his face was emerging from its wound, which slanted red down across his cheek, Garet saw a short nose, crested with freckles, and frank brown eyes, an intent mouth, a shock of brown hair. Garet shook his head.

"I'll go, Garet. I will. I'll find some way."

Garet broke a stick into eight pieces. Then he said, "I know what my father would say. He'd say, 'Try, Gamwyn, try.'"

"I will. It's all I can do. You'll see. It will work out."

 IV

THREE days later, a guardsman stopped at Gamwyn's door and announced that he was wanted by the Protector. The boy was puzzled. He wondered, as he walked through the echoing stone hallways, if Garet had told. He was not being taken to the Protector's room off the Judgment Room, but to her quarters.

He was ushered into a sitting room. The Protector sat at a round table drinking tea. The guardsman stood at attention. She looked at him. "Thank you. You may wait outside, please." The guardsman left. She did not invite Gamwyn to sit. "I have sent to Threerivers by message bird. They will send guardsmen for you. We will not use our guardsmen. How is your cheek?"

"It—it . . . not your guardsmen? They will tie me, Protector."

"Perhaps. I know I would if I wanted to get you all the way there. Now, come here and let me look at your face."

Gamwyn complied, walking around the table and turning his cheek. Sagan frowned at it. She rose and went to the window, asking him to follow, then turned his head to the light. "There will be a scar, but not a bad one. Aven has cared for you."

Gamwyn felt a throb of despair now that it had come over him he was returning. Already the guardsmen were on the river coming for him. Why had Sagan done that? Garet had told her. He must have. The Protector was now leaning on the windowsill, gazing out. Her face was impassive.

"What will become of me, Protector? What will I do?"

"You will have to go through what you will have to go through, Gamwyn."

"Can't you help me?"

She turned to him. "You mean we haven't?"

"Oh, yes, Protector. I am very grateful. But I wouldn't really like to go back to Threerivers, except for my family. Pelbarigan is not the same at all."

"I was there once. I remember the inscriptions of Craydor on the walls."

"Yes."

"Do you read them? Do you think about them at all?"

"Not much, Protector. They've always been there."

"I remember one statement well: 'The genius of the past may be of much help, but our real strength comes from our own inspired genius.' Have you read that one?"

"Yes. It's on the front-stair hall."

"I like that one."

"I have no genius, Protector. I'm only a boy. I have always worked and fetched things."

"When you go down the river in the canoe, you'll have time to think. Will you keep saying to yourself what you don't have? Or what you do?"

"What do I have?"

"Then there's no help for you, is there? Not because you have little, but because you refuse to see what you do have. Now. I am busy. I'll probably not see you again. I have two presents for you." She handed him a little leather bag. Inside he found a bag of white powder and a small length of wood that turned out to be a folding knife.

"The knife is perhaps symbolic. It has a ring, see, so you can get a thong and wear it around your neck. The powder —well, in case you have trouble sleeping, that will put you to sleep. I have had it mixed with salt to make it tasty."

"But I don't have trouble sleeping. I don't understand."

"Then you don't want my present?"

"Oh, yes, but I . . . I . . ."

"You must not tell anyone that I gave these things to you. No one. After all, you are a reprobate, a ghastly little brat, right? Somebody a Protector has no business chatting with. Now, two more matters. Gamwyn, do you ever lie?"

"Lie? No—only when I'm kidding with Brudoer. Why?"

"Curiosity. I've been thinking about it lately. Lying is very complex. Those who hold others by brute force, against reason and justice, often seem shocked when the helpless lie to them, and all the while they are living a lie in the eyes of Aven and never noticing it."

"I don't understand, Protector."

"No matter. If they put you in prison, you'll have time to think about it. Now, one other thing." She turned him and put her hands on his shoulders. Her eyes fixed his. "I haven't lied to you in any particular. I want you to promise to remember everything I've ever told you and to think about it. Everything. Every word." She shook him lightly.

"I promise," he said. She embraced him. He could hear the steady thump of her heart as his ear pressed against her tunic. She let him go and rang for the guardsman. Gamwyn walked down the hall bewildered, holding his small bag of gifts.

Gamwyn's remaining time at Pelbarigan passed rapidly. Garet was always with him, and he became less and less sure about whether the boy had told his grandmother. When the boat arrived from Threerivers, it contained two men and a woman from Udge's own guard. As he had expected, Gamwyn was bound and set in the center of the canoe. A crowd gathered on the bank as it prepared to push off.

The protocol of Pelbarigan's guardsmen seemed strict, quick, and impeccable, until at the last moment a Pelbarigan guardcaptain waded out with a folded sack and snugged it in behind Gamwyn's back, where he rested against a thwart. Then he turned to the Threerivers guardcaptain. "Take care of the boy. He isn't wholly strong yet. He may have trouble sleeping. Keep him comfortable."

The Threerivers guardcaptain merely saluted, while the Pelbarigan guardcaptain shoved the canoe into the river, and the deep voices of the men on the bank took up a short hymn of hope for protection and safety. The Threerivers guardsmen seemed nervous, stroking out into the current quickly and settling into the channel at a pace they could never keep up. When they reached the proper place, the guardsmen's horn sounded from the city towers, and in reply the paddlers flicked their paddles upward only momentarily.

Gamwyn wormed his hips forward so he could lie down once they had glided well away from Pelbarigan. The morning radiated late-fall chill, and he wanted the slight shelter of the boat. High overhead, a ragged line of ducks moved southward, changing leaders constantly. It all seemed unreal. The last normal thing to happen in his life was his running down the stairs with Brudoer.

Protector Sagan had puzzled him. What had she meant by all she said? Why had she sent for Threerivers guardsmen to take him? Was she washing her hands of him? Then why had she embraced him?

Once the canoe was well downstream, the guardsmen talked with each other occasionally, and even laughed. Gamwyn was left to his own thoughts. Driving downriver with the current, they made good time—too good, he felt, his dread growing. The current would carry them. Why couldn't they relax? He began to feel that he himself was drifting—allowing natural forces to carry him along to the shame awaiting him. How could he take hold of his life? By relying on his own genius, as Craydor had written? Sagan had quoted that to him. Why that? What had she meant about lying? Why had the guardcaptain made that remark about his having trouble sleeping? The Protector had asked him to trust her, then given him nothing to trust her about.

She had made him promise to remember everything she had told him. He began to go through all those things. In a flash it came to him, and he sat up with a little cry. The guardsman ahead of him turned to look at him, but he simply saw a boy's startled face. Gamwyn lay down again. She told me to rely on my own genius, he thought. She gave me a knife that doesn't appear to be a knife until it is used. She told me that was symbolic. She gave me a sleeping drug that tastes like salt. She got guardsmen from Threerivers to take me so that whatever happened on the way, Pelbarigan could not be blamed. I couldn't really escape from her guardsmen, but I can from Udge's. Then Garet did tell her. But he didn't betray me. He knew she would do what she could. She has herself agreed to my traveling to the sea for another shell, but only if I have the strength to do it myself. What about the lying? She admitted that was complex.

At that point the woman behind Gamwyn remarked, "I don't see why we should do all the paddling while he lies there dreaming. How about a break? Let him paddle."

"We'll have to release his hands. And they said he was still weak."

"We'll try him." She poked Gamwyn with her paddle blade. "You. Sit up and paddle."

Gamwyn sat up and held out his bound wrists. The woman untied them. Gamwyn took up the paddle and began to work, directed and chastised by the guardcaptain. Soon he stroked well enough, in unison with the men ahead. But he tired quickly. At first he thought to stroke on grimly as long as he could, but then asked himself why he should. After no more than five ayas, he rested the paddle across the boat and said, "I am too tired."

"Tired? You just started. Get going." The woman thumped him in the back with her foot.

"So your tortures start now. Well, you might as well get on with them."

"Tortures? All we are asking is a little work. You've been trouble enough."

Gamwyn thought of pitching the paddle out into the water, but decided to be compliant and limp.

"I'm sorry," he said. "I'm too tired."

The woman kicked him harder in the back. Gamwyn lurched forward, dropping the paddle in the water. She reached for it as they went by, but missed it. They had to backwater and turn to catch it.

"Guardcaptain," said the man in the bow. "We might make better progress if you did your own job."

"You are talking to your superior."

"I know it. Superior in every way but one. I am paddling and you are not."

"Watch your tongue."

"Yes, guardcaptain. But scolding won't make him stronger. We were ordered to proceed as fast as possible. If you report insubordination, I will report delay."

"It's true, Ret," the middle man said. "We need you and your paddle. I'm nervous on this river."

The guardcaptain spat in the river, then bumped Gamwyn again and said, "All right, wilted lily, lie down."

Gamwyn did. They didn't retie his hands. Was this what a lie was? Were they in a hurry and careless, or did they really regard him as helpless? Thinking about that, he fell asleep, then woke in noon warmth as the middle guardsman shook his leg and handed him a round cake of travel bread. They allowed the canoe to float as they ate and drank from a bottle of cold, honey-sweetened tea. As Gamwyn passed the bottle, he caught a strange look from the man ahead of him. Was it sympathy? He couldn't tell.

"What's in your bag?" the man asked.

"A small folding knife they gave me, and—and just some salt."

"Salt?"

"Yes. They said I should take a pinch with each meal. I don't know why." Gamwyn opened the little bag and took some between his thumb and forefinger, then put it on his tongue. The man reached for it and tasted it.

"Nice," he said. "We'll borrow some for our stew tonight." He handed it back.

"Just leave me some, please," Gamwyn said. "That's all. Until the Ursana tells me what to do."

"She's been replaced."

"The Ursana? Why?"

"Because of you, disrupter. You've changed a number of things."

"Gind," the guardcaptain said. "Let the brat be. We'd better be paddling if we're going to make it to Pigeon Island tonight."

Gamwyn lay back again, thinking that he now understood the Protector's whole plan. Ret reached up and took his small knife from the bag, slipping it into her tunic pocket.

Sunset and a chill wind came early, it seemed, and it was dusk before they reached the island. In midafternoon they had put their dried meat to soak, and Gamwyn had been set to work peeling potatoes they had gotten at Pelbarigan. Once on shore, Gamwyn was sent to dig ankleroot and wild onion for the stew. Gind dumped much of the Protector's sleeping drug into the pot, smiling at Gamwyn and saying, "I'm sure we have enough salt for you at Three-rivers—unless you cry too much."

Gamwyn smiled back and feigned drowsiness. When Gind finally thrust a bowl of steaming stew at him, he seemed reluctant to take it, but did and ate a little, managing to scrape most of the stew out into the dry leaves behind him, covering it with them.

The guardsmen ate hugely, stretched, and settled down, first uttering the standard prayers to Aven. Gind tied Gamwyn's hands and feet and helped him into his sleepsack. "Sleep easy, boy, if you have any sleep left in you," he said.

"Gind, I'll take the first watch," Ret said. "I'll wake you a quarter before high night."

Gamwyn watched her feed the fire. The men nodded off almost immediately. Ret stood up and shook her head, then wandered down to the water and splashed some on her face. She came back, then, and squatted by the fire, throwing twigs in. Then she sat back, and before long slumped down in a dead sleep. Gamwyn wormed from the sleepsack and rubbed his bonds against the edge of the iron stewpot, which he carried out into the dark, crawling laboriously. He was soon free. Rolling it loosely, he threw his sleepsack into the canoe. He was about to shove it off when he remembered his knife. His heart beating fast, he returned to Ret and slipped it from her pocket. She stirred slightly. He took her sleepsack and gently spread it over her. Again she stirred. Gamwyn took two paddles out of the boat and stuck them in the shore sand, retrieved the salted drug, then shoved the canoe into the river, a raw potato in his mouth. As he paddled, he chewed it slowly. His cheek still radiated dull soreness.

He was still perhaps thirty ayas above Threerivers, and knew he ought to pass the city in the dark, even before false dawn. But after forcing himself as hard as he could, he saw the east grow light before he had come near the city. He continued to paddle well into the daylight, until he recognized a bend well above the city. He and his brother had often snagged driftwood for the city from the point there. He hauled the canoe out on the west bank and dragged it back into the woods nearly a quarter of an ayas, then returned to the river and traveled almost a half-ayas upstream, forcing his way into a willow thicket. There he spread his sleepsack and crawled into it exhausted. Chewing another raw potato, he drifted off to sleep.

He was still drowsing, at dusk, when the exhausted guardsmen walked and trotted down the east bank opposite him. Gind had finally awakened near dawn and roused them. They had paddled across to the east bank on a log and set out, angry and chagrined.

That evening, Udge greeted the confession of the guardsmen with rage, especially because it was the guardcaptain, the woman she had sent along to guard against any male treachery, who had slept and allowed the boy to escape.

Before high night, Gamwyn saw boats with torches

cruising along the banks and knew the guardsmen had made it back. One came close enough to his thicket to allow him to hear someone say, "This is a fool's parade. What can we see but our own torches?"

In spite of himself, Gamwyn laughed quietly. But he knew they would come back in daylight and inspect the whole bank with great care, so he groped his way to the canoe, dragged it back to the river, and after the lighted boats eventually departed, glided downstream past the city. He could see small lights in its towers and through several windows. A swirl of fear and longing blew through him as he passed, far toward the west bank, crouched low. He had cut branches and propped them up in the bow, sticking high up, imitating a floating tree.

Unknown to him, two guardsmen, standing on the middle terrace, noticed. "Ssst," one said. "Look there. There he goes. Go, boy. Hurry."

"Shhh," said the other man. "Are any boats below yet?"

"I don't think so."

"I hope he has the sense to leave the river."

"He's done well enough so far. But don't tell anybody at all, no matter what you think they feel."

"Me? Tell them what?"

By the following noon guardsmen had retrieved the floating canoe far downstream. It was laden with debris, and a rock tied to the stern with vines dragged in the water behind it, in Gamwyn's attempt to keep it in the channel and make it track straight. The guardsmen took it ashore and emptied it, finding in the process a long note from Gamwyn to the Protector, written on a flat stick he had shaved white.

It was late in the afternoon before the guardcaptain of the detail reported the findings to Udge, in the Broad Tower, and handed her the note, which she read aloud to the four quadrant counsels:

> Protector: I am much better now and am grateful to everyone for sending me to Pelbarigan and takeing such good care of me. I know I am the cause of al the problems. Pleese don't hurt Brudoer. He didn't do it. Pleese tell the Sowthcouncel, Bival, how sory I am for what I did. I am going to make it up to her and have thout of a way. Pleese tell her. I hope to see you

somtime when I have done this. This is from your divoted citizen, Gamwyn.

Udge set the stick down on a table by her chair. "Guard-captain," she said, "see that the contents of this note are not divulged to anyone."

"Protector, forgive me, but it was not private, being open, and many of the guardsmen read it."

"Go, then, and see that it is kept confidential."

"I fear it is too late for that, Protector. They are with their families by now."

"Try. Go."

The guardcaptain bowed and backed out hurriedly. Udge stood and walked to the window, muttering, "What sort of muck-heap guardsmen do we have? A gang of food-swilling, drooling carcasses, blind as eggs, waterskins full of swamp ooze. They let a sick child escape from them. A sick servant child."

"Perhaps it is better, Protector," Cilia said. "Perhaps we can free Brudoer when his thirty days are up, and let the whole problem die. There are tensions."

Udge whirled on her. "No. If that is done, we would have lost. I don't intend to lose. I know authority. It doesn't work like that. You assert it. If there is opposition, you don't draw back. You overwhelm them with your power. You strike. All of Threerivers is near cracking. Lax ways did it. My election is proof of a majority desire for the strictness that has kept us orderly. No. It is Brudoer who must make up for this. Let them chuckle a moment about this escape. Brudoer has continued to act out-rageously, even in prison. With a little effort we can tempt him into a further attack and then punish him so severely that the point will be made."

"What point, Protector?"

"That we are not a slack city, smiling at attacks on our counsels, tolerating unruliness in the males."

Bival looked at Udge, somewhat startled. She hadn't quite wanted this. Udge seemed fanatical, spitting as she spoke. Bival's anger had faded long ago. She wished it were all over. She missed Warret and alone in the room, felt his accusation every night. But the Protector had done so much on Bival's account that she could hardly object now. She felt a rising sense of disaster.

Udge continued. "In two days Brudoer is to be released,

yet the scars he left on Bival have barely healed. There were sixteen separate cuts, I believe, several deep. We will complete his punishment with one lash for every two wounds he inflicted. Surely that will be merciful enough. And when we see defiance from him, as I'm sure we will, we'll place him in the second cell for another thirty days."

"Protector!—"

Udge held up her hand. "That's how it will be, West-counsel. Now all of you go and leave me."

Later, the sense of dread growing on her, Bival wandered into the central Judgment Room of the city, unused now since Udge took office. It stood at the focus of the arcs created by the terraces and occupied four city levels. The floor was perfectly round, divided into quadrants by black, zigzag tiles radiating from a triangle at the center, continuing on up the walls, which rose and curved in elliptically, meeting at the central skylight, which protruded from an upper city level, underneath the Broad Tower. The central triangle, Bival knew, was the tip of Craydor's sealed tomb, which lay under the floor. A previous Protector had had the jutting pyramidal apex leveled because it was an inconvenience.

The walls were circled with inscriptions from Craydor. Bival's eye wandered around them idly. One of the longest, "The hawk, which spirals high over us all, split and forgot the egg which warmed him," was quoted at every wedding, indicating the freedom of the newlywed woman from parental control even while she worked within the family.

Bival felt a flick of recognition. Here was another shell. Craydor was speaking of a different sort of shell. And the room was shaped like a bird's egg. Even the quadrant patterns could be seen as stylized cracks, illustrating the inscription.

Calling a guardsman, she requested him to bring Warret to the hall—a command from his quadrant counsel, not his wife. She sat alone in the dim light, wondering. This new insight complicated things. Craydor constructed the Broad Tower on the model of the shell those wretches had broken, but here she seemed to advocate the breaking of a shell.

Eventually Bival heard footsteps as the guardsman escorted Warret to the Judgment Room, then bowed and left. Warret stood, arms clasped behind him, facing his wife.

"Please sit down," she said.

"Is that a command?"

"No. As you wish. Look what I have discovered." She explained her musings to him.

"Is that what you brought me here for?"

"Warret, don't you see? What did Craydor mean? She was trying to tell us something. Don't you see how important the shells are? I am trying to explain to you why I needed that shell so badly. I meant you no personal harm. Can't you trust me even a little?"

"Aside from your temper, I trust you. But I don't regard you as very wise, and I can't trust your limitations."

Bival clenched her hands, but stifled her anger. "How can you say such a thing to me? Have we shared nothing? I don't deserve this from you."

"That all passed away, Bival, like cottonwood fluff floating by."

She was silent for a long time, finally saying, "Cottonwood fluff? All your eternal promises? Our life together? You can't deny all of it."

"Like your precious shell, it was smashed when you wholly disregarded all my hopes. It has been ground to powder by my weeks of lifting water. I see how you had regarded me all along—as a tool, a device for your use."

"How can—well, then let it be. I will request the council for a formal separation, permanent and complete. I can't suffer this embarrassment any longer." Again she fell silent a long time. "Don't you feel anything?"

"According to your explanation, we are in an egg. Look. The crack runs between us, splitting the whole city, not only us. How can I feel? We all know that one poor child lies in prison and that Udge intends to lash him in public. And the other, still weak and wholly unused to the outside wilderness, now is struggling to survive so as to make up to you something that he never really owed to you in the first place. No. I am the boys and the boys are me. You are the others. I should have seen it long ago. We have nothing, you and I. What egg of ours ever split? What hawk of ours ever broke free to soar?"

"A child would have only hindered us."

"Hindered you and your rise to power. It's over. Now may I go? Let it happen, whatever will. I can do nothing about it. All I can do is lift water to the tower. At least that isn't cracked."

"No, and it won't be. It has a true design. The whole

city has a true design. It has worked well. We have to trust it."

"People are being destroyed in this precious design, Bival. You see the theory. I'm concerned with people."

"How are your hands? I'm sorry what I did to them."

"They're all right."

"I am afraid for us all."

"Well you might be."

"Warret, would you at least . . . if I waited on the formal separation, might this not pass?"

"You'll have to decide that yourself. Don't you see yet? It has already happened. You're concerned with official things, but the actuality is over with. Done. Finished."

"Is it? I know you worked long, extra quadrants for your pellute. I'll make it up to you. In any case I will. I am not a bad person, Warret."

"What is bad? Things good people do are often horrible. May I go? Aren't we through?"

"I suppose. I don't see how—May we not embrace once more at least?"

"If you wish."

Infuriated by his patronizing tone, then suddenly tired of anger, she walked to him. They embraced formally across one of the black zigzags, and the meaning was lost on neither. Then they came apart, holding hands a moment before dropping them.

"For the sake of us all, you had better help Brudoer."

"There is nothing now, nothing I can do."

"You can. You just don't see that far."

Her anger rose again, but again she sighed it out. "Well. Leave me now please." She dropped her eyes for a time, trembling, and when she lifted them again, he was gone. Again she looked around the walls. Had Craydor contradicted herself about this shell? An egg had to break away for life to grow. A shell protected mature life. What did it all mean?

Far in the north quadrant, Prope, an elderly family head, again was scolding her servant. "Mall. Look. Again the folds are not sharp. How can I serve when the napkins are so wretchedly arranged? I shall have to put you on wood detail again and use the funds you earn to hire a replacement."

"Yes, of course," Mall said, bowing. "But, if you'll forgive, I think the wood detail will not have me anymore. My hands scarcely grip, I regret to say."

"Yes. Willfulness. They surely do not grip napkins, or grip them like a maul or axe. The Protector was right. But I shall have to tolerate you since there seems little alternative. You are not, however, justifying your existence."

Mall's eyes blazed momentarily. "No, certainly not, I regret to say," he murmured.

"Well, all the city is asleep," said Prope, rising. "Old as I am, I suppose I shall, too. I trust you have turned the bed down properly." She didn't wait for an answer. Mall glared at her retreating back.

 V

IT was early morning two days later that Brudoer heard voices, then the bolts thrown back on his cell door. The massive, steel-sheathed portal swung open, and five guardsmen entered. He flattened against the far stone wall.

The guardcaptain stepped forward and announced, "Your period of incarceration, as prescribed by Craydor, is over. The Protector has determined that you may be freed after public punishment, provided your attitudes are correct. Now, come."

Brudoer moved away down the wall as the guardsmen advanced and took his elbows. He struggled, silently, until a come-along grip pulled threads of pain down his arms. Still he said nothing.

Emerging onto the lowest terrace, he saw a rack erected near the edge. Massed guardsmen lined the terrace and stood stationed above on each level, and much of the city also lined the walls arcing above him. He was jerked and wrestled to the rack, stripped of his tunic and shirt, and tied on. As he struggled, Brudoer scanned the crowd for the Protector, but she seemed to be nowhere. He did see a whip with three tails.

The guardchief read from a roll. "By order of the Protector and inner council, having served your thirty days, you may be freed after suffering public punishment for attacking a council member. You are to receive one lash for each two wounds you inflicted on the council member, eight in all. After that, if you humble yourself to her, and beg forgiveness, you will be reinstated in the community."

A mixed murmur rolled through the crowd. Many clearly approved, cheering and clicking their tongues. Brudoer, turning his head, thought he heard a different undertone, a hesitant, dark muttering of protest. Twisting his neck farther, he yelled out, "One lash for each two wounds? Look at the whip. It has three tails, you flea-ridden heap of old fish guts! You—" The guardchief thrust a gag into his mouth. On the terrace above, a great drum stood on a platform, and as a guardsman brought a heavy, padded stick down on it, Brudoer felt the first slashing cuts of the whip burn across his back. A surge of sound rose from the crowd. A second drum sound brought the lash again. Brudoer tried to scream, fought the gag, dashing his head from side to side.

At the third drum thud, Brudoer braced himself again but felt nothing. Wim, the deposed guardchief, had been assigned the task of lashing him. She threw down the whip. "I will not beat a child any longer on anyone's orders," she shrieked.

From high above, the Protector stepped to the edge of the top terrace and called down, "Then strap her to the rack over the criminal and let her take the lashes until she agrees."

Three guardsmen seized Wim, but she never struggled. Her tunic was split down the back. She held out her arms to be tied down. "I am deeply sorry, Brudoer, for what I did to you," she said in a loud voice.

"Gag her, gag her," several voices called, almost all older women, but no such order was given. Udge stood high above now, her mouth down.

"Commence," the Protector called down. The drum thudded. The guardchief with the whip swung it hard, and Wim screamed piercingly. The crowd sound fell to a murmur at the shriek, even the most inflexible citizen subdued before the reality of revolt's painful consequences. The thud came again, and another lash brought a new scream, long and lingering. The guardchief again drew back the whip, grim and sweating, but also willing. Suddenly, like a sun flicker from a buckle, an arrow flashed from somewhere and took her through the neck. She turned, her arms fluttering up, her silent mouth open, then she staggered back and fell soundlessly off the terrace to fall to the rocks far below.

"Guardsmen, arm yourselves," a guardcaptain shouted, but the crowd had already begun to scream and flee, pouring through the doors into the city and running down its corridors. Guardsmen soon sealed off all the entrances, while others stood with short-swords at the ready. From the second terrace, an old woman, with her hair up in two tiers, turned upward and yelled, "See what your tyranny has brought us, you bloody old wretch!" It was the Ardena, an old opponent of Udge's.

"Arrest her," the Protector called down.

A guardsman moved toward her, but she flashed at him, "On what charge? I am a family head, a member of the full council, and I have merely expressed my opinion."

The guardsman hesitated.

"Arrest her immediately," the Protector again called.

The guardsman turned. "What is the charge?" he called back.

"Will no one arrest her?" Udge screamed. "She has opposed the proceedings. She is under suspicion of aiding in the murder of the guardchief."

The Ardena looked up at Udge and laughed derisively. A guardsman reached for her arm, but she shook him off. Another stepped to her side and murmured, "Auntie Unset, please. She will harm you. She'll find a way. You must go. She will really harm you." The old woman glared at him. "Please?" he said. She turned and left with dignity.

Above, Udge did not press the point. She would bide her time. "Release Wim and remove her guardsman's insignia. She is remanded to the first cell. Put the criminal in the second cell. All guardcaptains report to the Broad Tower immediately," she called. She turned and left.

In the hallways, the Ardena scolded her nephew unmercifully, but he held his ground. She turned into her quarters, attempting to shut the door, but he followed her in. "Sit down," he said. She was amazed but complied. He shut the door. "Listen. You don't know how far she has extended her control. She has done it by the general fear of disobeying Craydor's wishes, which she claims to understand. You are in danger. You must send her an apology."

"What? Never."

"Then I will send it in your name, Auntie. I mean it. I won't allow you—"

The Ardena stood and interrupted him. "You—you send in my name? You would dare?"

He took her hands. "Are you Brudoer? Will you lie down for her lash? Aren't there different ways of winning? Don't we need you in this family more than ever before? Can't there be one clear spokesman for the opposition? This is a crisis. What's happened to your subtlety?"

The Ardena sank back down, and he released her hands. "It seems so dishonorable."

"About as dishonorable as for Gamwyn to escape, Ardena."

She looked up at him. "I will send an apology," she said. "It will hurt, but I will do it. You are right, after all."

"Make it sycophantic, Auntie."

The old woman suddenly wept into her hands. Then she lifted her eyes to him again, fiercely. "Yes, curse her bones. It will be so sycophantic she will choke on it." The two laughed quietly with each other, and as the guardsman turned to go, the Ardena said, "This is not the end of it, though, you know."

"No. No, it certainly is not."

In the evening, as Brudoer lay on the stone floor of the second cell, still unwashed, throbbing with pain, he heard the door open. Turning his head, he saw his mother and two guardsmen. "I am allowed to wash you as long as I don't talk to you. Otherwise, they will send me away," she said.

Brudoer groaned. As she worked, he lay still. He could see her knees and the boots of one guardsman. She worked slowly. The pain shot through him like sheet lightning as she moved slowly over his back with warm, slightly soapy water. He set his jaw and allowed no sound to escape. She took great, almost exaggerated care, and through his pain, Brudoer saw that she was talking to him with her hands. They meant love, forbearance, defiance. He felt them tremble slightly. On his part he decided to tell her by perfect silence that he still was strong.

Finally she stood and said, "It is finished." Then she looked around and remarked, "What a strange room. I suppose if Craydor designed it, it must mean something."

"Silence."

"Yes. That is it. Are you a father?" She put a strange accent on "it" and "father." After they left, Brudoer lay without moving for a long time. What had that meant? "It" and "father." What father? His own, of course. A thought darted into his mind. She had told him it was his father who had shot the arrow. Brudoer didn't even know he had ever handled a bow. Amazing. But was it true?

Eventually he sat up slowly. The lofty light that burned until the guardsman drew it out from above at high night showed a room very different from the first. It had the usual band of letters, apparently meaningless, around it. Below that, the word ANGER repeated itself in a complete band around the room. Under that series of reliefs illustrated faces and bodies obviously in states of rage. Brudoer turned his head slowly upward, and saw two large heads in relief, a man and a woman calmly looking at each other. He sighed and rolled back on his stomach, drifting off to sleep.

Three days later, in the morning, a guardcaptain announced himself at the Broad Tower and was admitted. He saluted Udge.

"Well?"

"It is Wim, Protector. She is not in her cell. She is gone. We have checked. Five boats are also missing, and we cannot account for twenty-one young men."

"From her family?"

"From all four quadrants, Protector."

"When was she last seen?"

"All three shifts of yesterday's prison guardsmen are missing. It would have been yesterday afternoon. What should we do?"

"Nothing."

"Nothing?"

"You may go now. Thank you for your report."

"What does it mean, Protector?" Cilia asked as the guardcaptain exited.

"Don't you see? They have taken her to Pelbarigan. It is of no use for us to follow. They have made too much distance. Pelbarigan showed with the boy that they are not in sympathy with us. It begins to happen."

"What?"

"The weak and unruly are leaving. This perfect city will

always be self-sustaining. Perhaps it is time the scum bubbled over."

Bival shuddered as the Protector said this. She wondered if Warret had gone. No. It had been all young men. She knew too that this move would only strengthen Udge with most of the populace, so fearful were they of initiative and so shocked at defiance. Sympathy also extended to the family of the slain guardchief. Murder was almost wholly unknown in Threerivers. It would generally be assumed that the murderer was among those who left. Bival was less sure all the time, though, of her own position. She stared out the window. A winter eagle turned lazy circles over the river. She felt as alone as the bird. She thought again of Craydor's statement. It had left the egg behind. So had those who fled. But it was not the same, surely.

After he abandoned the canoe, Gamwyn struck out across the land west of the river, trending southward. He was cold in the late-fall weather. Unused to the outdoors, he hardly knew how to care for himself, but tried to live on ankleroot. At last, when he was quite sure there was no pursuit, he returned to the river, constructed a crude raft of driftwood, and set off on it. Loneliness bored into him. He felt the foolishness of his journey, but it never occurred to him to turn back.

Finally he passed the mouth of the Oh, with its dark water running down the east bank. He stopped to fish occasionally, using rough Pelbar traps of willow twigs. But he was not able to feed himself properly and sometimes felt light-headed. Once or twice he spent most of the day in his sleepsack, with the raft drifting and slowly spinning down the river. Somehow his plan would work out. It had to. He tried to pray but seemed not able to get through a thought without his mind drifting.

Far to the north, the Protector of Pelbarigan visited Wim in the infirmary. The younger woman was by then sitting up, though not leaning back as yet.

"You will not send me back, Protector, I beg you."

"We have not been asked."

"Not asked? Surely they must have surmised that we came here."

"Your Protector is a shrewd woman. She has managed

to dispose of a problem. In Threerivers you would always be a goad to her. What would she do with you? I imagine she wishes she could rid herself of Brudoer as well."

"I'm not sure of that. I think she has been strengthened by all this. The conservatives are shocked, and they tighten up. So there is use for the boy. She will try to make his rebellion seem so monstrous that the family heads will cluster to her."

"This world asks a great deal of its children, it seems. I wonder where Gamwyn is now. Far down the river, perhaps." She sighed slightly. "I know you will not tell. Gamwyn told my grandson he would go to the sea to get another shell for Bival. He told him that. It is hard to believe. He thought it would make everything right again."

Wim looked at Sagan. "And you let him, Protector?"

"Let him? He seems to have done it on his own. Would you rather that he were at Threerivers?"

"No. But is that the only other option?"

Sagan looked pensive. "I'm afraid it is. Pelbarigan has sent out other young men, in different circumstances, with staggering results. But never quite such a boy before. I wonder if he will survive."

"I hope so, Protector."

At that moment, Gamwyn lay on his back watching a red-tailed hawk flying in slow circles. He was cut with hunger. As he watched, it seemed to describe the shape of the shell in the air. "Shell? Shell?" he murmured. Then he heard voices. Rolling onto his elbow, he saw a long boat approaching, paddled by a gigantic young man. A small black-haired girl about his own age sat in the bow looking at him. They swung alongside the raft, and the girl jumped on.

"Hold the boat, Jamin," she said. Then she knelt by Gamwyn. "Hello," she whispered, frowning. "Are you all right? My name is Misque. Are you well? Come. Get in the boat with us and we will take you to Jaiyan's Station. That's Jamin, Jaiyan's son. Do you know of him? Who are you? What a strange haircut. Come on now, can you get up? Here, Jamin, I will hold the boat, and you get him and his gear. Come on. You'll be all right. You look hungry. What's your name? You aren't a Sentani. Have you come far? Here. We will get your things."

"Gamwyn," he murmured.

"Gamwyn? What is a Gamwyn?"

"Me. My name."

"Oh. Yes. Well, come. You are a skinny person, all right. Here, Jamie, pick him up."

Jamin had said nothing yet. He picked up Gamwyn like a sack of dry leaves and laid him in the boat, scooping up the boy's things. Then he heaved himself into the stern seat, shoving off from Gamwyn's raft, which he left to float downstream. Gamwyn watched it, then turned to look at Misque's penetrating eyes.

"I know," she said. "Your hair. You are a Pelbar. A real Pelbar. I've never seen one. Look, Jamie, a Pelbar. Are you from Pelbarigan, or maybe that strange city—what is it?"

"Threerivers. Have you anything to eat?"

"Yes, that one. Threerivers. I've never seen it, but they say it is tall, silent, strange, and shadows live there. But Ravell has been there, and he knows people there."

"The trader."

"Yes. You know him? Look, Jamie, he knows Ravell. We are almost neighbors then. What are you doing here, anyway?"

Gamwyn didn't reply. She pursed her mouth. "Well, no matter. Look, some of the old people are at the bank already."

Gamwyn turned. On the near shore was an assemblage of people, some dark-skinned, some light, a few with red hair were outnumbered by those with gray. All were dressed in dark Sentani tunics and rough pants, their breath steaming in the cold air. Gamwyn felt faint as the boat grounded. Jamin stepped onto a thick plank, took hold of the bow, and easily dragged the whole thing up onto the bank. Gamwyn felt himself lifted, amid chatter, then carried by many hands up a hill.

Looking up, he saw a door frame as they passed into the darkness of a building. A piece of baked apple dipped in honey was thrust at his mouth. It nearly burnt. Another piece came. He was lifted onto a couch, where he ate, looking up at a circle of weathered old faces that laughed and speculated until he drifted off to sleep.

Gamwyn was eventually awakened by a gentle shaking on his arm. He opened his eyes and found himself in a shedlike room of rough boards, with three bunks. An old man bent over him, and as Gamwyn blinked, he said, "Wake, young one. Time for evening song."

Yawning and standing, Gamwyn found himself led by the arm to join a number of others, all old, all moving through a maze of rooms to a central chamber that Gamwyn dimly recognized as the one he had been first brought to.

The building was a strange structure, large and circular, with palisaded log walls about three arms high. A high, conical roof capped it. In the center of the room stood an enormous pillar, made of one whole tree trunk, against which all the rafters leaned. Almost half the room was taken up by a complex and bizarre device.

"That's Jaiyan," the old man whispered and pointed to an extremely large man seated at the edge of the device with his back to the small crowd, facing rows of light brown blocks, which arced around him. He seemed surrounded by upright tubes, of a great variety of sizes. Off to the side, toward the back, stood a row of enormous bellows. A number of the old people went to them and began pumping them up and down.

Jaiyan reached out his fingers and depressed the blocks selectively. Gamwyn was startled at the sudden growth of sounds from the device, sounds becoming music, intricate and varied. Jaiyan began to move his fingers faster, jerking his head in emphasis, as he created racing sounds. Then Gamwyn noticed Jaiyan's feet sometimes moving, too, depressing a series of wooden rods, as he rested his hands. The old people pumped the bellows faster and faster, and soon others moved to take their place. All who were not working sat as a polite audience. Low tones seemed to shake the whole hall, while high ones flitted among the rafters like sparrows. Gamwyn sat fascinated. It sounded as loud as the whole Threerivers choir singing at once, but this was more varied, though it had no chords.

At last Jaiyan stopped, stood, bowed, and laughed a guttural guffaw, extending his arms and thanking the workers at the bellows. Then he frowned and said, "Somehow it isn't full enough. Needs another row of whistles. Something much deeper. Hmm. I see our new recruit is awake." He walked toward Gamwyn and, practically kneeling, gave him the Sentani greeting, palms against each other, foreheads touching. Then he stood straight, looked down at the boy, and laughed again. "Hungry again?"

"Yes, thank you," Gamwyn said softly.

"Misque? Misque. Take care of this bent reed. Feed

him." Then he turned to Gamwyn again and asked, "Can you build? Got any skills?"

"A few. I have done woodworking and some work as a mason's helper. But I have mostly just done labor—as much as a boy can."

"Wood turning?"

"A little. How shall I address you?"

Jaiyan laughed. "Misque calls me chief. That's amusing enough."

"What is that device, uh, chief?"

"That? An organ. Have you heard of an organ? Probably not. It's the only one in the whole Heart River Valley, I imagine. I dug up an ancient building and found one. Took me years to figure it all out. It was called an organ—stamped right onto the brass. It makes music Atou himself would gladly listen to. Now, I'll give you to Misque."

She stood ready with a bowl of thick soup. She led Gamwyn to a side table and sat with him, prattling at him endlessly as he ate. Gamwyn felt something enigmatic about her. She wasn't a Sentani, surely.

Finally, he asked, "What are you? Where are you from?"

"Oh, I was lost, like you. I'm from far away. To the east. Jaiyan took me in, like you. I live here now. I take care of Jamin. His son. I like it here, like you will."

"From the east? East of the Tall Grass Sentani?"

"Much."

"That's Peshtak country."

"Some of it is. There are other people. I am from far east of that."

"From the eastern cities? Innanigan?"

"How do you know all that?"

"Some of us Pelbar have been there, you know."

"Yes. The famous Jestak. But none since?"

"How did you get through the Peshtak without getting killed?"

She laughed. "I didn't know they were there. It was mostly forest, you know. It's an awful story, and I don't want to tell it again. Maybe sometime. Now tell me how you came to leave Threerivers."

"I have to go to the sea and get a shell."

"The sea? A shell? You mean a seashell? Are you mad? That's impossible. The Tusco would stop you. You? Such a spindle? Go to the sea?"

Gamwyn said nothing, just ate. Misque found Jaiyan

and brought him over, and they got Gamwyn to tell his story. He summarized it, with traditional reticence about Pelbar affairs.

Jaiyan was silent awhile. "I can't let you do it, little one. The Tusco would simply enslave you. You would come back here when you are as old as these people. It's silly." He waved his hand. "They're all former slaves. Once they were Siveri. The Tusco took them and worked them until they were too old to be of use."

"How did they get here?"

"The Tusco used to kill them, but I agreed to buy a number. I give them a home, and they work for me."

"And pump the bellows?"

Jaiyan laughed. "Yes. Without them, I couldn't play my organ. So we benefit each other. But you can't go any farther. It's a silly idea. You'll have to give it up."

"But . . . but, chief. Threerivers is my only home. All I know is there. I have to make right the wrong somehow."

"Doesn't sound like a wrong to me. You wait. The Tusco will be here in a few days with cotton to trade north. I am trading them tanned leather and other stuff. This is the one place the Sentani trade with the Tusco. You'll see them. A swampy lot. Just ask yourself, then, if you want to hoe cotton and maryjane for them all your life—or until they throw you out because you're of no use."

Gamwyn felt utterly bleak. He began to sob even though he fought against it. Jaiyan stood, put his hands on his hips, turned and walked away, turned back and stared again. "I can't let you do it. We have plenty of work here. You can help me with the new whistles. The Siveri are too backward to help."

Gamwyn continued to sob. Jaiyan glared at him. Then he turned away again, saying over his shoulder, "Misque, take care of the child."

The girl put her arm over Gamwyn's shoulder. He looked at her. Her eyes were hard as the sun on metal. "Stop it. Stop it," she hissed at him. "You don't have to do that. You water-lily stem."

"I'm trying."

"Trying! Show some control. Look at you, blubbering like a baby."

"You can go away. You don't have to stay here."

Misque sighed dramatically but said no more. Nor did she move her arm until Gamwyn regained his calm. Then she said, "Listen. Don't think I'm going to baby you. You'll have to pull your own weight and stand on your own spindles."

"I never asked anything from you."

"Remember that."

Gamwyn looked at her, wondering, and saw hesitation and trouble in her expression, which she tried to hide. "I'm going back to bed," he said.

At that time, Brudoer, now able to lie on his back again, rested in the sleeping alcove in the second cell at the base of Threerivers. On the low, curved ceiling over his head was a grotesque face, and again the word ANGER chiseled into the rock. At the foot of the bed, facing the other direction, was the faint word PEACE. Again, fury at his situation boiled over in him, and he struck out at the grotesque face, skinning his knuckles. He sucked at them, still furious. Suddenly it all seemed stupid. He closed his eyes, then opened them again to the word ANGER.

Slowly he took his bed apart and remade it so the angry face was at the foot. As he lay staring up at PEACE, he noticed a gull in flight very faintly etched into the curved stone. He reached out his hand to it, but it disappeared in the new shadows. He couldn't really feel it distinctly. He drew his hand down and the image renewed itself in the sidelong light.

Another of Craydor's ideas, he thought. It began to dawn on him that she was talking to him. He rolled over and looked around the cell walls. Most of what he saw was obvious, but the rows of letters were simply enigmatic and meant nothing at all. He would study them the next day.

At Jaiyan's Station, Gamwyn quickly merged into the strange community. Like all the others, he had standard duties, but because he was small, quick, and bright, Jaiyan frequently used the boy as a helper in the endless adjustments and additions to his gigantic instrument.

The others took the enormous eccentricity in stride. It had taken over the trader's life. With great pains and skill, he had deciphered the initial instrument he dug up and had recreated his version of it with a boy's pure joy. He played it, with the Siveri at the bellows, three times a day, and between these times would tinker with it. Because it needed leather parts, he had built a tannery, and now bought skins from the Sentani, not only for his own use but for trade. His wood shop, too, employed the old people, who worked slowly and seemed content with their lot. They looked at him as a father. Long enslaved, they took everything mildly. They were free to leave, but since it was far to Siveri country and the Tusco slaving parties were everywhere, the old ones saw little to gain in returning after all the long years of their captivity.

Gamwyn enjoyed the quietness of the Siveri, but chafed at their bovine complacency. Really heavy work was done by Jaiyan himself, or by Jamin, his hulking, simpleminded son, the one person Misque seemed genuinely devoted to. She watched out for him, directing and harrying him the way a kingbird does a hawk, or, the way a mother does a child.

One afternoon, just as ice chunks began appearing in the river, Gamwyn heard a horn. Looking up, he saw three long, flat-bottomed boats coming up the river. "It's the Tusco," Misque said.

Gamwyn stared, as the laden boats, rowed by slaves, slowly drew up to the bank, where Jaiyan greeted them, holding up both hands. The sign was returned by a black-haired man in the bow of the lead boat. This man was dressed entirely in black leather, even wearing a tight leather helmet with cheekpieces.

Gamwyn shuddered. The man's curved sword hung longer than the typical short-sword of the Heart River peoples. A quirt dangled from his left wrist, and as the slaves unloaded large bags of cotton, he flipped it idly against their backs. A line of guards, similarly dressed, stood in bow and stern, as well as on the bank. All were armed with bows.

Very little talk was exchanged as cotton was traded for leather, Pelbar ceramics, turned wood trays and cups, salted meat, and a large quantity of cattle bones. Near the end of the exchange, Gamwyn became aware that the leader stood next to him. Suddenly he took the boy's cheeks in his hand and turned his head. He stared at Gamwyn.

"What he?"

Gamwyn reached up and with a guardsman's thrust stuck his thumbnail into the man's wrist. The man yelled and let go, and at that moment, Jamin stepped between the two. The Tusco retreated several steps.

"Not in deal," Jamin said. "Not in deal."

Jaiyan strode over and put his arm on the man's shoulder. "It's all right. He's only another waif I've taken in. Only a boy." The man's glare softened slightly. "Come into the hall and we'll settle our account," Jaiyan added. The matter seemed ended, but Gamwyn didn't like the way the Tusco bowmen looked at him. Jamin stayed right with him, but Misque was nowhere in sight.

The Tusco stayed the night, but in their boats, as was agreed. The whole time, a taste of danger hung like acrid woodsmoke in the air. Gamwyn was glad to see them cast off in the morning, their Siveri slaves wearily taking up the long, scarred oars to begin the downstream voyage.

Only then did Misque reappear. What did that mean? Gamwyn wondered. "How long have you been at Jaiyan's Station?" he asked her.

"Awhile. Why?"

"No reason. Do you plan to stay here always?"

"Why? Want to marry me?" She laughed lightly at him.

"You never tell me about yourself."

"About as much as you'll tell me about Threerivers."

"Why do you want to know about it?"

"Why do you want to know about me?"

At Threerivers, Brudoer whiled away long periods staring at the letters mingled on the wall. He could make out the word THE obviously worked into the pattern, but that was all. That was obvious. He was sure now that it was a pattern. He was so absorbed in deciphering it that when the two guardsmen came for his dishes, and to give him dinner, he scarcely noticed them. They were wary since he had been so unpredictable. One looked at the other and raised his eyebrows. Finally Brudoer glanced at them but seemed uninterested. They left, a little bewildered, deciding to report the change in the boy to the guardchief. Again Brudoer stared at the inscription, which read, THEPD. UERCPNOASHENOEFETBHEIRSOSFHEERLELHTTOE. OFIISLTEOC-ENNAH. It must mean something.

His eyes tired from looking, and all seemed to tremble and blur. He passed his hands in front of his face, and as he turned his head, the word SHELL seemed to jump from the tangled sequence of letters. He stared again, but couldn't seem to find it. He carefully went over the list again. Wetting his finger in his water bowl, he spelled patterns on the floor, methodically going over the list again and again. The word wasn't there. But he was sure he had seen it. Why that word? It seemed to mock him.

He looked again for the letters, then found only the first three, SHE, as before. No. That was not it. Then, at the third S, he found them again, each separated by a letter. SHELL. It was there. What else was there? He went back to the beginning, which he took to be THE, an easy clue to the fact that there was a code, then took every other letter as in the pattern. What came out was "The purpose of this shell too is to enh." What shell? What of the rest?

Then he saw the two periods, one near the beginning, one nearer the end. Skipping the letters he had not used did no good. If periods were a clue, that meant to go backward. He began, but at that point the guardsmen took away the lamp, for it was by this time high night. Brudoer yelled for them to bring it back, shouting repeatedly, his voice resounding in the high cell, but he was plunged into darkness until the morning and had to crawl to his bed. He lay awake a long time pondering what Craydor might have meant. What shell? He thought ahead. In eight days he would again be taken from the cell. He was sure that Udge would try some pretext to put him back again.

Brudoer then began to wonder what he had missed in the letters of the first cell. And he began to look forward to the third cell, though the thought of another whipping made him bead with sweat. He now had a secret—he alone with Craydor herself. Somehow that seemed momentous, and he stared and strained to see in the dark, knowing the faint gull image lay just over his head.

As she was chuckling again over the roll of "The Loves of Aliyson," Prope heard a crash from the direction of her small pantry. She sighed, rose, took her stick, and walked down the short hall to the room. Mall, her old servant, was on his knees, cleaning up the tea from a small crock he had dropped.

"Again! The best tea, I suppose."

"No, not the best, but again I am sorry. I regret . . ."

Prope brought her stick down on his bent back with a solid whack. "Again!" she shrilled. "And again and again and again." She whacked him with each word, then grew slightly faint with the effort and grasped the doorframe, panting.

"Are you all right, Turana?"

"Leave. Leave at once. When I am going out, you may come back and clean this. And don't save that filthy tea."

"Oh, no. Of course." Mall squeezed by her, being careful not to touch her, and hobbled toward the outer door. With gritted teeth she watched his back then blew out the lamp he had left lit in the pantry, and, leaning on her stick, returned to the sitting room to look at her sand watch.

 VI

FOR the first time in some months, the whole council at Threerivers met in the Judgment Room, where Bival had last talked with her husband, Warret. The issue at hand was Brudoer, whose whipping lay two days ahead, at the end of his second cycle of punishment in the cells.

Udge opened the session by stating her position unequivocally. That is, Brudoer's public whipping was to be continued or the decision of the Protector would be compromised by opposition and the unknown terrorist, who had never been caught. However, she proposed that this time only guardsmen and family heads be present, and all access to the terraces be blocked. At the conclusion of punishment, if Brudoer expressed full contrition, he would rejoin the community.

Udge maintained a clear majority in each quadrant of this most traditional of Pelbar cities. The tight faces of the old family heads almost universally expressed support. Rigidly maintained law was a tradition at Threerivers.

Almost cursorily, the Protector asked for expressions of contrary opinions, expecting none. Unset the Ardena rose and awaited recognition. Udge stared, then sighed, and said, "The Ardena wishes to speak. I thought, after your apology, that you would no longer oppose the clear will of the council, Ardena. I suppose, though, you have the right to speak."

"I suppose so, Protector, since you did call the council, and that is the established rule of procedure. However, if you wish to contravene the rule, I shall not appeal to the laws of Craydor."

"Well, proceed."

"There are several points, Protector. First, it seems to me that the original offense has been more than punished already. The boy defended his brother, who had been cruelly hurt. Surely it was a grave thing he did, but when he saw the blood of his twin gushing he probably didn't think. He reacted. He is only a child. I believe that standard Pelbar forbearance should lead us to forgive him—on the condition that he expresses public contrition for his act and begs forgiveness of Bival.

"Second, we have seen how the males regard him as a martyr. If we hurt him further, it will only exacerbate that feeling. I sense rumblings that I have never noticed before —rumblings that sound almost like the beginnings of revolt. I'd hope that control could be maintained by some means other than force. After all, many of us are married and wish to live in peace and harmony with our families, including the males. We don't want to taunt the males with the fact of their inferiority. We depend on them, and those of us who are happily married wish to enjoy their company. Though it may seem surprising, some of us actually love them.

"Third, the terrorist who killed the guardcaptain has not been apprehended. Keeping the populace away from the act of punishment will not prevent his acting again at some other time, since revenge must be a part of his motivation.

"Fourth—well, I wish I could be more definite about it. I feel a nameless foreboding, jutting up into this council like the tip of Craydor's tomb. We are becoming a divided people, we who so depend on unity. I fear for us. The true cement of this society has always been justice, mutual regard, and love. It's now becoming force and intimidation. That will split us. No outside hostility keeps us together anymore. We've already lost the young guardsmen who took Gamwyn to Pelbarigan. Surely their dissatisfactions aren't isolated. This foreboding I have, it hangs like a fall mist over the river. Surely some of you have felt it."

"A foreboding, Ardena? I feel no such thing. I see only the clear flame of pure justice at work, burning away the impurities," said the Protector. "I might add, Ardena, that we must be safe in Craydor's eyes, since an inscription on her tomb entrance reads, 'This city will never fall until I rise out of it.' The entrance is permanently sealed, and she seems safely in place as usual." The Protector smiled wanly, scanning the room. "Are there any other comments?"

Bival rose. The Protector looked a little startled. "Protector, with your permission, I only wish to say that I deeply regret being close to the cause of all this trouble. Any anger I had toward the boy is gone, but I do wish to obey the law the Protector has invoked in my behalf. As she has pointed out to me, I erred in taking the boy for special training in mathematics and geometry when I saw what I felt was promise in him. Undoubtedly that made him familiar enough to take such shocking liberties."

As Bival talked, she stared at the triangle in the floor which had been the tip of Craydor's tomb. Was there more to that design than she had realized? She determined to think about it further.

The Protector coughed, and Bival realized that she had remained standing after she stopped talking. "You may resume your seat, Bival," said the Protector. "Now, if there are no more regrets or poetic contemplations, may we adjourn." She clapped her hands. As she rose to leave, the Ardena appeared at her side.

"I beg a favor, Protector."

"You seem to have spoken your mind, Ardena. You wish more favors?"

"Only to visit the boy in prison and inform him of your decision—in order to convince him to be contrite."

The Protector hesitated. She could see no harm in the request. "All right, Ardena. You may do that." She turned away smiling, sensing the obligation under which she placed the Ardena.

A full quarter of the day later, Brudoer, who was staring at the curious geometric patterns on the wall, sure that Craydor meant something by them, heard the grating of the door. He stood and turned, and saw, to his amazement, the Ardena entering. He did not bow as courtesy said he should have. She stiffened her back.

"Boy," she began. "Am I safe with you if the guardsman leaves?"

"You, Ardena? Of course. You did not beat me. You didn't carve my brother's face."

The Ardena gestured to the guardsman, who left, shutting the door. Both Brudoer and the Ardena glanced at the door, seeing the shadow of the guardsman by it, close enough to hear.

"You are a stiff-necked child, boy. You know your courtesy. You'd do well in your position to practice it."

"Did you come here to teach me courtesy, Ardena?"

"I don't need your irony. I came to advise you and help you, and you are making it very difficult."

"I am?" Brudoer laughed.

"You seem devoted to your dingy cell, then. Perhaps you'd not like to hear me."

"That's up to you, Ardena."

The old woman was stunned. The boy showed no anxiety or gratitude. "I'm not saying this for you, then, but for the good of the city. Further punishment is coming in two days. If you express full contrition, that will end your incarceration here."

"What good will that do the city, Ardena? Will it help the city to have sliced up a boy? What can help the city with Udge the sludge running it?"

"I see you're in no mood to listen. Then you will have to suffer your own consequences." She turned to leave, but Brudoer advanced and put his hand on her arm.

"My family. Are they all right?"

"They aren't doing marvelously, child. Your father has lost his position, and is now cutting rock. Your mother lives in seclusion. You are the one who can help them."

Brudoer leaned close to the Ardena and whispered, "I'd just as soon be put in the third cell." She drew back, startled, then glanced at the door.

"Come over to the light," she said, "and let me see your back. You will have another whipping, you know." They walked across the room to where the high window cast down a wintry gray light. "What are you talking about?" she whispered, as he removed his tunic and undergarment. She winced as she ran her hands across the scars.

"It just ought to be that way," he whispered back.

"You must tell me why."

"I ask a favor, Ardena. Please get me a copy of the inscription from the first cell—the letters that run around the room in rings and make no sense but are only letters."

"Why?"

"I need them."

"I'll get them for you if you tell me why you have to be put in the third cell."

"I just did tell you."

The Ardena pushed the boy away. "You are a rude child," she said aloud. "You refuse to communicate. Well, then, I shall leave you to your fate, and Threerivers will have to get along as well as it can."

"Please? The letters? And some paper for me? Please, Ardena?"

She looked at him and saw he was in earnest. He took her hand, his eyes brimming. She squeezed his hand and smiled, slightly. Then she called the guard, and remarked to him, "It has done no good. He will not bend, even to someone who means him only well."

"Yes, Ardena," the guard remarked. "You could only try, however."

They left Brudoer alone, and he sat down again, facing the inscriptions on the wall. Craydor does nothing for no reason, he had come to feel. No decoration is a mere decoration. Everything has some meaning.

But the remaining two days passed before Brudoer had determined anything from his study of the diagrams. He steeled himself when he heard the guardsmen coming to take him to his punishment.

The scene he saw on the lowest terrace differed startlingly from the previous one. The curving walls were ringed with guardsmen, as was every high corner. All held strung bows, with arrows nocked. The Protector stood in a covered pavilion on the second terrace, in her winter cloak, surrounded by the four quadrant counsels. As Brudoer cast his eyes across the landscape below he saw that the trees stood stark and bare. A light snow lay across the landscape.

Brudoer was brought to face the Protector from below. "I believe that the Ardena, in misplaced kindness, has informed you of the conditions of your punishment. You may now humble yourself to Bival and express your contrition. Then the lashing will end your punishment. Is that understood."

"Understood? Ridiculous things are not understandable, Craydor says, you pitiful old crow," Brudoer returned. "I'm sure there is a dead fish or two down by the water. Why don't you croak down there and eat them? And you, Bival, you snarling, wretched salamander, why—" The

Protector had raised her arm, and the guardsmen gagged Brudoer.

The Protector gestured upward with her hands. "It is clear that we can never let such hostility loose in our city again. Prepare the miscreant for punishment. Then he will be remanded to the third cell."

She sighed and rose to leave. One of the guardsmen by the wall shouted and pointed, and she turned back to see a number of boats, heavily laden, being launched into the wintry river. Men were hastily boarding and shoving off, paddling out into midstream.

"Guardchief, stop them!" the Protector shouted. The guardchief yelled and gestured, and the guardsmen on the walls poured down the stairs toward the river bank. "Shoot them. Shoot them from the walls," the Protector shouted, but the guardchief only turned, amazed.

"It's against the code, Protector. We cannot do that." Then she turned and ran through a door toward the stairs, as the Protector opened her mouth to reply.

In a matter of a sunwidth, the terraces were deserted except for the two guardsmen holding Brudoer, the Protector, her own guardsmen, and her council. One of the guardsmen remarked, "It's hard to believe that two boys could cause so much trouble." The Protector glowered at him, and he dropped his eyes.

Bival descended the stairs to the first terrace and walked to Brudoer. She looked at him sadly. He looked at the sky above her head. Reaching out, she removed his gag. "He's shivering," she said to the guardsmen. "You'd better put his tunic back on." Then she turned away, looking from the wall to see if Warret rode any of the boats now reaching midstream.

The guardsmen found the remaining boats holed, so a detachment quickly gathered winter gear and prepared to follow the boats, running on the bank. The guardchief was worried. How many guardsmen might have planned the pursuit itself as their own way to Pelbarigan? Finally she chose twelve men she thought loyal and ordered them off. Soon they jogged north along the bank, frowning and squinting into the winter glare.

VII

FAR to the south, Gamwyn stood on the slanted roof of the main building at Jaiyan's Station, sawing a large rectangular hole according to Jaiyan's directions. He paused a moment for breath and glanced at the sky, which hung raw and gray. He shivered in the cold wind then resumed his sawing. The hole was to accommodate new whistles for Jaiyan's organ. The big man had been so delighted at Gamwyn's skill with tools that he pressed the boy into immediate service.

The plan was to cut through the roof, then build an enclosure over the cut to cover the hole yet leave room for the tall whistles. The location of the new pipes demanded that two main support rafters be cut in half. But Jaiyan weighed too much to climb on the roof and do the job himself. New framing would restore the strength of the roof later. Just before completing the large cut, Gamwyn drilled a large hole in the sheathing to be removed and looped a rope through it, tossing the end down to Jamin, who waited outside on the ground.

"Be careful, Jamie," he called. "It's going to be heavy. Better snub the rope end around something. Be sure and wear your gloves."

"No worry. I hold it."

Gamwyn wasn't sure he could, but when the splintering of the last shreds of wood fiber began, the rope pulled taut, and the square of roof swung down and hung, then lowered easily and slowly inside. There seemed no limit to Jamin's strength. Looking down at the swinging roof square, Gamwyn felt the rush of warm air from inside, then the first pebbles of sleet from a new storm on his neck. He could see the upturned faces of Jaiyan and the old people inside watching the square descend. Jaiyan reached up for it and lowered it.

"It's beginning to sleet, chief," Gamwyn called down.

"I was afraid of that. That means we will have to erect

the roof extension now. Wait'll I loose this rope, and you can have Jamie tie on all the pieces."

Gamwyn studied the gray sky, cupping his hands around his eyes. It was after high sun and his arms ached from the sawing. Now he would have to build a great wart onto the roof, perhaps into the night. He ducked his head down through the hole again, studying the underside of the roof structure.

"What are you looking at?"

"I hope this will be able to hold all the new weight."

"Of course it will. We'll brace it soon enough."

Gamwyn set to work, cutting and framing, then pegging siding and eventually roofing it over. Fortunately, almost all the material had been ready cut below. Soon the sleet fell steadily, and Gamwyn had to tie himself with a rope to keep from sliding off. Jaiyan would not hear of stopping. It would waste heat and allow sleet and melt to drip in, perhaps on the organ.

As it grew dark, Gamwyn called for a lamp, and eventually two more. It was the third quarter before high night when he finished, throwing a large cloth over the new structure and tying it down. He could pull it off in the morning to recheck his workmanship in the light without ice or snow getting in the way. The roof felt spongy. Cold and wet had invaded his body, and he shivered continually. Once on the ground, he almost staggered inside, where old hands reached out to him with a blanket and a hot drink, leading him to the fire.

After his drink, when he still could not stop shivering, he went to his sleeping shed to change into dry clothing. Misque's face seemed watchful with worry. He returned to the main fire still cold. By then everyone but Misque had gone to bed. She took his hands and felt their cold, then put another cup of hot soup in them.

"I don't see how you stood it."

"That's what the chief wanted."

"Still. I don't." She turned his head in her hands, feeling his cheeks, then rubbing them.

"Your hands are soft."

"I don't have much to do. I watch Jamie mostly. There are so many people here to do everything. They seem so happy to do it."

"Are you happy?"

She looked startled. "Happy? I . . . I . . . That's an unfair question. What is it to be happy? I don't know."

"I don't know. It has something to do with having people to do things for, and knowing that they appreciate it. And to love—to love something. People, or Aven—or Atou, as Jaiyan calls him."

"That's what you want?"

"I want to be home."

"You can't go on your fool's journey, Gamwyn." He looked at her. "But maybe . . ." She took his face in her hands again, then kissed him, not a short kiss of friendship but a long, searching lover's kiss.

Gamwyn sat startled, then gave himself to it, returning it, wondering, What am I doing? I'm too young for all this. I don't want it. He felt her warm breath infusing him.

Then she sat back. "Perhaps you'd better go. In the spring. But I . . ."

Gamwyn lay back on the stone floor, and she lay next to him, cradling her head in his shoulder, her arm around him.

"You have sympathy for the helpless, don't you," he said at last.

"Yes," she said into his shoulder. "Some. I think."

Some meaning hovered in the air, slowly settling on Gamwyn. What was she, coming from the east, passing through Peshtak country unnoticed, arriving alone, to be taken in by Jaiyan as another stray?

"Why do you want to go back there—to Threerivers— when they were so awful to you?"

"Threerivers? It was not so bad before the present Protector. We were controlled, but we were all like a huge family. And everything about the city is so finely made. It is Pelbar work, not only that but Craydor's way."

"Craydor?"

"She designed Threerivers hundreds of years ago. She set a standard we still try to keep up. At Threerivers they always try to do everything well. I see a little of it with Jaiyan and his organ. He'll go to any amount of trouble for it. But the rest of this place is just a sort of shed—or a stack of sheds leaning on each other, almost like what we dry fish on."

"Things aren't good, now—in Threerivers? What's wrong?"

Gamwyn felt his natural Pelbar defenses go up. The

Pelbar seldom told others anything about themselves. The habit was a carryover from the old time of hostilities, when such silences were protection. "Oh, it'll pass. I hope. The older people, especially the women, want the world to stand still. With the election of the new Protector, all their old feelings came welling up, and they now control the city the way it was before the great peace, but still it lacks something. They don't listen. They only tell, tell, tell. That's all."

"Is it weakening, then?"

"Weakening?" Gamwyn sat up and looked at Misque. "You're a Peshtak," he whispered. Her face became hard and a momentary hatred blazed out of it. He raised his hands to his face. "Will you hurt them? You won't let them hurt Jaiyan and the others, will you?" Misque rolled away and started to stand up, but Gamwyn held her.

"Let me loose," she hissed. "They'll never believe you. You just try. You—"

Gamwyn kissed her, as she had him, holding his mouth hard against hers, asking himself, Why? Why am I doing this? This is crazy. She is a Peshtak.

Finally she wrenched her face away, gasping, "I don't understand. You don't make any sense at all."

"I won't tell anybody. Look, Misque. Jaiyan is only like a Pelbar woman to me. I'm only a tool to him. He sharpens me, uses me, and when I wear out, he'll throw me away. Look at me. I'm still cold to my bones. You saved my life on the river. I owe you. I won't tell. But you can't let them be hurt."

She sat beside him, looking distant and distracted. "None of this has turned out as it was supposed to," she said dreamily.

"Maybe that's better. But you'll have to help me go on downriver now, and that'll make sure I'll never give your secret away."

"The Tusco will hurt you or enslave you."

"It would be the same if I stayed, wouldn't it? Your people would come."

"Not if they turn north."

"To Threerivers? That'll do them no good. They could never get into Threerivers. And if they did, they'd only die. Why, Misque? Why don't you Peshtak just stay in the eastern mountains?"

"The Innaniganis and the others are driving us out."

"Why?"

"They want the coal in the mountains. And they are afraid of the disease."

"The disease—the one that rots away the face? Do you have it?"

She looked at him, startled. "I . . . I don't think so. It is too early to tell. It comes later." She began to tremble and bit her lip.

"What is it?"

"Who knows? We've always had it. Since before anyone can remember."

"Why don't you send somebody with it to Pelbarigan? We have a physician there with the knowledge of the ancients, a very old man now. But he could maybe find a cure, then all of you could be free of it."

Misque laughed lightly, almost hysterically. "Who would do that for a Peshtak?"

"A Pelbar would. They'd hope to gain your friendship and add you to the Heart River peoples. Then we could travel unhindered to the east, and trade with the eastern cities."

Misque sat silently for a long time as the fire hissed. Finally, looking down, she said, "None of this would work. Everyone has always been against us and hated us."

"You murder everybody you meet—even women and children. You are feared. In fact you're the most ferocious people anywhere."

"It's the only way to be when you have to live the way we do. It keeps the easterners away out of fear—and the Sentani."

"Maybe they don't have to be enemies."

"You don't know the Innaniganis. None of those things you say could ever work. It's just dreams. We've got to deal with realities."

Gamwyn took her hand and kissed it. She seemed so desolate. She looked down at him and held out her other hand for him to kiss. Then she looked at her hands. "Now I'll always be afraid here," she said, rising.

Gamwyn stood up, too, and they embraced. "Not of me," he said. "Don't be afraid of me. It's got to work out. It's got to." She pulled away and left the room.

In the morning the sleet continued, and Jaiyan played a long series of melodies for the old Siveri in a relaxed atmosphere. Misque stayed away from Gamwyn. Finally the big Sentani turned to Gamwyn and asked him if the Pelbar had any music.

"Oh, yes. A whole lot of it, chief."

"Whistle me a melody."

Gamwyn whistled softly Craydor's hymn of the flowers, and Jaiyan picked it out on the organ. "Can you sing it? Does it have words?"

"Yes. It has four stanzas." As Jaiyan began to play, Gamwyn sang:

> Just as the small composite flower
> in every part cooperates,
> conspires with air, agrees with shower,
> passes through several perfect states,
>
> each petal with its opposite,
> each structure functioning with all,
> so let our people interknit
> in Aven's perfect protocol.
>
> So—

The organ had stopped. Jaiyan turned. "What wretched doggerel," he said. "Don't you have anything better?"

"It doesn't sound too bad when we sing it in parts."

"Parts?"

Gamwyn walked to the organ and reached out. He had studied it when no one was around and figured out where the chords would be for some simple melodies. He played a sequence of five or six chords. "Stop! What are you doing?" Jaiyan yelled, knocking his hands away. The boy stepped back. The sudden eruption of incredible music had stunned the group.

"I think the machine may have been meant for this," Gamwyn said. "Like our choirs."

"Get away. Don't you have any work to do?"

"Yes. Yes, chief. I'll bring more wood." The whole group of watchers melted away in embarrassment, while Jaiyan sat stunned, facing his organ. It had instantly been evident that the boy was right. The organ was meant for more complex music than he'd been playing on it. But to be shown on his own creation that way nearly overcame him. His mortification grew to anger, even as he knew it all to be senseless. People stood attentively at the bellows, but finally he dismissed them and disappeared into his own sleeping shed.

Misque looked across the main hall at Gamwyn. "You shouldn't have done that," she said.

"I see. Too late now."

She turned away, too, leaving Gamwyn momentarily alone. He stood thinking for a few moments, then went for the wood barrow to feed the main fire.

At that moment the guardsmen from Threerivers were ahead of the party in the canoes. Snow was falling, and they stood around a big fire on the east bank waiting for sight of the fugitives.

"Here they come," the guardcaptain said. "It must be cold out there. Look at the ice cakes."

"Good. They deserve it, putting us through this."

The party in the canoes slowly drew nearer, though far out on the water. Several even waved. Then one pointed and shouted.

"What is that? Quiet. I can't hear. Look, they're turning."

The canoes headed directly for the shore, the men leaning into their strokes.

"I don't understand," said the guardcaptain. "String shortbows and nock." A man in the middle of the lead canoe stood with a two-arm longbow and sent an arrow out, high, far over the heads of the guardsmen and into the forest. As the guardsmen turned to watch it, the air seemed full of arrows coming at them out of the woods. Two guardsmen went down, the rest ran for the trees. More arrows came from the high ground, and a peculiar high-pitched cry. "Not Shumai," the guardcaptain called. "What, then?"

As the boats grounded, men ran down the slope shooting more arrows and yelling strangely. One man from the canoes went down, but the fugitives had six Pelbar long-bows, which only a strong man could pull, and soon long arrows flicked among the advancing men.

"There must be at least seventy," the guardcaptain shouted. "Form a perimeter. Use the trees. If they break through, draw back. Put the longbows in front." Two more Pelbar fell. The hostiles used the covering trees so skillfully that they had taken only three arrows.

"Conserve your arrows," the guardcaptain shouted. "Pick sure targets."

Another Pelbar guardsman took an arrow in the leg, grunting and writhing as he fell.

The yell went up again, and the hostiles advanced, but this time, two longbowmen found targets.

"Should we get to the boats?" one man shouted.

"Too late. We'll have to stand here."

"Good Aven, they're Peshtak," one man said. "See the skunk-fur hats?"

"Peshtak?"

The hostiles again advanced, but suddenly a series of sharp slaps, like trees breaking under ice, came from the hill behind them, and Peshtak began to fall. They turned, wavered, then advanced, hoping to gain the Pelbar canoes. A sharp fight ensued, first with bows, then short-swords, but always punctuated by the sharp slaps from the hillside. Figures could be seen advancing down the hill. Pelbar guardsmen. Some Peshtak turned toward them, caught between two forces but making no attempt to surrender, fighting now in utter silence and grim determination. The new guardsmen had strange weapons. They looked along a tube, there was a flash, and another Peshtak would drop. Finally, with a yell, the Peshtak all came in a tight body toward the boats, massing inward.

"Let them through," the guardcaptain shouted. The Pelbar ran aside, putting arrows into the hostiles when they could get a clear shot. Then the Pelbar closed in behind, and in their initial rush, the Peshtak swamped three canoes just offshore, sinking and struggling in the icy water. With silent discipline, the others formed a half-ring, backing slowly, and loosing their remaining arrows as the boats were filled with men and shoved off.

The Pelbarigan guardsmen, arriving with the new weapons, formed a broad circle around the shrinking Peshtak one, loading and firing the loud tube weapons from just outside the range of the Peshtak arrows. They called for surrender, but in reply got only a derisive gaggle of shouts full of obscenities. The Peshtak dropped like sodden rags, dwindling but fearless. Four laden canoes moved well out into the river, but then they too slowly settled as they were holed by the new weapons, the men struggling and flailing briefly among the ice chunks before going under.

Finally only three Peshtak remained standing on shore, their long knives at ready. The Pelbar slowly moved in on them, and the Pelbarigan guardcaptain stepped ahead of the perimeter.

"Throw down your weapons," she called.

"Come here and I'll unravel your insides," one of the men returned, in a sharp but understandable dialect.

The guardcaptain took two more steps forward, and suddenly two men rushed at her and were caught in a roar as all the new weapons fired at once, dropping like old fruit. One jerked slightly.

"Look for wounded," the Pelbarigan guardcaptain said, panting. "Try to keep them alive. Don't touch them before I see them." She turned to the Threerivers guardcaptain. "I'm Ahroe Westrun, guardcaptain. I'm glad we found you in time."

"I—I don't understand. How did you know?"

"Your Protector sent us a message about the, ah, the refugees. We were looking for them, but one of our wood parties was massacred, and all the signs were Peshtak. We shut up the city, then looked south, found a sign that some of them had holed up in an ancient tunnel up a side valley only about three ayas from Pelbarigan. How they found it, I don't know. It was almost wholly sealed up. We knew then we'd better try to intercept you. Only this morning we ran into the tracks of the larger band."

She turned to a man in a furred coat, the only Shumai with them, a rangy man with freckles, his blond hair pulled back in a single braid. "Blu. Are there any others?"

"I don't know. Don't think so. We'll run an arc. Don't like this. This is so many to be so far west. We ought to call back to the city."

"When you get your wind, take ten men with rifles and make your arc. All right?"

"Right. We can go now. You've got seven of them wounded, Ahroe. Two clearly have the Peshtak disease. One other is near dying."

"Good. They will do. Too bad about the canoes. We'll have to carry the wounded back."

"The diseased ones—what will you do?"

"They have to come. Royal will look at them. And Celeste."

Blu shuddered. "I hope you know what you're doing. There are several without faces—like at the burnt valley." Blu turned and began his arc with the guardsmen, walking slowly up the steep incline. They were all still tired from their run.

Ahroe watched him as the rest of the Pelbarigan guardsmen gathered wounded and dead, lopping off branches with their short-swords to use for hooks to drag the Peshtak up under the lip of rock outcrop. The Pelbar dead and wounded were brought to the shore. One guardsman carrying a long wire climbed a tree, and the astonished Threerivers Pelbar watched as the Pelbarigan guardsmen sent signals to the city and received others.

"Guardcaptain, they're sending a Tantal ship," the signalman called.

"Good. We'll wait, then."

"They say to bring all the Threerivers people."

The Threerivers guardcaptain stiffened. "I protest," guardcaptain," she said. "We are to return with these who ran away."

"We just saw them save your lives, guardcaptain. And we will not return them for the sort of punishment that Threerivers is dealing out now. They've done no wrong now that we have peace."

"Peace? You call this peace?"

Ahroe looked hard at her. "You can take it up with the Pelbarigan council," she said, turning away.

In the weeks following Gamwyn's inadvertent revelation that the organ could be played in chords, Jaiyan grew increasingly frustrated. He installed most of a new row of whistles, but Gamwyn could see he yearned to try playing several notes at once. His pride would not allow him to. The result was irritability, and hard work for Gamwyn.

One day at the beginning of the firstmonth thaw, Gamwyn had spent most of the morning gathering wood chips and blocks for the fire into rough cotton bags. The bending was tiring him. He had begun humming to himself, feeling whimsical in the warmth. One of the big, brown bags had two ragged holes in it that struck the boy as eyelike. He put it over his head. Two of the Siveri laughed and pointed. Gamwyn shucked it off, took a piece of charcoal, drew in the rest of a face, enormous, grimacing, coming to below his waist. Then he put it on again. The watching Siveri laughed again.

Feeling giddy, Gamwyn set out for the central building to surprise Misque. He stumbled in, finding her with Jamin.

Gamwyn let out a loud moan, raised his arms, shambled forward at them, and grunted. Jamin whirled and shrieked, turning white. Then he heaved his big body upward, leaped back, blundered into the great central pillar of the structure, and fell down. The pillar cracked in two, splintering, bursting suddenly with groping, winter-stiff black ants.

The roof slumped together at the center, slowly twisting, cracking at the extension. As Gamwyn looked, horrified, the roof began to sink. He yelled, running through the sheds to get the old Siveri outside. But in a long moment, the roof fell inward on the highest whistles of the organ, then sections of the palisaded walls slumped outward, and all the leaning sheds also began to go. Jaiyan, who had been turning a whistle in the farthest shed, came rushing up, shouting, "The organ. My organ. Quick, get all that wood off the organ."

"The old people," Gamwyn shouted back.

"They can all get out. Save the organ."

But all had to retreat, as the structure and all the attached sheds groaned, lurched, and slowly crumbled. Black ants were everywhere, and most of the wood was riddled with their chambers and the dirt-filled tunnels of termites.

Finally all that remained standing, with pieces of wall and roof leaning against it, was the gigantic organ and two stone chimneys. Then the weight grew too much for it, too, and the tallest ranks of whistles twisted and fell. Jaiyan let out a yell and ran into the tangle, lifting and throwing logs and boards off the organ. Soon the Siveri began to help, stacking the wood that had just been their home.

Suddenly Jaiyan stopped. He turned and called out, "Who did this?"

"I," Jamin said simply. "Gamwyn scare me. I did it."

Jaiyan's face seemed to pause, blank, and then shrivel like a baked apple. With a bellow, he ran at Gamwyn, picking up a large board. The boy staggered back, holding up his arms as the big man brought the board down on him. It disintegrated in a shower of rot, and Gamwyn turned and ran for the river as Jaiyan cast around for a more effective club, then lumbered after him.

The boy fled out onto the ice, which still reached across the water to one near island, and Jaiyan took several steps out before the sudden cracking of the ice forced him to retreat.

Gamwyn stopped far out on the ice and turned to look

back. For a long moment they simply looked at each other. Then Jaiyan yelled, "Is this what you give me for all I've done for you?" He threw the long board he'd picked up. It spun in a high arc and then fell and stuck into the rotten ice near where Gamwyn stood. The boy was crestfallen, especially as the old Siveri began to arrive at the river bank, and Misque and all looked out at him across the ice. He never said anything, but turned, and began walking southwest across the ice toward the long island. He would survive somehow. Maybe Jaiyan would see his own responsibilities eventually. As Gamwyn reached the shore of the island, now well below Jaiyan's Station, he turned again and saw two figures, one large, one small, still standing on the river bank. That would be Jamin and Misque.

Well, I've done it again, Gamwyn thought. And oddly enough, he laughed to himself, thinking that if he couldn't get Jaiyan another organ, at least he could get Bival another shell.

☐ VIII

BRUDOER lay at ease in the third cell, studying the walls, which were much more extensively covered with letters and designs than those of the first two cells. Low on the wall, a circle of oval shapes alternated with images of small river clams, which Brudoer easily recognized. Above that, a row of land snails alternated with turtles, all aiming to the right. The third band showed the four familiar shapes of a changing butterfly—egg, caterpillar, pupa, and flying insect. Above that another band depicted Threerivers itself, followed by a troubled face, followed by a miniature image of the third cell, and finally a running man.

As Brudoer studied the troubled faces, he found each one was different. They seemed to show anger, frustration, worry, pain, moody introspection; each sixth one showed the face covered by hands. Brudoer easily recognized himself in each of them. But the meanings of the whole eluded him. He also found that the four bands of letters were not in the same cipher as the ones in the previous cell.

As he studied them, the door ground and swung open, and the Ardena entered. She ordered the guard to close the door after him as he left. Brudoer stood to meet her, bowing courteously. The Ardena raised her eyebrows at that.

"It's dim in here," she said. "Come and sit below the window." Once they were seated she looked at him closely, then sighed. "Well, young one, do you know of the people who fled when you were about to be whipped?"

"Yes, Ardena."

"Five of them are dead, and four of the guardsmen who followed."

"Dead? Nine dead? How?"

"Peshtak. They encountered Peshtak and were saved by the Pelbarigan guardsmen. They killed sixty-three Peshtak with their new weapon. Three Peshtak wounded survive at Pelbarigan.

"This is amazing."

"Pelbarigan will not return the fugitives; three of the guardsmen who followed have also chosen to stay." She looked at him. "You have started something, Brudoer. It may spell the end of Threerivers. Only you can stop it now."

"Me, Ardena? What about the Protector?"

"She will not. Her party is strengthened because all who left disagreed with her. You must see that."

"But if the Protector herself will not stop the destruction of the city, how can you expect a boy to?"

"If the boy is wiser than the Protector, he might." Brudoer looked at the door. "Don't worry," the Ardena added. "My nephew is guard."

"Did you bring the letters from the first cell for me?" The Ardena reached into her sleeve and withdrew a paper, then sat as Brudoer unfolded the paper and frowned, studying the letters.

Finally she said, "I assume that you will have time to do that after I leave. I wish I understood you."

"If I tell you what I see in these walls so far, what would you do?"

"Do? What would you have me to do?"

"Nothing."

"Then I will do nothing."

Brudoer looked at her. "The rows of pictures have a pattern," he said. "So far this is what I have seen. At the bottom are eggs and clams. Both of them are shells. Bival was right, you know, about the importance of shells. Above them are snails and turtles. These are creatures with shells, too, but they carry their shells. They can move. Next are the changes of a butterfly, which we all learn about. The first stage is also an egg, and then the caterpillar comes. Then in the cocoon the butterfly is in another sort of egg. Finally it emerges into a butterfly. That's the first really free creature so far. It flies.

"The row above it I'm not sure of, but I think it repeats the pattern of the one below. Threerivers is the egg. Like those on the bottom row, it cannot move. Then comes the troubled face. I see my own in it. But it could be anyone put in these cells. Then comes the cell itself, which is like the cocoon stage of the butterfly. Finally the man runs free like the butterfly."

The Ardena stared at the wall, at first humoring the boy, then seeing ramifications in what he said that he never could have seen. She started, rose, went to the wall and reached out to it, touching some of the figures. At last she asked, "How do you know you have read the top row in the right order? Perhaps Threerivers comes last."

"No, Ardena. See the small dot in the lower right of the butterfly? It's also on the blocks with the running man. I think that is a period. We know that the butterfly has to be in that same order, so I think that Craydor is telling us that I have to become free of Threerivers."

The Ardena slumped back down. "The letters, then. I suppose they say something as well."

"They did in the last cell. I haven't been able to work it out here. There they said, 'The purpose of this shell too is to enhance life. Therefore, be enhanced.' I haven't really come to understand that yet."

The Ardena sat as if stunned, her eyes glancing across the walls of the cell. "Brudoer, do you know what the Protector has in mind now? She means for Pion, your own father, to take the whipping for you. You'll just have to apologize, then, to be released."

Brudoer jumped to his feet. "Father? My whipping? No. She can't condemn an innocent person. Let her do it to me, not him. Damn her, the pile of old fish entrails. What can be done?"

"If you apologize before your father is beaten, then she assures me that the strokes will be very light."

Brudoer seemed to lose all his stiffness. "I must not be taken from these cells," he said.

"Then your father will be beaten."

"I cannot allow that." He looked up at her. "He's my father," he said, simply. "Maybe she's won after all, then." Brudoer began to cry, covering his face with his hands. The Ardena put her hands on his shoulders.

"Think it over, then. When I came down here I was sure what you should do. Now I'm not so sure," she said, looking around the room. "Brudoer, you're not to tell me what these letters mean, if you learn it. I'm grateful for your confidence, but this is your own job, not mine."

"Tell my father everything, then, and ask him what to do. Please?"

The Ardena kissed the boy's forehead and walked to the door, rapping on the barred window with her ring. As she slipped through the doorway, she waved at the boy, who waved back.

Brudoer returned to the letter code from the first cell and solved it easily. It was simple and innocuous, merely repeating the beliefs of Craydor as learned by all first-year schoolchildren. Why had Cradyor designed it that way? He could only speculate, but it seemed, after he thought of it, to fit her pattern. If a prisoner in the first cell solved it, he would feel it had been put there only in a kindly attempt to amuse and instruct him. If he were then put into the next cell, against traditional and lawful Pelbar rule, he would be prepared to work on that code by knowing of the first. It hadn't worked that way for Brudoer, but he'd had to calm down and begin to reason again before patterns began to open to him. He thought it odd that Bival's instruction was paying off now in a way she had never imagined it would. It seemed a supreme irony, somehow.

As night settled on the west bank of the Heart, over a half-ayas downriver from Jaiyan's Station, Gamwyn built a fire, using a trick the old Siveri, Odsem, had taught him. All he needed was his folding knife for whittling and a tunic lace to make a bowstring. The rest he had taken from the dry underside of a dead tree. He felt proud of himself. In the morning he would start south after a fish breakfast. He was confident of finding fish in his new weirs because

he had tended Jaiyan's with good success. Well after dark
he heard a slight sound toward the river, and, getting up,
he found Misque with a bundle.

"Misque? Will he find out? What's he doing? How is
everyone staying warm?"

"They've built shelters of the boards. They'll be all right.
Here. Don't worry about him. He half expected me to
come here."

"He won't hurt you?"

"No. He knows that you didn't put all the rot in his
house. He's still angry, but he can see through it now. He
is angry with the organ now. He knows he neglected everything for it."

"I'm sorry. I wish he could build it at Threerivers, in-
doors there. It would be a great contribution."

Misque laughed, bitterly it seemed to Gamwyn, then
handed him the bundle and turned to go. He took her arm.
"Can't we kiss good-bye?"

"No, Gamwyn. Let me alone." She turned to go. Gamwyn simply stood, watching her as she slid her feet out
onto the wet ice. She stopped and turned, then came back
and put her arms around him, holding him tight against
her. "I wish . . . I wish . . ."

"When I come back, where will you be?"

"Come back? Will you, then? Do you think you really
can? If you do, I'll be on the far side of a lot of awfulness."
She pushed him away and left, walking out into the darkness.

"Take care," he called out after her.

Brudoer wiped the sweat from his face after his exer-
cises. He was in a quandary. He had less than two weeks to
work it out now, and he hadn't even decoded the message
on the wall. Perhaps Udge would win. He looked again at
the wall, again used the paper the Ardena had given him.
The letters formed three groups, separated by stars:

TM. TOTIWPCMAEHFIHSHLVADELRWDOEOOEYTEIVIMOSES. EIS-
TPNLDINI * HIUTLAHSHOSEUSTNHTLOYNFLCDOGN.SMRTDRM-
EHULEHAHGNMODGMLW * EHRNELIIHDSRTISEEE.MLBAOIEO-
PN,SAAOHNISRFSLLSRTEIYENAL *

He worked at it once again. He realized already that this
was a much more difficult cipher than those he had already
deciphered. No clues flashed into his vision this time.
However, after many trials he noticed that the first letter of

each group formed THE. Was that a start? After all, there was another THE in the last group. He tried the next three. MIH. Perhaps it was an accident. What then if Craydor was working this cipher from both ends, as she had the last one? Brudoer decided at last to assume that. This would mean that every other letter in each group would be every third letter in the message, though he would have eventually to work from both ends to get it all.

He worked much of the day, the letters blurring before his eyes again and again. At times he forgot what he was doing and had to start all over again. But at last what came out of the letters read; THE TURTLE WHICH HAS SHUT ITS SHELL MAY BE FORCED OPEN. SO MAY THE RIVER MUSSELS. A RIGHTMINDED MAN WILLINGLY OPENS THE SHELL OF HIS MIND TO REASON, GOODWILL AND LOVE. THEN HIS FREEDOM IS PLAIN TO HIM.

Brudoer's heart sank. All that work and worry, and it seemed to mean nothing. But perhaps this too was Craydor's challenge. He was being tested by the difficulty of the cipher; she didn't want anyone merely good at ciphers to understand her. He had to look further. But as the days passed, nothing came to him. At last he walked slowly around the room examining the reliefs of the turtles and shells, testing each with his fingers. He felt nothing.

Several more days passed, and he sank into a desperate, almost frantic state. He knew he had to calm himself. Something ought to be plain. After his meal one late afternoon, he walked around the room again, tapping at the reliefs with his spoon. One turtle rang differently. He tapped again, carefully. Yes, he was sure of it. Carefully he worked the handle of the spoon around the stone, but it seemed tightly in place. He continued over a quarter period from sundown to high night, but it was no use. It was a typical, mortarless Pelbar joint.

He gave up, then lay back in his bed musing. After high night, when his lamp was removed, he recalled the message once more. ITS SHELL MAY BE FORCED OPEN. Perhaps it was not the whole stone, but only the shell. He had seen nothing. He groped toward the wall in the pitch blackness, but, unable to find the right stone, he gave up until morning.

When the daylight filtered down through the thin window of his cell, he again went to the stone, and with care hooked the handle of the spoon here and there into the shell of the turtle. Working around the edge of the plastron, he felt a slight grating, and at last the fitted piece worked its way loose and came out in his hand. Within the stone lay a large metal box with a hinged lid. Brudoer reached in and took it out. Beneath the box lay a small roll of the seven essays of Craydor, which he had been taught as a child. It was crisp and its edges were crumbling, but he found he could unroll it enough to read it.

But his immediate attention went to the metal box. It, too, was shell-shaped. The curved lid was plain and dull on top, but the edges were finely decorated with a motif of turtle and mussel shells. The sides of the box curved down and around to complete the strange shell shape, which Brudoer recognized as that of the Protector's Broad Tower again—the same as Bival's shell, which he had helped to break. Strange feelings blew through him, but in his eagerness to study the box, he stifled them. It seemed reasonable that he could open it as he had the wall box, so he put his thumbnail under one of the turtle shells and lifted. Nothing gave. He continued around. As he tested the third turtle, the lid lifted.

Inside lay a gold bracelet of incredible beauty, decorated with the motifs of the cell, turtle and mussel shells, the stages of the developing butterfly, and the running man. Brudoer lifted it from the box. A note written on thick parchment fluttered out with it. Brudoer took it over below the window and smoothed it out. In faint, brown ink was written:

This bracelet is for him who has been in all of the first three cells for a full term of punishment. Read the inscription inside it, put it on and do not remove it. You will know how to put it on. May it bless you in your quest for freedom. Plainly you have suffered by now. Likely you will continue to suffer. Please replace this note in the stone. Give the box as a gift, unopened. Do not tell its secret. Do not tell the secret of the stone unless forced. You are learning what I had to learn. Design is not complete unless it includes all within its scope. There is no healthy body if the eye, the hand, the liver, the stomach are denied. All the parts must be cared for. Take my love with you and remember that you will have to bear up under many things. Remember too that you have only begun to learn. Continue.

Craydor, Founder of Threerivers

Brudoer held the note a long time, trying to memorize it. Then he knew it was nearly time for the guardsmen to bring his water for washing. He put the note back into the stone, replacing the turtle and hiding the box and bracelet in his bedding.

Almost immediately, the door bolt ground back and the massive door swung open. Three guardsmen entered with warm water, soap, and towels. As usual, they stood silently as he washed himself and poured the water down the drain. But as he handed back the bucket and basin, one said, "Haven't you caused enough trouble? You would do well to apologize to Bival and stop this viciousness."

Brudoer looked at him. "I still have to bear up under many things," he said enigmatically.

"You little snot. You will apologize or it won't go well with you. Or your father. We have the beating of him. We can manage it so he will feel it cut to his ribs. Don't forget that."

Brudoer blanched. "This isn't Craydor's way," he said.

"Nor Craydor's time. We've lost guardsmen because of you. The city is in turmoil. It's going to stop in two days. Is that understood?"

The door, which had stood ajar all the time, moved slightly, and the Ardena and Warret entered. The guardsmen started and the one shouted, "Out. This is guardsmen's work. You were not given permission. Out now."

"Yes, we will leave for now," said the Ardena. "Nevertheless, we heard."

The guardsman smiled grimly. "You did? And where is your sword?"

The Ardena said nothing, but turned and left.

Again the guardsman turned to Brudoer. "You see? The trouble continues. Remember what I said. Remember if you have any regard for your father." They turned and left, slamming the heavy door behind them.

Brudoer sank down and found himself sweating. The thin shaft of sun moved slowly across the stones of the room, but he barely moved. Finally he stirred himself and went to his bed, uncovering the bracelet. In the sunlight he looked at it and read the inscription inside, which said,

"This bracelet is the gift of Craydor to someone who has been in all of the first three cells for a full term of punishment—proof of his misuse by authority. It is for no one else. The rich and powerful will seek to have it, but if they gain it from him, it will be by force and injustice alone. Craydor, Founder of Threerivers."

It was too small a bracelet to slip over the hand, but Brudoer again put his nail under one of the small turtles on the design and snapped it open, slipping it on and shutting it. It was impossible to see how it fastened. It might have been forged on his wrist. He would have to hide it, he thought, when they took him from his cell. But then he remembered the note. Craydor had commanded that it be put on and not taken off. Well, that was fine for her, but Brudoer knew it would cause him endless trouble.

But then the bracelet had its inscription. It was his. Brudoer could see that Craydor had something in mind. He would keep it and wear it. But what about his father? The boy again sank into thought, wondering what would ever happen to them.

As he mused over this, the guardsman reported to Udge in the Broad Tower. "He seems as unrepentant as ever, Protector."

"You did mention again what would happen to his father."

"Yes, Protector. He recoiled at that. But then he said, 'I still have to bear up under many things.' The little snot."

"He said that?" Bival interposed.

"Yes, Southcounsel."

"It's from Craydor's fourth essay."

"Enough, Bival. Yes, yes—the one about what would happen to Threerivers if we ever stop respecting one another. I've heard far too much about Craydor lately. I assume the boy learned that in his schooling, as all do."

"It makes me uneasy."

"You needn't be. You have your responsibility in this, but the trouble was surely present before you lost your precious shell." Udge turned to the guardsman and dismissed him. He bowed and left. Again the Protector turned to her four quadrant counsels and her crony, Dardan.

"This next few days may well be the ultimate crisis for the foreseeable future. I have sifted the guard and determined the absolutely faithful ones. There is rebellion abroad. This city will operate only when the supremacy of the Protector is unquestioned. It is like a beehive and will swarm if a new queen is bred in it. We have already had some swarming, but it has served to bleed off the drones. Perhaps a few more will go, but we cannot afford a large exodus. The boy's father will not budge. I would welcome the chance to cow him with a good beating. The boy is as stiff, and an apology from him may serve as well.

"But we don't want a reconciliation at this point. We need to stifle the opposition, to overwhelm them. I know I have the support of the family heads. Too many have suffered through this crisis. They can see a rebellion and know how to deal with it."

"But Protector," Bival said, "Craydor herself said that reconciliation is the best—"

"I don't need to be told what Craydor said, Bival. If you should ever become Protector, you will understand that Craydor is all right in her place. When you have opposition, you find some statement of the founder that will support you. Then you honey it all over the opposition and go on with business. *That* is the chief use of Craydor at this point. You have to remember that she herself said that no generation can rest on the genius of the former ones. Each must rely on its own, because no generation is stronger than those who are in it. Craydor is fine, and undoubtedly she was a genius herself, but *we* must progress. She isn't around to direct us. Now. The guard is doubled. All are standing double watch and will continue to until well after the punishment. I have heard of murmurings among the fuel-bearers, the mushroom-culture workers, the water-lifters, and even the beekeepers. But they are only workers and it is only talk.

"We will keep it there, and stifle even that. This city has always operated well because there was no crack in it, no chink for a mouse to get in or heat to escape. We'll see that it continues. Prepare your quadrants. We have only two days now. You may go."

After the counsels filed out, Udge called for more tea and sat brooding. She was less satisfied with Bival than ever. Though the Southcounsel had started the trouble, she was not working in unison with the Protector. Udge saw the woman would have to be replaced. She would ask Dardan to move into the south quadrant immediately so that she'd be an established resident in time for the next election.

For her part, Bival went to the fourth essay of Craydor again, and read the passage Brudoer had quoted and the surrounding material. The goodwill and wisdom of the founder began to flood her spirit, and she saw increasingly the abomination of the present situation. Things were intolerable. She would try to see the boy. She left her room and descended the long winding stairs to the base of the city, stopping to get the Ardena's nephew, Arlin, to accompany her. As she entered the anteroom of the ice caves, she came upon a small meeting of men seated on the floor, playing dice, each with a small lamp. She paused. They looked at her silently. Warret was one of them.

"Warret," she began.

"Later. I am in the middle of a game."

"I'll wait."

The men looked at him. He stood and dusted himself. "Well?"

"Come with me. Only a few sunwidths. I wish to see the boy for a moment. But I wish to talk with you first."

Hostility hung in the air like the smoke of wet leaves. Warret gestured to the men, then walked aside with her, out under the arches that led to the row of cells.

"This has gone too far, Warret. It is out of hand. I need no apology. I want to draw the city together again. I—"

"You picked a strange way to do it."

"I was wrong. I know it. I know I have a temper. But now I see that all along Udge has seized every advantage in the hope of gaining complete control over the city. It's only in theory, though. She doesn't know how false she is. She believes herself right. Can you keep them from an open break? We must. We owe it to all the history of the city."

Warret said nothing. She reached out to him. "Come with me to see the boy," she said. "I can go. I can bring you. I have the right by law."

"It will change nothing. As you say, it has gone too far. If they take Pion, people will die."

"Die? You mean that they will fight the guardsmen?"

"No. Just that they will die."

"Will you come up with me again?"

"What for?"

"It's time for reconciliation."

"Only when things are set right."

"May this not help?"

"I doubt it, but I will come see Brudoer with you."

* * *

Brudoer was so engrossed in the roll of Craydor that he did not at first hear the voices at his door, or the clang of its opening. But as Warret and Bival entered, he stood, still holding the scroll in both hands. When he saw Bival, he drew back. Arlin carried a chair for her, which he set down opposite the boy. The Southcounsel sat down and composed herself.

"Brudoer, the whole city is in great tension. Will you not apologize to me? For the sake of Threerivers? In public? I no longer care about apologies myself. It's for the city. I beg it of you. I am unsure of what will happen if you don't."

"No."

"But why? Are you so arrogant?"

The boy hesitated. "No. Maybe. I don't know. It's my mission now."

"Your mission? Who gave you a mission?"

Brudoer longed to say, "Craydor. Craydor herself gave it to me." But he said nothing. Finally, he held up the roll. "I've been reading the essay on government. I think that Craydor says that you cannot whip my father instead of me. Here: 'Punishment must in every case fit the fault. If it is to be inexact, it must be merciful, not harsh. Harshness simply breeds opposition. Every care must be taken to identify the criminal and not to punish the innocent, for no society which punishes recklessly will be able to maintain the internal cohesion that it must have to survive.'"

"We all know that passage, boy. It has been determined by the Protector that your father is responsible for your rebellion. He raised you. He has not helped. He also has a rebellious nature."

"Then if you agree with that, I have no more to say to you. Do what you want to. I can take it, any of it."

Bival stood, her fury rising in her again. Warret put his hand on her shoulder. "Bival is seeking reconciliation, Brudoer. You're not helping her."

"You would say that? You, whom she has also wronged? You heard what the guardsman said. What of that? Don't you see we are under a tyranny—a fist with a club calls itself a government?"

"You are a child. I am afraid myself of what's happening. We can't let the whole city fall apart. If they won't pull back, maybe we have to."

Brudoer sank down, feeling a sudden despair. "No one

will obey any of the laws. It's all here. I've been reading it. What's happened? Nothing is the way Craydor said it should be."

Bival thought to say, "Craydor is an idealist, but we have to do what must be done," then as the thought took her, she realized that was Udge's view. Instead she went to Brudoer and took the roll from his hand, gently, seeing it was old, and sat back down to read the essay. They were the words of an idealist, but a very canny one, and it seemed to proceed so limpidly, so reasonably, that reading it calmed her. "Underlying all government must be a mutual regard by each element of society for every other element," Craydor's words read. She came to a familiar passage: "Just as the body staunches its own wounds through properties in the blood, so the society . . ." She stopped. The word "properties" was interlineated. Below it, crossed out, was "elements." Bival uttered a light cry and stood up."

"What?"

"This is in Craydor's own hand. It's Craydor's copy. Look." She held it out to Warret, who studied it. "Where did you get it? Did someone actually take the original copy from the library vaults for you? Steal it?"

"No. Nobody stole it. It's mine." He said it so quietly that she paused. "However," he added, "I suppose you'll take it from me. I'll not be seen as worthy of what has been given me. Right? It must be someone else's. Perhaps so. I have a present for you. I owe it to you, I think. It's not an apology—just a restitution. You may have it if you leave me my roll. Is that agreed?"

"This is precious. It will be destroyed here. You can always have a copy of it, just by asking the guard. I'll see that you do."

"Then you will not leave me my property?"

"Such treasures belong to the city, boy. You must know that the real point of the essays is the ideas."

"If you thought that," Warret said, "you would let the boy have his roll. Come. Take it from him and give him a copy. Let him keep his present. After all, he's only a male, isn't he. You've learned nothing after all, have you."

Bival's anger blazed up. To leave a precious manuscript in prison with a boy was insane. Then she sagged back into the chair. What did it matter? She saw Warret's logic and his point. "Keep it. And keep your present."

"You don't mind, then, if I give the present to Warret? It is really owed him more than you."

"Do as you please with it. This was to no purpose. I will go. Warret, come."

Awaiting Brudoer's gift, Warret didn't move. Brudoer took it from his bedding, brought it over, and placed it in the man's worn hands. "It is mine to give to whomsoever I wish," the boy said. Warret looked at it and uttered a low murmur.

In the flickering light of the lamp, the dull metal form of the Broad Tower shell and its precisely wrought frieze took Warret's eye with its beauty. "Where—" he began, then checked himself. "Thank you. It's beautiful. I've never had anything so beautiful."

"It's for you because you accepted it. I believe Craydor held it in her own hands."

At that, Bival turned and looked, then cried out and ran to it, taking it from Warret's hands. Again it was the shell, mocking her. "My shell," she murmured.

"Your shell?"

"This is important. Don't you see? Look. It—" She turned to see the two staring at her. "I— Will you let me study it, Warret? It will be yours. I only want . . ." Again she felt the surge of anger in her—and a sudden desire to smash the box. The other two saw this, but neither moved. Then she handed it back to Warret. She sat down. "I don't understand. Why am I always to be thwarted?"

"Thwarted? It was offered to you, and you refused it with anger. You'll be able to look at it anytime you want to. You're beginning to understand that others also preserve some inherent rights, even though you rule."

"Rule? All I have ever done is serve the city."

"And gain the credit. Many have served and gained nothing."

"Here," said Brudoer, holding out the roll. "You may have Craydor's writing. Please give me a copy."

"No. You— Well, I will put it in the library. I will bring a copy. Yes."

"You may have it if you will keep it."

Bival looked at him, then took it. "This changes nothing, though," Brudoer added. "I will not apologize. However, I would like to ask you a favor."

"You will not apologize but you wish a favor? Boy, I am

more bewildered by the moment. Everything is on its head."

"I am only a boy, Southcounsel, but I have had time to think. I think things ought to be on their heads. I'll tell you my favor, and you may help grant it as you see fit." Brudoer then hesitated, but added, "No, I won't ask it. Things will have to work out as they will." As he had been going to ask Bival to be sure he was put into the fourth cell, he had been unable to. He knew he had manipulated the council and Protector to get himself moved, but that depended only on their severe response, their willingness to punish a boy for words, and words that were no doubt provoked by undue severity.

He longed to tell somebody of what he had learned so far, but he knew he should not. The city may have it within itself to heal its own spirit, and he should not interfere.

They palmed good-bye, in a wholly different atmosphere, and the couple left. Arlin shut the door and fastened the long bolt, saluted the door guard, and left.

Warret and Bival found the men still sitting in a circle, awaiting Warret's return. "Look. See what Brudoer gave me." Warret held out the shell. Bival winced as it went around the circle, held tenderly by the workmen's rough hands.

"I cleaned that room," one man said. "These things are what are on the walls. It must have been in there all the time. I saw them when I scrubbed the walls for the boy's coming." Bival started. She had never explored the cells, as so few ever went there. She reached for the shell and took it, turning it over and over, and wondered. Then she handed it back.

"These patterns also are found around the walls of the Protector's private inner room," she said. "I've cleaned that room, as only counsels are privileged to do. But they are there." The men fell silent, staring, awkward. Somehow they all saw that Craydor had connected the Protector and the prison in her mind.

"He gave me this roll of Craydor," she said to them. "Craydor wrote it herself in her own handwriting." A man reached for it. She hesitated, then gave it to him. He looked at it, holding it close to his lamp, then passed it around. Each man took it gently, then passed it on. Finally it returned to her.

"Well, Southcounsel. What's going to happen now?" an old man asked.

"I don't know. I don't know. Whatever, I fear it. Warret, will you come with me?"

"Not now. When this is all over."

"Take care of the shell box."

"I will. Ason, will you accompany my wife back to her room?" A hulking young stoneworker stood and walked to Bival, and the group watched them ascend the winding stairway.

"What good will it do, Warret?"

"For the city? Little, I think. Our source tells us Udge means to replace Bival anyway. But for me? I think some good will come of it." Warret smiled slightly, then added, "After this is all over, perhaps."

In her room, Bival found the Ardena waiting for her. At first they eyed each other coldly, but Bival held out the roll of Craydor to her visitor. "The boy, Brudoer, gave it to me. Look at it. It's in Craydor's own hand."

The Ardena started, then looked at it closely under the lamp. At last she put it down. "So he has been reconciled to you. He has apologized then? This is all going to end?"

"No. He didn't apologize. He said he would refuse to. I need no apology now. This has cut too deeply. Even if I lose my place, I don't care anymore. I am afraid for the whole city."

"I've also been to see the boy, Bival."

"So I've heard."

"Yes, the Protector has her spies. I think you must insist that the boy take his own lashing, and that his father not be lashed in his stead."

Bival whitened. "The boy? You want the boy to be lashed? I—"

"It's like this. As I sense it, the men are outraged by any lashing, but far more at the lashing of Pion, because, after all, he has done nothing. The boy did attack you. And he has insulted the Protector. He can be given three more lashes and the rest put off for the sake of humanity. If I know Udge, she will simply continue his incarceration. She wants to crush him utterly. Brudoer can bear a few lashes at a time, but the Protector must not be allowed to hurt him too deeply. Besides, if he is to be released, we must give the Protector time to do it through forbearance, not complete victory. The atmosphere of the city depends on her learning this, if she is to learn it."

"But the lashing."

"How much worse to lash Pion. I feel you must call a council meeting for tomorrow. Insist. Craydor was explicit on not punishing the innocent."

Bival thought a long time. "I know the men are planning something. If I do this, what will happen?"

"I have no control over them. But I can talk to them. I will ask them to forgo violence. I will tell them it is Brudoer's wish."

"Then?"

"I don't know."

"I will tell you this. The remaining guardsmen are generally loyal to Udge. She is anticipating trouble. She will not spare the citizens if they begin any trouble."

"All right. We surmised as much." They embraced briefly and parted, both somewhat bewildered.

Far in the north quadrant, three women were having a late tea.

"Ossi," said the hostess, "it seems clear that we must back the Protector, extreme as she may seem to you. She is our only hope of reestablishing the old order. All of this change!"

"I didn't want to see it in my lifetime. Before the peace . . . well, things seldom went so distressingly awry."

"Quite," Finge said. "This tea is bitter."

"Yes. I agree." The hostess, Prope, rang a small bell, and an ancient, bent man slowly came from the anteroom. "The tea, Mall. It's bitter." The old man bowed, remaining silent, looking at them stupidly. "Well, Mall. Make new. You must have hot water."

"No. No hot water."

Prope shook her head. "You may prepare some then."

He bowed slightly and turned, saying, "I shall put more honey in it this time." He left, rubbing his knobbed knuckles.

"I recall," Finge said, "the old midwinter festivals, with the choir, the rows of shining heads, the best purple tunics, the lacework, even the workmen scrubbed and agreeable. Everything has sadly faded away."

"But we must stand by the Protector. That has always

saved us. Udge may be somewhat new, but she has had full training. I have confidence in her."

"Quite. Where is the tea?"

At the first quarter of the morning, the Southcounsel called the full council meeting, as was her right. Udge objected stiffly, but knew the right was a check in the law against supreme power, and she had not yet been successful in removing or circumventing it. She convened the council with her guardsmen thumping for silence.

"We have been called into session by the Southcounsel," she began. "It is the opinion of Bival that the boy, Brudoer, should take his own punishment, rather than our bestowing it on the sturdier body of his father, who undoubtedly is largely responsible for the boy's aberrations due to the child's deficient upbringing. But first, to keep proportion and decorum, I will call for two sunwidths of silence and prayer for citizen Prope, who suddenly died in her sleep last night, without known cause. Prope is well known to you all as the retired head of ceramic manufacture and wax products. She was found as if asleep this morning by her servant, Mall. We will hold a memorial service for her this evening."

A general murmur arose from most of the council, who had not heard. Bival was irked because Udge was diverting attention from the matter at hand. What did she hope to gain from such tactics?

At last the sunclock announced that the time for silence had passed, and Udge asked Bival to speak. She rose, viewing the council, who sat on three sides of the hall, with their hair in two tiers, save the quadrant counsels, who bound it up in three. She saw impassive, quizzical faces, somewhat withdrawn and disturbed by her.

She dropped her eyes, beginning, "Members of the council, I realize that I am the unwitting cause of our present troubles, though I believe that they have had a somewhat wider and older origin. I have thought over the decision to punish Pion in place of the boy tomorrow. I have concluded that this is a mistake, even though it has had the highest origins, both in wisdom and desire for harmony. The desire has been to give the punishment to a body more able to bear the lash. The reasoning is that Pion, being the boy's father, is certainly the cause of his attitudes. He is known himself to be a person of unwavering tendencies and not one to maintain strict proprieties.

"However, in the present state of tension among the workers, I believe they would take this as an injustice. They know and have heard Brudoer's vile tongue. They cannot defend it. They can hardly oppose his punishment. If the lash is too severe for him, I recommend that only three of his six remaining lashes be administered, and that, as before, he be allowed to proceed to the next—the fourth —cell, as Udge has decided to be proper, until his healing progresses enough to allow him to take the rest. Those could, of course, be commuted if the boy is genuinely repentant. Otherwise, I hardly see how we can release such a mad creature into the freedom of our city again."

"Are you attempting to draw out his punishment, then, out of fear for yourself, Bival?" the Protector asked.

"No. I had not thought of that, Protector, though I can see that you might reasonably suppose it. There is another side to the issue. Craydor has expressly written, 'While punishment must be merciful, it must also be immediate and exact. Waywardness in punishment will never produce a sound city.' She also writes, 'Every care must be taken to identify the criminal and not to punish the innocent, for no society which punishes recklessly will be able to maintain the internal cohesion that it must have to survive. If the right hand stabs the left with a knife, then it does not have the use of that hand.' While the Protector has determined that Pion is the real cause of Brudoer's guilt, and I do not want to gainsay that, still it may easily be seen that the working population itself will not view the matter in that light. It's a matter too subtle for them. I fear rebellion. Already the men gather in small knots, and stand aside when we approach. I feel we must not be overly soft, but we ought to be merciful as well."

Bival looked around at faces either reserved or wondering, occasionally hostile. Then she bowed to the Protector and sat down. Udge looked at the full council with a slow swing of her head. "Is there any commentary?"

The Ardena rose and said, "Protector, for once I find myself in agreement with the Southcounsel. I have only one contention. Several days ago I was in the base level of the city, and seeing the door to the third cell open, I investigated. I overheard some of the guardsmen threatening Brudoer with severe harm to his father and perhaps himself if he didn't comply. I believe the guardsmen must be kept in line and instructed to use moderation."

Udge raised her eyebrows. So the Ardena agreed to the just punishment of Brudoer. What did that mean? Was she part of an active opposition? Udge felt uneasy. What the Ardena supported probably ought to be opposed. But perhaps she had won, after all. It was not a bad plan, then, to have proposed the punishment of Pion. Perhaps all would draw together behind the proper rule of law. And if Brudoer remained recalcitrant, beyond the whippings, he could be excluded as an incorrigible. Surely that was reasonable. Or she could keep him on in the cells.

"Agreed," said Udge. "It shall be as Bival requests unless I hear any further objections." Udge was greeted with silence. The Protector's guardsmen rapped to signal the end of the meeting. Udge rose and retired through the Protector's door. Several of the council noted that Finge did not rise. One nudged her. The old woman slumped over, and was sustained by her neighbors.

"I . . . I . . ." she murmured. Guardsmen were summoned to take her to the infirmary.

That night, Bival sent Arlin for Warret and met him in the darkened Judgment Room. He entered on the guardsman's arm, unwillingly, and stood opposite his wife. "So you did it. All that talk of goodwill, and what you did was to arrange to have the boy whipped. You and Udge. And you made it look like mercy."

"Trust me, Warret."

"Trust you? You've played me for a fool. You know what you are. An unkept promise. Like all women."

Bival turned away, almost thought to leave, then said, "Perhaps you saw a promise in your own mind, one that was never really made."

Warret laughed bitterly. "It's the same in the end. To me. It's a story told by an old servant maundering on. Wind howling in the towers, inarticulate except for its threat. That's what you are to me."

Bival put her hands to her face, then dropped them. "The Ardena . . . agrees with me, I think. It is the best for the boy. I don't see any other way. You must believe me."

"The Ardena? Even she has betrayed us. She found out we meant to defend Pion."

"You did? You agreed to that?"

"Of course. I don't plan to be led around by the nose anymore."

"This is sedition."

"Sedition against injustice is perhaps just."

"Perhaps. Warret, I see you have gone too far. Listen. Please listen. If anything comes of this punishment tomorrow, it will be bloody. The guardsmen are ready. Please. Do not resist. If you plan to do anything, just wait a few days. If you're going to leave, do it then. Udge will think she has won. She can't watch everyone all the time. No one will be hurt then—if you plan it right."

"So that's your strategy. Get us to wait, then when we prepare, you'll be waiting for us, and you'll have had your little party with the lash. No distractions."

"No. No strategy. I know you'll do nothing for me anymore. I've given that up. Please go to the Ardena. I'm sure Arlin will take you there. Ask her. Tell her what I said. If you're going to leave, just wait three days or so. Please."

"Leave? You want me to leave? What do you have in mind?"

"Nothing. I don't stand to gain in any way. You must see that. Isn't it obvious? By calling the council meeting this morning I know I have alienated Udge. I expect to be replaced soon enough. I may leave myself. There's nothing here now. Is there? Threerivers is empty—a body full of sickness, feeding on itself."

Warret looked at her. Was she sincere? What was she up to? "I'll talk to the Ardena," he said and turned to leave. Bival motioned to Arlin, who accompanied him.

In the morning, Brudoer heard the cell door open. It was the guardsmen ready for him. He made no attempt to resist, but simply mounted the broad stairway in the middle of the body of guardsmen, watched by faces at each landing. As before, he emerged onto the terrace. It was still winter, but he could see the channel clear in the river far below, though the banks were still bound with ice. As they brought the boy out onto the terrace, an eagle, cruising the bluffs, floated overhead, then veered aside and glided well out over the river. Brudoer watched it, saw it mount on a gust, teetering, mastering the air, free and alone, until he was roughly jerked around to face the Protector above.

"You will have time enough to watch birds when you

have apologized and received your punishment, boy. Now, have you an apology for Bival?"

"I need no apology, Protector," Bival blurted out. "I wish all this to end."

Udge glared at her. "I understand your concern, South-counsel," she said benignly. "However, we are dealing with a matter of law and justice here, and with a very difficult person. We cannot let him loose among us unreconciled to our ways. Now, boy. What do you say?"

Brudoer laughed. "I say you are the remnants of old vomit, occupied only by maggots. You mistake your or-dure for ideas. Your breath is a pile of fish entrails. The vile ugliness of your entire being might make one mistake you for rich fertilizer, but you would kill any garden." Brudoer paused. Why were the guardsmen not stopping him? He had run out of the insults he'd planned. But he added, "You are an offense to justice, to mercy for the young. Craydor would have hated you and thrown you out of here a long time ago."

"Is that all, boy? I'm glad to see you are on speaking terms with Craydor and know what she would do. Have you no more insults to add to your offenses? Perhaps you would like to compare my speech to something."

"Your speech? It's the rumbling belly of an old wild cow. An odorous wind, Protector."

"Indeed, that is good, but somewhat of a cliché. What else? Surely you have prepared further provocations."

Brudoer looked down. "No, Protector. Will they not do? I had expected to be gagged before now."

"That is all, then?"

"All? Isn't it enough? We all know that you're destroy-ing this city. I'm only a boy, and I see it well enough. You and this ghastly crew of old women with their minds all gone to ashes."

"Ah. Yes. And have you anything to say about them?"

Brudoer looked around on rows of severe faces. "Only that you are all mindless. Nothing I ever say will make any difference to you. Your minds are made up about every-thing and are about as changeable as the fossil shells in the bluffs. You obviously think you're made fit to rule simply because of your sex. That's absurd."

"You are articulate for a child, Brudoer, but surely you cannot evoke Craydor and still claim that men should rule.

Perhaps you would prefer the Shumai way, where the men rule."

"Of course not. Any idea that being a man or a woman will make somebody better able to rule is silly. You have to look at the person."

"Indeed. Well, friend of Craydor, now that you have spoken nonsensically but at least civilly, are you ready to retract your insults?"

"No. I have thought of another. You never had a child, Protector, because you are such a loathsome old bag of guts that no man would ever look at you. You couldn't even force them into it."

Udge's hands tightened on the arms of her chair. "Yes. I see," she said. "Enough of this, then. Guards, give him all six strokes. I see no need to prolong this. Then we will return him to the cells and after thirty days exclude him."

"No," the Ardena shouted. "No. The council has decided."

"Do I hear any other objections, now that you have seen him again?" Her eyes swept across the rows of severe but troubled faces. No one said anything. "Proceed."

The guardsmen stripped Brudoer's tunic and undershift off. His gold bracelet glittered in the winter sun. A guardsman looked at it. "Protector, it's a gold bracelet. Very fine."

"Gold? Take it off. Let me see it."

The guardsman struggled with the bracelet for some time as all waited. Brudoer began to shiver in the wind. "Boy," the Protector called. "Remove it for the guardsman."

"It's mine. It stays where it is."

"Then break it off with your short-sword, guardsman."

"It's Craydor's work. You'll break that like everything else you touch of hers—her city, her people," Brudoer shouted.

"Craydor's? And you say it is yours?" Udge laughed. "Remove it, guardsman."

The woman looked at it closely. "It is very beautiful, Protector. It may be Craydor's work. It's extremely fine. I am reluctant to destroy it."

The Protector frowned. "Brudoer—I will give you your choice. You may remove it so we may see it. If it is really yours, we will return it. You see, you have many witnesses. If you don't, we will destroy it."

"I will remove it, Protector, if you agree to have Bival read the inscription to the assembled council."

Udge frowned again. What did this mean? "Cilia will read it," she said, shooting a look at the compliant Westcounsel.

Brudoer hesitated. Turning, he looked at the Ardena. She nodded slightly. Twisting, Brudoer deftly removed the bracelet and snapped it together before anyone could see how he did it. He handed it to the guardsman, who passed it up to the Westcounsel. She held it up to the light, and, squinting, read it: "This bracelet is the gift of Craydor to someone who has been in all of the first three cells for a full term of punishment—proof of his misuse by authority. It is for no one else. The rich and powerful will seek to have it, but if they gain it from him, it will be by force and injustice alone. Craydor, Founder of Threerivers."

Cilia turned to see hatred burn from the Protector's eyes. Udge reached out for the bracelet, took it, and held it to the light. "This is a poor time for such a joke, Cilia. It says no such thing. You should be ashamed. It says nothing. This is some trick. How would he get it? He has confederates. It must be from the museum."

"Let me see it, Protector," the Ardena shouted, across the crowd. "Let us all see it."

There was a moment of silence, then Cilia said, her voice trembling, "I was only joking. It says nothing."

"You stinking convenience!" Brudoer shouted. "You know you read it right. You know that's what it says."

"Enough!" the Protector said. "We have had enough. Tie him, guards."

Brudoer was wrestled up against the wooden rack that stretched his arms. The guardsman took up the whip and as the drum sounded, lashed it across Brudoer's back. The boy grunted. The drum sounded again, and the lash stung again across Brudoer's bleeding back. Brudoer said nothing, but as the third lash fell, he let out a wild yell of pain and anguish that seemed endless. The guardcaptain hesitated and turned to look at the Protector, who didn't move. The drum thumped again, but the guardcaptain was staring over the Protector's head.

"Guardcaptain, do your duty," the Protector said.

"Fire," the guardcaptain shouted. "The Broad Tower is on fire." She was looking over the heads of the crowd. The guardsman at the drum whirled and said, "Good Aven, it is. Guardsman, sound the alarm. " All stood and turned. Udge saw thick smoke pouring from the windows of her private tower.

"Guardsmen, dismiss this body! Return the boy back to prison. Quick. The city must be saved."

"The city?" the Ardena shouted. "The city, you old leak in the roof? You. You mean you, just the way you stole the boy's bracelet for yourself."

Udge turned toward her momentarily, but hurried off, anxious about her things.

The guardcaptain looked at the drum guard. "Come. Help me take the boy down. I think he's had enough now, anyway."

As they worked on the ropes, the drum guard asked, "Was there writing in the bracelet?"

The guardcaptain grimaced. "Yes," she said.

That night, Rotag came to the fourth cell to bathe Brudoer again. "We can talk," she said. "The guard is one of ours."

"Ours? Ahhhhhhh. Don't. Not there."

"We have to clean it. Can't you apologize? Must you drag us all through this?"

"What does Father say?"

"Father? Listen to me," she said, shaking him slightly. Brudoer drew in his breath. "I'm sorry. Listen. You are tearing the city apart."

"I? That old rot Udge is. Look. She even stole my bracelet. With all she owns."

"Yours? What was that story about an inscription? Where did you get it?"

"In the third cell. You will not tell? Craydor left it there for anyone smart enough to find it."

"The inscription?"

"It was there just the way Cilia read it."

"I don't understand. Hold still."

"What about the fire? What was that?"

"A fire. Somebody piled a lot of old food sacks in the Protector's front room and lit them. They were dampened and made a lot of smoke."

"Who?"

"Who? Who knows? I don't know how to get in there."

"Yes. Of course. I will be all right here. Don't worry about me."

"How could you talk to her like that? Where did you pick up all that bad language. You are making it so hard."

"I don't care anymore. I don't care about anything. Look. Gamwyn is gone. We are all discredited. I am learning things down here. Let me alone about it."

Rotag sighed and gently patted her son's back dry. "I can't take much more of this."

"I can."

"I could hear you cry out from the second level. My heart almost stopped. Is that how you take it?"

"I tried not to. It was easier to."

Eventually Brudoer's mother left. Reasoning with the boy had been like talking to her own husband. Her hands were trembling from her inability to make him see reason.

Brudoer lay for a long time in pain. Then he lifted his eyes to the walls. They were nearly bare, with no inscriptions, just a frieze of river mussels like that in the previous cell, and some of the stone patterns, though much larger. He sank in disappointment. No. Craydor's messages meant something. He would have to see what.

 IX

GAMWYN walked downriver on the west bank, having crossed on a log. He made slow progress because he had to feed himself, largely by fishing and by gathering the few winter seeds. Penetrating deeper into Tusco territory, he tried to estimate how close he was to the U Bend settlement. Finally he decided to strike westward from the river and walk south well out of the range of the black-leather-clad police patrols of the Tusco.

Jaiyan had said they called themselves the Nicfad, that they had dogs that could trace the scent of a man as if a road led to him. He described them as large and short-haired, with long, hanging ears, generally well-behaved, but ferocious when urged on by their handlers.

The Pelbar boy moved south about eight ayas west of the river, as well as he could tell it. He had no weapon but his folding knife and a wooden spear with a fire-hardened tip. Several times he crossed ancient tracks of artificial stone—concrete, the Pelbarigan people had begun to call it.

Winter was moderating. Already the early duck flocks moved northward. An unseasonable thaw brought mud and discomfort, since Gamwyn had no way of keeping his feet dry. Then another snow brought him even more misery. He walked on, wondering how soon he could go east to find the river again. Suddenly, as he capped a rise, he saw it, not a half an ayas east. He had unknowingly drifted toward the river. Frightened, he began moving west again, plowing through the fresh, wet snow, his feet soaked. For food now he looked to the small, tough roots of the wild carrot, which he located by their dried tops.

At last he made a camp and set rabbit snares, finally falling into a shivering sleep, only to wake early to find the shapes of a man and a dog standing over him.

The dog let out a low, throaty growl, and Gamwyn cringed from it, but the man jerked its collar and it sat. He was a Nicfad. He prodded Gamwyn with the end of a long, iron-tipped stave.

"Up. Up, you," he said.

Gamwyn stood, still cold. "What? Who are you?"

"You come," the man said, slipping a black, braided-leather noose over Gamwyn's head and jerking it. Gamwyn fell, and the man jerked him upright. "Come."

Gamwyn dumbly obeyed, walking through the snowy prairie, utterly miserable. Ahead five black-clad men were approaching, with three more dogs. When they met, the men set the dogs around the boy and stood aside to confer.

At last one of them, larger than the rest and wearing a white crest on his hat, walked over and stood opposite Gamwyn. "You boy from the Sentani's river station. He see you." He jerked his head slightly. "Peshtak, eh. Come to spy?" Then the man laughed a long, evil laugh. "Good. You come to stay then." His voice was slow and thick. Gamwyn could scarcely make out his meaning.

"I'm not Peshtak and I've done nothing. Let me go."

The man stared at him, then swept up the end of the leather rope and jerked Gamwyn off his feet and dragged him through the snow about fifty paces, then dropped the rope and stood over him as the boy gasped for breath. "We talk. You listen. Now, follow."

The party set off at a brisk pace. Gamwyn had a hard

time keeping up. Soon he saw the river again, and realized that they were very near the U Bend settlement. He had strayed nearly into it, the river having meandered westward.

From the hill they were descending, he could see the river did make a large U-shaped loop to the west around a fairly narrow neck of higher ground surrounded by a palisade wall, on levees. In the neck, Gamwyn could make out concentric circles of buildings from the center of which rose a large, white tower. Beyond that were fields laid out for farming. Much of the loop of the bend also lay in fields, and at the tip of the loop, behind more palisades, which had small log guard towers, stood rows of buildings, low and nondescript. Those would be the slavehouses, Gamwyn thought, his heart sinking.

Eventually they reached the river's edge. It was largely ice-free now. Gamwyn was shoved onto a log raft, which the Nicfad poled and paddled across the broad stream. The boy stood flanked by the dogs, who seemed to pay no attention to him.

When at last they reached the east bank, below the palisade, the tall man again picked up the rope and led Gamwyn off the raft, then turned and faced him. "Take good look around," he said. "This your home now forever. You try to escape, we capture. We always capture. Dog smelled you many strides away. We never kill when we recapture. We cut off your foot." He laughed again. "Then we fit you with wood stump so you can work in fields again. Now, you come."

Gamwyn was led around the palisade wall to one guard tower, where a ladder led over the wall. He was made to climb the ladder, then thrown down into the mud inside. He hit with a sickening jolt. Inside, another Nicfad took the noose from his neck and tossed it back to the tall man, who waited above.

They shouted a brief conversation, then the new guard looked at the boy, pointed to a long, low building in the center of the group, turned him, and kicked him toward it, saying, "Go there." Gamwyn fell again, but got up and hurried ahead of the guard. The door was low, and Gamwyn had to stoop to open it. As he did, the guard shoved him into the room with his foot and slammed the door again.

The room had no windows and was too low to stand up

in. No one was inside, but Gamwyn could see, in the very dim light from one chimney at the end, that many people used the building. The floor was lined with straw and the room divided by logs laid parallel to each other on the floor. It smelled very heavily of smoke. Gamwyn suddenly felt tired. At least it was dry in the building. He knew he should try to get out as soon as he could, but instead he sat down, took off his wet boots, and tried to dry out his feet. Gradually he grew drowsy and faded off to sleep.

A quarter sun later, near evening, he was awakened by the sound of men entering the building, mildly stumbling and cursing. They paid little attention to him, but lay down on the straw in parallel rows as one old man lit a fire on the hearth that lay at the far end of the building from the chimney. Soon the building began to fill with acrid smoke. The men lay in it singing a slow, dreamy song. Gamwyn lay as still as he could, keeping his face near the straw where the air was clearest. Slowly he began to feel light-headed. A strange sense of well-being sifted through him. He felt like laughing. It was a summer evening on the terraces of Threerivers. He was cultivating corn and beans with Brudoer, and joking with the old beekeeper, Sepp. No. That was wrong. He was at the U Bend Tusco settlement in a smoke-filled building with the other slaves. Well, that wasn't so bad. He would talk to them. They would let him go in the morning.

Eventually most of the smoke drifted out, and the men slowly roused themselves and went outside. "You new?" one man near Gamwyn asked. "Come now. Time for supper." Gamwyn went out with them and stood in a line in front of another building. The line inched forward, and at last he was handed a large wooden bowl filled with steaming liquid. Gamwyn tasted it. Fish stew had never seemed so good before, even though he knew it was poor.

"Come," said the man behind him, the same one who had spoken earlier. "Come with me. Room in our hut." His words seemed a slow, dreamy chant. He led Gamwyn to one of the rows of smaller buildings and stooped inside. Straw lay on the floor of this building, too. By the light of a small fire, Gamwyn could see it was marked off into small living areas. His new companion gestured to one. "There," he said. "Was Ount's. He's dead. Yours." He sat in the adjoining area, separated by a barrier two logs high. All the men silently ate their stew. Again Gamwyn felt sleepy. The stew had a faintly rank odor. He didn't care. It tasted too good.

"We've been cuttin' wood. You'll come with us. But first they'll ask you a horde of things up in the circles. Don't worry. Just tell 'em everything. Won't matter. You're in it now. We never get out. You're in it for life now."

Gamwyn's hope dropped again, despite the uplift he felt from the smoke and food. He was drowsy, but he knew he had to think the situation out before going to sleep. Though he seemed to fade into and out of sleep, he had long periods of mental clarity in which he set his direction, his design for action, he thought, borrowing Craydor's terminology. First he would never resign himself to being a slave. He would take every opportunity to thwart the Tusco, but never at the cost of undue personal danger. He would never betray his fellow prisoners. He would try somehow to slip away unnoticed, but if this was not possible, he was willing to undermine the entire false design.

He remembered back to his talk with Sagan, Protector of Pelbarigan. She told him that the oppressed had the right to lie to the oppressor. Didn't she? As he recalled it, he wasn't so sure. Did he have that right, or did he owe them the truth? Even desiring to escape was to them a lie, though. Then he did have the right, though he would use it judiciously. He would not bring danger onto himself with it.

He recalled a bitter old servant in Threerivers, a tall, spare man who had once confided in Gamwyn as they worked on a bank stabilization detail together. Grasping the boy's forearm fiercely and fixing his eye, the old man hissed at him, "Listen and never forget this. We live in the worst kind of oppressive society. Don't forget it. Remember this. Don't thwart them openly. They run things, these stupid old women. Circumvent them. Do what they ask, but do it slowly and stupidly and live your own life to yourself. Nod and accept their insults. There isn't any other way. You have a family. I don't. You have some help. You are young and have freedom from the hostility of the outside tribes. That will help, too. But it will not cure. Remember this. Live like a spy among them. You don't have to respect them even if you do comply. There are ways to attain your own fulfillment." The fellow had spat forcefully on the snow, then turned back and said again, "Remember that."

Gamwyn didn't think the fellow was right about Three-rivers. Things weren't so bad there. Perhaps the old man had created his own aura of tension and bitterness. But, now that Udge was in power, things really had changed. Perhaps the old servant had seen it coming all along. He was a secret ornithologist, too. He knew an immense amount about the birds of the Threerivers region, both the migrants and the natives. He showed Gamwyn his volumes of notes with sketches once—endless observations, noted in a tiny, neat hand. He had sworn the boy to secrecy about them. The woman for whom he worked, when not sent on outside details, knew nothing of his hobby but thought him merely a stupid old man.

Gamwyn knew his own most immediate problems were two. First, he had to become anonymous, acquiring the shapeless clothing of the slaves. Next, he had somehow to avoid the smoke. He saw the debilitating effect it had on the others, dulling them to the facts of their situation. Gamwyn had the typical Pelbar admiration for clarity of mind, an attitude that made them avoid all stimulants to jollity, even at times of feast and celebration, if intoxication would result. Avoidance of excess was a part of Craydor's code. "Do not think of it as balance," she had written, "even though it is in a sense a balance to live moderately, eating neither too much nor too little. Think of it as the harmony of the Pelbar choir, in which each note contributes to the whole impression, sounding out and combining in a perfection of individual clarity, agreeing with the whole. A muddiness of the individual note or a hesitancy or an excess mars the brilliance of the whole."

Gamwyn eventually fell wholly to sleep. It seemed to him he was aroused only a moment later, but it was dawn. A heavy Nicfad opened the door to the hut and shouted them all into wakefulness. In his hand he had a collar made of leather, with metal loops sticking out of it. As the dull group filed out, heading for the smokehouse, the man took Gamwyn by the hood of his winter coat and threw him aside, then buckled the collar on him, snugly. Only then did the boy notice that all the slaves wore such collars, though their shapeless coats hid them.

"Now, go get your smoke," the man said, throwing the boy forward and chasing him, kicking him as he went.

Gamwyn dove into the room, tripping over a man near

the door, and in the dimness found a place to lie down. Already the room was filling with the acrid smoke. Everyone there lay on his back, placidly drinking it in. Gamwyn turned on his side, parted the straw, and thrust his face down into the pocket there, hoping to minimize its effect. Eventually he thought, Well, maybe this life would not be so bad after all. It could become a routine. My trip downriver was a silly thing, after all. I could settle into this society just as I did into Threerivers. No. I've got to resist. It's the smoke talking. But then again . . .

After breakfast stew, the slaves were led out toward the downriver side of the circular Tusco community. But as they neared the hill below the outer wall, the same Nicfad who had brought the collar took a long staff with a small hook on one end and stuck it through one of the loops in Gamwyn's collar, yanking him from the line then leading him up the hill. They passed through a gate into an outer ring of houses where Gamwyn saw a number of Nicfad with women and children. The boys all dressed in the black leather of the elder men. They stared at him with contempt. One threw a glob of mud. Gamwyn tried to dodge, but the staff holding his neck made it impossible.

Almost immediately, Gamwyn was led through another gate in a wall partly composed of another ring of houses. No Nicfad loitered in this area, but a number of people in brown, shapeless garments, all carrying things, hurried busily along the circular corridor. Gamwyn raised his eyes to the white tower in the center of the ring ahead. He could see its whiteness came from a surface of bones fastened to it. He stopped with a slight outcry as he recognized a number of human skulls, but the Nicfad jerked his collar, leading him to a long, nondescript building and thrusting him inside, unhooking the staff.

Gamwyn found himself facing a table at which a middle-aged man sat. Before him lay shallow wooden racks with pebbles in some of the squares into which they were divided.

"New slave. Put in uniform," the Nicfad said.

The man peered up at him nearsightedly, then rose and walked around the table to look again. He regarded Gamwyn intently from close up, then felt his coat and parted it to look at his tunic.

"Not Siveri. Who?"

"Peshtak spy," the Nicfad said.

The man drew in his breath sharply and stepped back. "Another Peshtak," he whispered.

"No worry. They stand no chance with us. Remember dogs. This one half-starved. Only boy. Other one already good slave."

The two made Gamwyn strip off his coat, and then the warehouseman fitted him into a quilted slave suit. It was shapeless but surprisingly comfortable. The warehouseman turned him to the light and surveyed him. "Strange hair. This fits all right. Fine weaving in his clothes. Lovely work." Reaching out, the warehouseman took up Gamwyn's folding knife, which hung on a lace around his neck. "What this?" he asked.

"The sign of Grogan, the beast-god," Gamwyn said impressively. "Go ahead. Take it and die."

The man dropped it. "No matter," he said. "Only decoration. Take him for questioning."

"Not need you to tell me that." The Nicfad hooked his staff in Gamwyn's collar and jerked him toward the door.

"Good-bye," the warehouseman said.

"Good-bye," Gamwyn replied. The Nicfad jerked him along roughly. They walked through another gate into the innermost ring before the tower. Here, too, Gamwyn saw people busily walking around, carrying sticks with marks and notches in them, as well as the racks of pebbles. Again the Nicfad thrust Gamwyn through a door into a dim interior. Again a long table faced the door. But this time, seated at it were seven people, surrounded with marked sticks and racks of pebbles.

One man, tall and severely dressed in a high-collared robe, gray with black piping, stood and walked around the table with his hands behind him. He snapped his fingers. "Release him," he said. "Wait outside."

In removing his staff, the Nicfad threw Gamwyn to the floor, stood for a moment dusting his leggings, then slowly sauntered off, as the tall man looked at him from under raised eyebrows.

"Stand," he said. Gamwyn stood up, rubbing his neck. "New Peshtak. You will tell us, then, of intentions of Peshtak. They move this way, then? They plan attack?"

"I know nothing of any Peshtak."

The man thrust his face up to Gamwyn's frowning, and hissed out, "You will find it will go very badly with you to hide anything from me. Knou, bring the stick." A short, fat man came from behind the table and put a willow switch in the tall man's hand.

"Now, then, you will tell me everything." He cut Gamwyn in the side with the switch. The boy barely felt it through the quilted coat, but he plainly saw the man's anger.

"You will not believe, then, that I am not Peshtak?"

"No. Now no delays."

Gamwyn paused. "All right. I see there is no help for it. I am from the farthest Peshtak city in the eastern mountains. It is called Kitat. We are moving west. It is difficult to live there, and with the eastern cities and the mountains, as well as the rat famine."

"Rat famine?"

"Yes. We live largely on rats." The tall man groaned and sniffed. "Something has killed most of them out—perhaps the groffhawks, which seem to get bigger every year. They are even beginning to carry off children."

"Children?"

"Yes. Not any big ones. Nothing over six months old."

"Months?"

"That's about thirty days."

"Ah. You mean just over six moon cycles."

"Yes. We have to move west, you see. We are looking for a place. I was sent to see if you were a strong society which would threaten us. If you let me go, I will assure them that you are."

"Make him slow down," said one man behind a table. "We having trouble notching sticks. He talks very strange."

The tall man turned impatiently, then sighed and said, "Well, hurry."

"What are they doing?" Gamwyn asked.

"You primitive society. They recording your statements."

"Why don't they just write it down?"

"They do. What you mean?"

Gamwyn was astonished. They didn't know how to write conventionally, as all the Heart River peoples to the north did. Instead they notched the long, flat sticks in some pattern. "Nothing," he said. "We write in a different way."

"A lie. You know well you have no way to write. That why you cannot hold your own in your own land. Hawks indeed."

"Then there are the giant beasts."

"Giant beasts?"

"Yes. They have come down from the north country, beyond the Bitter Sea. They are white like snow, and they eat everything that has flesh—birds, fish, mice, people."

"Many of them?"

"They travel in herds, like the wild cattle of the west here, and leave the countryside decimated. In the summer they even eat insects. No, there are not many, but when they come, they tear down our strongest log walls, and if we shoot the first ones, the ones behind devour them, then keep coming, entering our towns. We have to flee or be eaten. There is no help for it."

"This truth?"

"Truth? That word again."

The tall man turned his back on Gamwyn. "You see," he said to the others. "He not even really know truth. That how benighted they, Peshtak." He turned again. "Many of you? Nearby?"

"No. Not many. Only about three thousand, and they are up near the Oh River. They are trying to decide whether to go upriver and attack the Pelbar, go west, or come downriver and attack you."

"Three thousand? How much that?"

"Don't you know how to count?"

"Count? To sum?"

"Yes. To sum." Gamwyn explained at great length how many three thousand was, using his hands, as one of the men moved pebbles rapidly in the boxes. When he was through the tall man looked at the pebbles and turned back with a grave face.

"That many. That too many. Three ten hundreds."

"I think they will go west, up the Isso."

"What of Shumai?"

"Yes. But the Shumai are settling with the Pelbar along the river. The Pelbar cities are impregnable, and the people all together are too many. We Peshtak will seek empty land to the west and not attack. I assume you have other Tusco cities you can draw on for reinforcements."

"We not tell you anything. Do not seek information from me." The tall man cut him across the legs with the stick. This Gamwyn felt, though he gave no sign. "Now. You say they not attack? We have heard from Sentani what you Peshtak have done."

"We are a peaceful people, but we have been driven to

fight. We will seek to avoid it. You are too well defended here for us. I imagine the slaves will fight for you, too."

"You will never return to tell them anything."

"There have been others."

"Others? How many?"

Gamwyn held up the fingers of both hands, shutting them and opening them twice. "At least that many. Last summer."

"Then why they send you?"

"They were all from the Oh Peshtak. River people. They came in the water, swimming at night. They can stay in the water for days on end. We didn't wholly trust them. They might want the best places for themselves. I was sent to check on them."

"And they right, these river Peshtak?"

"Oh, yes. Completely. You don't have to worry. We will not attack you. The dogs are too frightening, and those black-leather men."

The tall man paced up and down for several sunwidths. "I inclined to believe much of what you say. You could not make most of that up. Remember what will happen if we find you lied."

"What will happen?"

"You will lose foot, just as if you escaped."

"Well, I have no worry, then, because I have told you all the facts."

The tall man rapped on the door frame for the Nicfad. "Take him," he said. "We have no further need of him. He incompetent boy sent by weak primitives."

As Gamwyn was led from the building, he looked up again at the tower and saw a plump girl of his own age, with light blond hair, gazing out a window. As he was jerked along by the neck, he smiled a little and waved. She banged the window shut as the Nicfad threw Gamwyn to the ground and stood over him. "You like to live? You never do that again. Never," he snarled at the boy.

"No. Sorry. I didn't know." Gamwyn was terrified.

"Never," said the Nicfad, jerking him back to his feet. "Now. To cut wood," he added.

Far to the north, at Pelbarigan, the three Peshtak captives were brought before Ahroe in the guardroom. Sun through the south window cast a harsh light across their thin faces. But their wounds were healed. Each one stood in front of a male guardsman, and two more flanked them. Their hands were bound behind them and their feet loosely shackled.

"You have told us nothing so far, not even your names," Ahroe said.

They looked at her impassively.

"But we have something to tell you, nonetheless. Only one of you has the Peshtak plague. The other two are free of it." The men started visibly.

"It has not shown up as yet," Ahroe added, "but it is present in your bloodstream. At least Royal says it is. He thinks it is curable, or preventable. You realize, of course, that you cannot mingle with the other peoples until this is under control. *Then* there would be no reason, other than your incredible ferocity, that you could not settle with us—or remain in your own region and trade with us."

The three looked at each other. "You can tell no such thing," one said.

"Is it you? You have felt the initial stinging in your nasal passages?"

The man shuddered. "No." Neither of the others would say anything.

"Summon Royal, please," Ahroe said. "Tell him to bring Celeste's microscope."

Soon the old physician arrived with the microscope, looking slightly apprehensive despite the guardsmen.

"Please explain to them, Royal. They still will have none of us."

"About the disease? Is it caused by a microorganism. That is, a living creature too tiny for the naked eye to see. I believe it was artificially developed, or else it has evolved since the ancient world fell. But it strongly resembles a spirochete artificially generated—according to our records in the dome and levels— by the U.S.S.R. for biological weaponry in ancient times. Unlike some of their microorganisms, which would sweep through a population, killing all, this one was meant to harass survivors who for some reason were not destroyed. It was to deny them animal food. For this reason I believe there is a cure, because the possessors of the disease could promise cure if the population agreed to submit to them."

Ahroe's expression mirrored her disgust. "Beastly. Please explain to them further about microorganisms, Royal. They are innocent of such knowledge, if of nothing else."

"Of course. They are tiny living things, as I have said. They are capable of inhabiting our bodies and are the causes of a number of our diseases, all the way from pimples to fevers. We can easily see them with a device like this microscope that magnifies. You have millions of them in your mouth right now. So, alas, do I since I have emerged into this world outside the dome and levels."

The Peshtak sneered.

"If I prepare a slide and allow you to look, will you behave decently?"

The Peshtak said nothing.

"Well, it is of no use then. You must return them to the ice caves, guardsmen," Ahroe said.

"Which one?" said the tallest, a red-haired man. "Which one is it?"

Ahroe looked down modestly as the men were led away. Then she turned to Royal and said, "I think they believe it. We need to let this knowledge soak in awhile. I have found no other hope of cooperation."

The old physician put his hand on her shoulder. "I believe it is absurdly easy to cure, you know. We must spread this knowledge to the others, even if they are hostile. It is only humanitarian."

Ahroe looked at him narrowly, but she said nothing.

In the depths of Threerivers, Brudoer's back was healing once more. He studied the walls without any further knowledge, patiently but a little desperately. After the removal of the lamp, he heard hushed voices outside and saw a slight light. He turned, at first idly, then in terror as he heard a whispered voice say, "At last we can blow out this nose-rolling once and for all. Give me some light." A torch flared suddenly.

Brudoer rose, in pain, and eased his way quickly to the door. Outside were three guardsmen. One had his shortsword drawn. Brudoer recognized one—the same man who had threatened him. He was helpless, trapped. His hands felt the inside of the door even though he knew the bolts lay on the other side.

He screamed out, "Help. Get away. Help me. They are coming." He ended in a long, incoherent cry, as the men rushed to open the door and silence him. Brudoer's hands beat on the wall above it, striking the iron decor, the bottom of the lamp bracket.

In a flash he saw its design, narrow and curled. He could draw it down twisting it around so the mussel-shell design overlapped the door and held it shut. None of the other doors had had such features. As the bolts were thrown free, the iron bracket, with its shell decoration, held it. The guardsmen outside cursed under their breaths and tried to wedge the door open with a short-sword, thrusting in through the barring with another. Brudoer continued to scream. He heard running footsteps and saw lights. The guardsmen turned from the door.

"Stand back," he heard one shout out.

"Are you the duty guardsmen? Why are there four of you?" Brudoer recognized Warret's voice.

"None of your affair. Get away before you get an arrow through you."

"Through all of us? You try it and we'll fry you slow on an open fire—take two or three days at it."

"What? You dare . . ."

Brudoer heard a rush and a confusion of shouts, but they soon were all subdued.

"We'll have to take them with us," a voice said.

Brudoer then heard a muffled protest and some thrashing. "Throw them in the river," a man's voice said.

"Brudoer, are you all right?" It was Warret.

"Yes. All right. Thank you for coming."

"Some are leaving. You come along. Have you jammed the door?"

"Yes. I found a way. No, I must not come. I must stay."

"Don't be a fool. The city will cease to function soon with all of us gone."

"Come close, Warret." Brudoer held his face next to the barring. "I have to stay. It's too important," he whispered. "Look. The ironwork above the door was designed so I could keep them out. Craydor did that. I'm certain of it. This is all a part of Craydor's purpose. You have to believe that."

"Stuff Craydor."

"No. Warret, go quickly. I have to stay here."

"I'm not going, either. But the others should. They know the bracelet was yours. That convinced a lot of the guard."

"You aren't going? Why?"

"Bival is here."

"Oh. Yes." Brudoer reached between the narrow bars. He felt Warret grasp his hand tightly, then let go.

Brudoer heard Warret say, "Come on now. Hurry."

The lights and voices faded, leaving Brudoer alone in the dark. He groped his way to the bed alcove and sank down, suddenly struck with deep fear. He could not stop his trembling.

 X

AFTER finishing his third day of cutting wood, Gamwyn, fagged out, sought the far corner of the smokehouse. He found that the drugged smoke lay thinnest there. By digging his face down into the malodorous straw, he could avoid most of its effect.

Another man was in Gamwyn's usual place, so he lay nearby, bone tired, only to have the man slide over to him and catch his arm in a tight grip.

"You. You're the one they call Peshtak. What is this? You're no more Peshtak than a squirrel."

"Who are you?"

"You answer quick." The man shook Gamwyn, who deftly caught his fingers and twisted them back in an excruciating hold. The man swung close and clamped the boy's neck, but Gamwyn tightened and bent, and with a low moan the man let go and writhed back.

Gamwyn eased his grip. "Who are you?"

The man spat at him. Gamwyn wrenched his hand again and the man screamed. Several of the others sat up and gazed at them. Gamwyn and the man lay quiet.

"Who are you?" Gamwyn repeated. "You must be the Peshtak that Nicfad ranted on about. What's your name?"

"I will say when you identify yourself."

Gamwyn sighed. "I'm Gamwyn, a Pelbar from Three-rivers. But to them I'm a Peshtak. That's what they assumed. They said they'd cut off my foot unless I admitted it. Naturally I did."

The man chuckled. "A Pelbar. Who would have thought to meet a hog-sucking Pelbar here?"

"Your name?"

"My name?"

"Even Peshtak have names. This time I'll break your hand. You'll have great fun working with a broken hand."

"Syle. I am Syle. Now. Let go." Gamwyn did. "Now I can tell the fish-gut Tusco you lied. You owe me. See? You won't get any sucker grips on me anymore."

"You'll tell the Tusco? I'll just say you want to deceive them. They absolutely know I'm a Peshtak. Look, why be enemies? We both need to get out. Right? Why not join together?"

"Join? With a Pelbar woman-slave?"

"Do you know Misque?"

"Misque? Where did you meet her?"

"Jaiyan's Station. I figured out she was Peshtak."

"And you told."

"No. She saved my life. We hugged good-bye."

"Faaaugh."

"I know I can't trust you. Too far, anyhow. But I'll swear to you by Aven now that I won't betray you—and if I find a way out, you'll be the first to hear of it."

"There is no way. No way at all. It's the dogs and the patrols. You could get out, but you wouldn't get away. The Nicfad are too good. Swill faces. They'd even find Peshtak. I'd like to see them, though, run across a good force of us. We'd skewer them all."

"There must be a way. Craydor would say it's a matter of design. Their whole society is a design—a very bad one. It's effective enough for the managers. But it has its flaws. It's got to. We only need to find them."

The two talked the whole time they lay under the smoke. Gamwyn learned that Syle was only eighteen. He had come from the mountains. He was also in despair. He had the usual guile and hatreds of the Peshtak, but his youthful anguish continually seeped around the edges of his bravado. The Peshtak roamed freely in the high forests, and the plodding life of slavery grated him terribly.

The signal for supper sounded, and as they crawled out toward the door, Gamwyn whispered, "Do you have the disease?"

Syle shot him a hard look, his jaw rippling. But he said, "I don't know. I don't know."

A few days later, a Nicfad again hooked Gamwyn's collar with his stave and led him toward the circles. The boy looked back at Syle, who was watching. The Nicfad said nothing, but marched him up into the innermost circle where a well lay, surrounded by square stone steps.

"Here. This the smallest one. He will go down," the Nicfad said to the circle of brown-clad workmen who stood around with stones and tools. The Nicfad threw the boy down with his staff and stood aside.

The workleader squatted down to him and turned his head. "This sapling?" he asked.

"He only small one. He Peshtak."

The man looked up. "Peshtak? Suffering catfish." Then he turned to Gamwyn and said, "This well fell in, boy. We need small person to go down and dig it out. Then we stone it."

Gamwyn was sent down a ladder into the caved-in well. He spent the day sending buckets of dirt and mud up the rope to the workmen above. They berated him for slowness, while he shivered and slipped in the semidark of the shaft. The whole structure stood in danger of caving in on him, and after much complaining he got them to brace it crosswise with sticks and rough boards, even though this slowed the work. At nightfall he came up, filthy and shivering. As he stood by the hole for a few moments, he looked up again. The pudgy girl was at her window looking down at him. He looked away carefully, but then let his eyes go back. She made a face and slammed the window again.

Gamwyn was not allowed to wash. Wet and shivering, he was led back to the compound. That evening, as he lay under the smoke near Syle, he said, "Now I know how to get out."

The young Peshtak rolled near him. "Out?"

"It'll take a long time. Maybe a year."

Syle muttered, "Bull dung."

"But no Nicfad will follow us. We'll be free."

"How?"

"You won't tell?"

"Tell? Who?"

"Them. You're Peshtak. I know you'd as soon see us all dead."

"Then don't tell me. Get away from me. Child. You're all mud."

They lay apart. Gamwyn suddenly began to cry. "It's all so miserable," he said.

"Curse you, tell me. I won't tell. I'll help. I swear it. I don't want to be here any more than you. Stop blubbering."

"Swear by Aven."

"Who is Aven?"

"Aven is God, as some other people call him."

"There is no God." They lay quiet again. Then Syle said, "I swear. I swear by Aven. Tell me."

"The well. The whole circle area does not rest on bedrock. All those buildings lie on dirt."

"I don't see—"

"Listen. I know about these things. Threerivers is by the Heart. But Craydor put it on bedrock so the river can't wash it away. The well caved in because the river really seeps through underneath—some, anyway. I noticed when I came up that the water level below is almost the same as river level. The walls are caving in because the whole thing is wet and unstable."

"So? How does that help us?"

"We go to the downriver side. At night. We get out over the palisade. Or under. There aren't any guard towers at the tip of the U because the Siveri slaves don't swim. We get under that boat landing and begin digging. We can put the dirt in the river. Only a few arms every night. We hide the entrance. The whole space between the rivers is only about a hundred fifty arms wide. We brace the tunnel. We use driftwood if we can. We put it all just above normal water level. We take it right under the tower. But *we* don't break through. The first big rise when we are done, and the river will break through. The whole center will end up in the river. It'll be the river."

Syle laughed. "You're crazy. That would take a lifetime." Then he fell silent. "It's too cold."

"It'll warm. Why do you suppose the river slices in? It is trying to cut off. You've seen bow lakes, haven't you? They are old river bends. We'll just help it."

"It seems impossible."

"Maybe. But I'm going to do it. Can we trust any of these Siveri?"

"No. They're completely enslaved by the smoke. You are, too, a little. So am I. I saw the Nicfad putting the weed in the stew."

"River snakes! Where do they keep it?"

"Ours? In the guard towers."

"We need to turn it on them. Mix oak leaves with it. Substitute oak leaves for it. Get it into their food."

"You're crazy. That is impossible. One old man brings it

for the fire. You watch him hurry. He can't wait to get it
lit and smell the first smoke."

"Then we intimidate him. Are the Siveri superstitious?"

"Yes, a little. They won't cross water without mumbling
something. They hold their fingers crossways when they
are out in a full moon."

"The Tusco are superstitious, too. Maybe we can use
that."

The Nicfad called them to eat, and the two separated.
The next day, they had no chance to talk at the morning
smoking, and Gamwyn was again led off to the well and
had to work most of the day up to his shoulders in mud
and water, so thoroughly chilled that he had to move continually to keep from going wholly numb. Eventually they
began sending shaped stones down to him, and he set them
in rings to hold the walls, even ducking under the water to
do it. When they brought him up, he fell and lay shivering
uncontrollably. The Nicfad reached out with the staff to
jerk him upright, but the workleader touched his arm.

"Easy," he said. "He has to stay alive to go down tomorrow. He's the only one small enough." The man got a dirty
old blanket and put it around Gamwyn, lifting him up.
"Bring it back tomorrow," he said.

Gamwyn staggered and fell again, but two workmen
lifted him up and supported him. Glancing up, the boy saw
the girl again, in her window, her hands held over her
mouth. The men led him all the way to the gate of the
slave compound, supporting him, then turned back. Gamwyn fell again.

The Nicfad kicked him. "Don't expect help from me,"
he said. Gamwyn rolled over and stood up, heading for the
smokehouse, trying not to fall.

Syle was waiting for him and led him to the corner.
Gamwyn shook so he could hardly talk, and the Peshtak
wrapped them both in the blanket and tried to warm him
despite the mud all over him. He dragged an old Siveri over
to the other side and held Gamwyn between them. Gradually the boy began to warm, but they were called to supper
before he felt at all normal. Syle stayed with him and led
him to his own hut, covering them with his own blanket.
He said little. Gamwyn finally fell asleep, with the Peshtak's arm still over him.

In the morning he felt weak and strange, but the Nicfad
again came for him, and he had to go to the well, clutching

the blanket. At the lip of the well, he said, "I can't go down again." The Nicfad rapped him on the ear with the stave, knocking him down.

"If you kill him now, we'll never get well stoned," said the workleader. Again he knelt by Gamwyn. "Come on, boy. You should finish today."

Gamwyn turned over and felt a flow of anger rise in him that he had never had before. "You may take the well and rot in it," he hissed. "It would take a Tusco to put a well in the middle of this sewer you call a society. May you drink from the river downstream."

The man stood and stepped back, spitting. He turned to the Nicfad, who stooped and twisted Gamwyn's arm back and around. The boy screamed. "Now? Get busy now?"

"Yes. Yes, I will," Gamwyn said, sobbing. The man stood away, and Gamwyn crawled to the ladder and began his descent, shuddering again as he reached the water. The stones began to come down in buckets, and he placed them carefully in rings working up. By midafternoon he had reached the top. It had begun to rain. He crawled away from the well platform and lay face down on the cobbled street. He felt the Nicfad's stave hook slip into his collar. The man began to drag him away.

From above a shriek tore the air. Gamwyn felt the pressure ease. He heard a high voice from high up. "You. You workman. You nearly killed him. Now you take him home. You—Nicfad. Get away, vulture. Stupid. Look at him. He has years of work left in him. You kill him now? Stupid."

"It not done. He—"

"You do it or you hear from Committee."

"You out of order. You not speak for Committee."

"Do it," the voice screamed again. From below there was silence. The workleader rolled Gamwyn over on his back. Looking up, the dazed boy saw the pudgy girl in the window staring down.

"All right. It on your head, not mine," the man said. Gamwyn felt arms lifting him and dragging him through the gate to the middle circle, then into the darkness of one of the houses. He felt hands moving over him, roughly scrubbing him dry, rolling him into a blanket in a corner padded with sacks of something like grass. Something hot came to his mouth. He felt himself cradled against a woman, her cloth-swathed ample softness against his cheek. Again the warm drink came. And again. He knew little else but was vaguely aware of arguing. But Gamwyn's mind whirled and sank. He no longer cared about anything. The woman's voice scolded and chided, but her warm hands arranged things around him and placed everything just right.

"Mother? Mother?" Gamwyn asked vaguely.

"No. Not your mother, you piece of dirt. We forced. Lie still. You get well."

"Piece? Piece of dirt?" Gamwyn said absently, then everything faded to black.

When he finally awoke, he looked up at a round, middle-aged woman's face, her hair straying, her eyes fixed on his. "There. Finally you wake up. Four days. It four days you lie here. A log. Now I demand you work for me to make it up. Four days."

"Mother? Mother?"

The woman shook him, then wiped the corner of her eye with the back of her hand. Gamwyn felt the warm drink come to his mouth again, and he took it gratefully in long swallows, finally gasping, "Four days? I'm sorry. I have been much trouble." Again he felt a total misery and began to cry. The woman held his head against her, spitting softly to her husband, who sat across the room sharpening a tool. "Look at this. Mere boy. Weak. Poor Peshtak spy cries for his mother. What this, anyway? Committee girl looking in all time. Nothing right. Why you not make well right first time, anyway?"

"It old well, Maatha. Too bad it not summer. Couldn't wait."

The door opened, and the pudgy girl entered. She was richly dressed in fine cloth, a sweeping tunic reaching to her calves, with high boots. The two stood, hands clasped in front of them, heads bowed.

"He awake now. You send him back? You satisfied, I hope."

The girl glared, then said, "Leave me with him. He too weak to hurt me. Wait outside."

The two went reluctantly. As Maatha went out the door, she poked her head back in and said, "He just woke. He needs to sleep again soon. Not ready to go back yet. Soon enough."

The girl turned toward the door but said nothing. After it closed, she stood close, looking down at Gamwyn. "You, Peshtak spy. What your name?"

"Gamwyn."

"Slave Gamwyn. What kind of name that?"

"The one my mother gave me. It's an old one in the family."

"You talk oddly. Strange words. Extra words."

"Thank you. I would have been dead but for you." Gamwyn's mind suddenly became clear for the first time in days. "If you hadn't stopped them, they would have killed me or let me die."

"You have many years of hard work left in you. Not very intelligent to let you die."

"You believe that, don't you—all this rot about making people slaves and working them until they die."

She snorted. "It scientifically designed society. Committee worked it all out. It functions beautifully. All needs taken care of. Better for you to serve such society than useless."

Gamwyn suddenly was tired of the conversation. He turned on his side. He felt her boot reach out to turn him on his back again. "Go away," he said. "There is no use trying to reason with you. Your mind is closed to truth and justice, except what is good for you."

"Truth? Justice? You spy say that? Peshtak? We hear about you."

"What's your name?"

She flounced toward the door, then turned. "Slaves do not ask names of Committee. You work. You not understand much."

Suddenly she came back and knelt down by him. He felt her warm breath reach down to him as she kissed his cheek. "You beautiful," she whispered.

Gamwyn reeled in bewilderment. He did nothing as she cradled his head against her. Abruptly she stood up again.

"Insult me! After all I do!"

"Please," Gamwyn said. "I don't mean to insult you. I don't know what to do. Want me to kiss you back? Me? A slave, worthy of working my life away, beaten and herded by those black-bodied beasts of yours, treated with the utmost cruelty, given nothing, no music, no reading, no kindness, all in the ugliest of societies, without a concept of decency, of worship, with no breadth of vision or depth of

perception, a society without real purpose, a surface ma-
nipulation of bestiality?"

The girl stood stupefied. "Where you learn to talk like
that?"

"At home, of course."

Gamwyn watched the girl's eyes dart around the room.
Something was sinking in. She reached for the door latch.
"I Daw," she said. "Daw, daughter of Central Committee
chairman. Good-bye." She left immediately, slamming the
door. The workleader and his wife reentered, then stood
looking at Gamwyn. Their eyes touched, and all registered
bewilderment.

Then a Nicfad entered without knocking. He wore the
white stripe on his hat and back, the mark of an officer. He
strode over to Gamwyn, glared down at him, and spat.
Then he whirled to face the workleader.

"Ahks," he said. "You will complain to Central Committee about this. In your own name. Not mine. That understood?"

"I? I have no . . . boy—"

"You will. This out of order. We cannot have dripping-
heart girls interfering with order." A knife snicked out
from his belt. He waved it in front of the man's face.
"Understood? Immediately." The man nodded. The Nicfad
slammed him against the wall and left.

The woman began to cry. "It wrong. Now all go wrong.
We between Committee and Nicfad. All wrong."

The two held each other. "No hope for it," the man said.
"I'll go now. They watching for sure." He left, and the
woman walked to Gamwyn and stared down at him. "You
trouble. Trouble from start." Then she reached down and
straightened the blanket over him, smoothing it.

The next morning, Gamwyn felt even stronger. He was
sitting up sipping the last of a bowl of stew when the door
opened and three Nicfad entered. The white stripe announced, "Central Committee hear your complaint now.
Come. Bring slave." The man and his wife exchanged
glances. One Nicfad strode to Gamwyn and snatched him
upright, then hurled him toward the door. He staggered
and emerged. The cobbled circle was scattered with people
watching in silence. They walked rapidly in through the
circle of the bureaucrats' houses and on across to a door in
the tower. Gamwyn, glancing up, saw it was surmounted
by seven white skulls fastened to the lintel. The Nicfad

shoved Gamwyn inside, and the group, joined by four other Nicfad, tramped down a corridor and through a wide door. Gamwyn noticed that all the construction appeared to be of wood, with stone pavement.

They emerged into a large room, and Gamwyn faced a dais at which seven people—hooded so that their faces were completely shrouded—sat at a long desk. A human skull stood upright, affixed to each end of the desk. Opposite the long desk were tiered seats, in which a scattering of people sat stiffly with hands folded. Gamwyn was thrust into a seat at a small table next to an old woman, who turned to him and whispered. "I your counsel. I will speak for you to Central Committee."

"I . . . I . . ."

"Silence," a Nicfad commanded. Then he continued, "Workleader Ahks has brought complaint. He has had to care for recalcitrant slave in his own quarters at behest of Daw, daughter of Central Committee. He wishes ruling from Committee on this."

The hoods leaned together briefly and conferred. One hood leaned forward and asked, "What says defense?"

The old woman stood, clutching the table. "The boy begs pardon for his recalcitrance. Says fatigue from work on well caused insanity. Wishes to return to slave camp and serve faithfully. Says Daw not at fault. All fault his. Says he will take beating from Nicfad to compensate. Says to thank Ahks and apologize. Says will do extra duty for Ahks to make up for all time necessary."

The hoods leaned together, and as the woman sat, Gamwyn looked at her with amazement. "Are you crazy?" he whispered. "What is this? I have—"

"Silence," she hissed. "It formality to please Nicfad. Let alone. You want Daw in trouble?"

"Daw? The girl? You do this for her, then. Oh. No, I would be dead but for her. No."

The hoods leaned apart again. "What says Nicfad-leader?" asked the one in the center.

A man with two stripes down the back of his leather clothing stood. "Respected Committee, we must agree with complaint of workleader. We have difficult task of maintaining order and discipline among working class. We know results of kindness always negative. Know order and strictness always go hand in hand down road of production. Ease brings disorder and loss of production. Brings thoughts of luxury to minds of workers. Social order demands our great watchfulness. Think, with all respect, kindness of Daw to slave misplaced. She still to grow, perhaps, to true views of Committee Statements. Has extended true family affections to unsuitable class. Wish all excused. Agree with Sandra of defense. Glad for agreement of worker."

Again Gamwyn stared in amazement. Agreement from worker? He? Again the hoods leaned together. Gamwyn turned and saw Daw sitting behind, beside a tall, thin man in gray, in a high collar. Her eyes were red and puffy. She caught his glance and tossed her head slightly in a sneer.

"What says Daw to this?" the central hood then asked.

The tall, thin man rose and said, "Honored Committee and others. Daw expressed great regret for incident but wishes to give her reasoning, which not inappropriate kindness, as alleged, but rather forward-looking economic thought. She observed worker repairing well because of small size on successive days. Observed he young. Observed that cold and water overcame him. Observed proper discipline rightly applied by Nicfad might in this case cost Tusco worker's life. Urges Committee to think ahead. Suppose worker to last another five years. Urges Committee to think of production of worker in this five years. Have calculated it. In terms of gross product of this year, the amounts to production of about ninety-two ten-hundreds of stones of smoke weed, cultivating of thirty-seven ten-hundreds of standard row crops, nine ten-hundreds of standard basket loads of earth for levee, eight ten-hundreds of loads of quarry rock for bank lining, cutting of two ten-hundreds of standard trees for fuel and walls, in addition to work on food drying and preservation and such. She thought it potential loss to U Bend. Bad to dispose of restorable resource."

The central hood leaned forward. "But have you thought of cost of maintenance of worker? Surely all you cite not clear profit."

"Have calculated that in, Central Committee, with respect, and deducted usual twenty-two hundredths for inefficiency. This resource young. If he lasts more than five years, then profits greater."

"That all statement of Daw?"

"Yes, Central Committee. That all."

Again the heads leaned together. They muttered for a

long time. At last the central hood rocked back and announced, "Here our judgment. We appreciate action of Ahks in bringing matter to our attention. Appreciate judgment of Nicfad in maintaining order so necessary for our community. Appreciate forward-looking calculations of Daw. Inclined to forgive worker his recalcitrance on grounds of conditions. We reassigning workleader Ahks to reward his alertness to head wood project in south swamp. Much responsibility. Ask Nicfad to forgo beating if worker complies—on grounds of loss to production. Wish to reward Nicfad for continued vigilance by additional allotment of service badges when trade allows. Committee stands adjourned.

"But while here, and for benefit of worker, who I understand new to us, I wish to make statement. We engaged here in scientific restoration of ordered society after shattering in ancient times. We split from Alats, who became corrupt, centuries ago, before their current decadent phase. Eventually, they will stagger to their fall. We will reconstitute them. We will spread north, then, carrying our ordered social system, with its balance of parts and assignment of tasks, its perfect state organization without messy individual wastes of effort, directionless and erring. We bound to do this by destiny and laws of history.

"If small adjustments like this necessary, then Committee glad to make them. Now it duty of each section of society to return to right place, give gratefully for good of whole." He paused and took a sip of some liquid from a jeweled metal goblet. "All must contribute willingly and with good heart. We insist on this. If sacrifice necessary, then sacrifice will have to occur. That all. Ask worker to stay for special counsel." The central hood then commanded the Nicfad to bind Gamwyn's arms behind him.

Gamwyn stood as the Nicfad lifted him up. Then the Central Committee left, all but the middle hood. Sandra also remained. Gamwyn turned and saw Daw leaving on the arm of the tall man. Finally the doors closed. The hood leaned forward, hands clasped in front of him. Gamwyn caught the gleam of a ring with a stone in it.

"You should not punish Ahks," Gamwyn said. "The south swamp? He did the least wrong of all. He only did what Daw said."

The hooded man leaned forward. "You judge then? You, who got off so lightly, got off with nothing? All because of my crying daughter, who would give me no peace if you harmed? Now I undergo suspicion of Nicfad for that, all for you—slave."

"I thought you were the head."

"They arms, and in arms weapons. Who you, anyway? You Peshtak spy?"

Gamwyn paused. Was this a trap? "I am whoever you wish me to be. I don't want to lose a foot."

The man reached up and flipped back his hood, revealing a cherubic face, balding and ruddy. He smiled. "You not lose foot. Just tell me. I need to know these things in my own city. Important. We care for needs of all."

Gamwyn didn't know what to say to that. He turned to the old woman and said, "Woman with the ancient name, what is to be said to that?"

"Tell him truth about yourself."

"Truth? What do you people know about truth? You make it whatever you wish it to be. You are without pity, without freedom, without real justice."

The cherubic face frowned. "Truth? Central Committee truth, boy. If you tell your friends anything, tell that. That truth. What Central Committee decides becomes truth." He reached a hand toward the skull on the left corner of the desk. "See him? That what remains of Ollo, former Central Committee. He still with us. Case of his skull held truth. Now case of mine holds it. Eventually I too will grace tower, looking out over our country, and another skull will hold truth. That truth."

Gamwyn looked at the man, then at the skull. "That's only the empty shell where a man was," he said. "He held thoughts, not truth. I'm only a boy, but I know enough to know that truth is more difficult than that. I have heard it said that 'truth is often beyond the reach of men because too pure for their self-interest, too permanent for their immediate demands, too difficult for their desires to struggle with. The approach of truth demands self-sacrifice, forbearance, forgiveness, an outreach of the heart and mind beyond all concerns even of the common good to the windless country beyond the stars.' "

The cherubic man drew back and frowned. Then he stared at Gamwyn and smiled again. "Only shell? Ollo only shell? Shells may contain in themselves same perfection of plan our society has. We have collection of shells here, many brought from sea. If you not slave, might show them to you." The man watched Gamwyn narrowly and saw him start slightly. The boy dropped his eyes.

The man folded his thick hands again. "You not Peshtak. You Pelbar. I learned this from Daw's account of what you say. Now I know she right. What you doing here? Why you tell them you Peshtak?"

Gamwyn looked up, stunned. He had talked too much. "I didn't tell them I was Peshtak until they said they would cut my foot off unless I admitted it. I am here because I was cast out by my people. If you know about the Pelbar, you know about that."

The man looked at Sandra. "I told you this trouble," she said. "They now allied to Sentani. What if they find we have him?"

The man shook his head. "No. They not find out. If they do, they not care. Pelbar not come here. He will fit in. You heard production figures. He may live beyond five years; then we gain even more. But for now he works only in slave compound. For at least year. We want no more contact with Daw. The silly girl. Need to instruct her slowly to correct views."

He turned to Gamwyn. "You, boy. You cause more trouble than you worth. Pelbar. Interesting. Woman-ruled. Another decadence. It all will pass. History commands Tusco will rule all."

Gamwyn looked up at him, thinking, Right now the river water is seeking a way under us, eating and flowing, and all your rock facing on the river bank will never stop it.

The Central Committee rang a bell, and a Nicfad entered with his staff. "It satisfactory. Untie him," the Central Committee chairman said. "For Sandra's sake, take him out by museum. See if he can read ancient writing. Then confine him to slave compound as agreed. Do not harm unduly."

Gamwyn was marched out a different way, through a series of corridors to a room full of strange objects, some from the ancient world. He was led to two small scraps of brownish paper with printing on them. The Nicfad brought a lamp, and Sandra fixed her eyes on him. "Read them," she said. She held a long stick and a knife to notch it with.

The first scrap was only a fragment. Gamwyn read, "Exclusions: This endorsement does not apply (a) to any loss arising out of the issuance . . . appropriation of any credit card in the . . . or the commercial pursuits of the insured, or (b) to any loss caused . . ."

Sandra notched her stick conscientiously, though they both knew it useless.

The other scrap was small and carefully cut out. In very faint ink someone had drawn a square around some of the writing. Gamwyn stared at it a long time. "Read," Sandra said. The Nicfad took his arm in a tight grip. The old woman frowned and removed his hand.

Gamwyn sighed. "I don't understand it all. This first word above the inked square, for example. The second is 'there.' Then this number is a nine. Then it says, 'If I take the wings of the morning, and dwell in the uttermost parts of the sea'; then this is a ten. Then it says, 'Even there shall thy hand lead me, and thy right hand shall hold me.' Then this is an eleven, but that is all."

" 'Thy'? What is 'thy'?"

"I don't know, but it must be an ancient word for 'your.' "

"Whose?"

"I don't know. It seems of little importance." But Gamwyn knew it was a reference to Aven. He had leaned over the scrap furiously memorizing it. He had it now. It was ancient scripture, even here in the middle of this slave community.

"You do know," Sandra said, shaking him.

"It means nothing." The Nicfad took his arm and began to bend it. "It is only a reference to Aven, whom some societies call God. I know you have rejected him as a falsity. So you see, it means nothing."

The old woman looked at him steadily. "God," she said. "That all?"

"Yes. That all."

Sandra snorted and turned away, saying over her shoulder, "Nicfad, take him."

The man hooked his stave in Gamwyn's collar and led him out, throwing him down several times before they reached the open. Then he led him through the circles and back to the slave compound. Once inside, he took him to a guard tower and hurled him through the door. Gamwyn sprawled on the floor at the boots of another Nicfad. The man raised his boot and set it slowly down on the boy's hand. Then he put his other boot on Gamwyn's other hand.

"You trouble," he said. "One more birdsqueak out of you and you will fry, Peshtak."

Gamwyn squeezed his eyes against the pain, gasping, "Yes. Yes, I understand."

The Nicfad let him up, then shook him. "You stay in compound. Don't worry. We find plenty for you to do. Come here in morning. Now go. Time for smoke."

Gamwyn found Syle astonished to see him. They had all assumed he was dead. In low voices they discussed all that had happened. Gamwyn kept nothing from him. "They're all crazy—staring mad," he finally said in summary.

Syle beckoned a young Siveri nearby, and the man rolled over. "This is Nim. The Nicfad brought in nine more Siveri while you were away. We've been talking. I've got them to resist breathing in the smoke. We've made progress. We found a way out, by digging under the boards in the gang privy and out through the levee."

"You can't do that," Gamwyn said.

"Can't? Why?"

"When the river comes up it will flood the compound."

"Oh. When is that?"

"If it rises, it will be in the fourth or fifth month, when the snow has melted in the north. It all depends on rain and how much snow there was."

"Then we have time. We'll fill the hole again and find another way when the time comes. We're already almost fifteen arms into the bank behind a large stone under the boat landing. Hog snouts. We're digging."

Gamwyn whistled low.

"I've learned something else. Almost all the Nicfad smoke the leaves. They take it from the guard tower supply. They really keep a lax watch. They depend on their dogs if anybody gets away—and they depend on the passiveness of the Siveri."

Nim snorted slightly. "They ain't all passive. You don't know. Not now, anyways. We got them busy, them we can trust. Just disrupting."

"Don't do too much," Gamwyn said. "It'll alert them."

"Nope. Just catchin' mice and lettin' them loose in the food barn. Just grindin' crystals into the dog meat when we can."

"You get to the dog meat?"

"One does. Yeah."

"Are the May apples up yet?"

"Just comin' a little. You mean mix some root in? They might catch us."

"They might. But we could kill one. Maybe the best dog."

Nim chuckled. The signal for supper came.

Meanwhile, at Threerivers, Udge stood in the Broad Tower, hands clasped behind her. All in all, she was satisfied. She retreated into her inner room as the workmen repaired the damage to her rooms from the fire set during Brudoer's punishment. But four nights had passed, and so far no violence had occurred. Perhaps it was all talk. Perhaps the boy had finally offended everyone and they no longer cared. Perhaps Bival had been right in insisting that Pion be beaten in place of his son. As the early light grew, the Protector stretched and yawned. A light knock came at the door. The sand clock had it still early. Udge frowned. "Come in," she said.

Cilia entered and bowed. "Protector," she said. Her face was pale.

Udge was instantly alert. "What? Something has happened."

"The men. Most of the men are gone. About a hundred, including at least half the male guardsmen. There are hardly any left."

Udge drew in her breath. "The other guardsmen. Are they following?"

"They're awaiting your orders, Protector. They are sure to be far outnumbered. All the longbows are gone. The shortbows that are not taken have almost all been destroyed. If the inside guard were to go, it would leave the city unprotected."

Udge sat down. "Is that all?"

"No, Protector. Some of the women and children have gone with the men. We haven't counted, but we think well over a hundred people left last night."

"I—I wouldn't have thought that of the guard."

"No, Protector. Apparently, though, a number were convinced by the bracelet."

"If you only hadn't read that inscription. That was stupid."

"I thought we agreed to. Besides, the guardsman that gave it to me saw it. Your lie was quite transparent to the others."

Udge's anger flared, but she saw only the compliant Cilia's worried face. She put her hands over her eyes, then looked up again. "Well, the city itself is impregnable, even with only a few. Call a council meeting for high sun. Bring the boy to it. We'll settle this once and for all."

Far below them, Brudoer was studying the cell desperately. He couldn't hope to hold off a hostile assault for long. He had to find the secret of the cell, or else find a way to get out. He had tapped on all the stones with the mussel-shell frieze, but none rang hollow. He sat back again. It was strange. The stones seemed arranged in a large diamond pattern, like the small ones in the previous cells, and one diamond seemed slightly darker. The bottom stone was a part of the mussel frieze. It too was darker. In an eyeblink, he saw it—if that stone were removed, the whole wall might come down. He went to it and pried in the crack with his spoon. It moved.

Then he looked again. If the wall came down, that would damage the city, opening a whole side, perhaps. That was too severe. With the present turmoil, it would leave them unprotected. Maybe that wouldn't happen. Brudoer touched the stone above and to the left. Perhaps if that one wasn't intertied, he could remove it and study the mussel stone. It seemed solid. He threw his weight against it, and it slid inward easily. Brudoer found he couldn't slide it back. It was square and flat and would have to be pushed from the other side. He pushed it farther and wormed into the opening. He was in a hollow in the wall, and a tiny upper opening admitted a whisker-narrow shaft of light.

Turning, Brudoer studied the stone he had first worked on, slowly realizing that the whole wall would not have come down, for it was intertied from the rear. But the large stone above would have caused a collapse. From his new vantage Brudoer could see it was a familiar wall trap design of the sort used to protect Pelbar cities from infiltration. It would have killed him if he had been willing to bring the wall down. Brudoer felt sweat bead on his forehead. At that moment he head voices. Quickly he moved the stone back into place with the iron handle on its back side. Was he free? He wasn't sure. At least he was out of the cell.

If they came for him, they would never find him now. Where that got him, he wasn't sure, but as he turned to look around, he realized that he was in a passageway leading upward—stairs. He turned and groped his way up inside the great walls of the tall city.

When the full council gathered, the usual buzz of talk was wholly absent. Silence dripped from the walls. Udge was very uneasy. After opening the meeting with a cursory prayer, she announced, "As far as we know now, a hundred and eleven people have gone. This includes ninety-three males and eighteen women and girls. Remaining in the city are thirty-four males, mostly old or boys, and two hundred thirty-two women. The guardsmen have informed me that the boy, Brudoer, has gone as well."

"Protector, I saw him in his cell early this morning."

Udge turned to the guardsman and raised her eyebrows, then turned back. "The boy is not in his cell. Now that the cancer is out of the city, perhaps we can begin again. We will need to reassign the work. We need not worry. The city is impregnable. Pelbarigan itself cannot interfere with us because they could never get in. Any Peshtak in the area cannot, either. We will have to work hard. Very hard. Women will have to do the menial work of the males until we can raise more. The quadrant counsels will have to assume much authority. In this regard I am announcing, in this emergency, that I am substituting Dardan for Bival as Southcounsel for obvious reasons. Bival's talents lie elsewhere. Perhaps we are in crisis, but we are also purified and can start over. The vision of Craydor will not be dimmed. This is only a clearing of the eye. We—"

"It is a gouging out of the eye," the Ardena said. "Your policies have finally wrecked the city, and you sit there bragging about it."

Udge turned, raising her eyebrows. "Were you addressing me?"

"Obviously."

"Use the proper form or be removed."

"The proper form? Yes. Of course. Destroyer of Three-rivers. It is like you. The proper form indeed."

"I see no danger to the city, no destruction. Only some trash removed from it. Now, guardsmen, take her from the chamber. We are orderly here."

Two guardsmen moved alongside the Ardena and lifted her, as she shouted, "That's like you, Destroyer. You see no damage to the city because a city is stones to you. It isn't people. What is a city with no people? A ruin. What are people with no city? They are still people, the essence of the whole thing. You and these blind cave crickets will have this place empty and—"

The guardsmen carried her around the corner beyond the Judgment Room. Bival rose and followed her.

"Bival," Udge said. "I don't recall adjourning."

"I have adjourned myself, Protector. It makes no difference. I am not on the council anymore."

"Return and sit."

"No. The Ardena is right. I should have seen it. You are set on a course to destroy Threerivers."

"Guardsmen, remove her and place her in the first cell." A murmur arose in the room. A guardsman followed Bival and took her arm. She did not resist.

Again the Judgment Room fell to silence. Udge said nothing for a time. Finally Cilia rose and said, "Protector."

"Yes."

"Might I suggest that we adjourn now? We can plan a division of work more easily in the smaller group of the inner council, assigning some to the cleaning, some to planting, some to the lifting of the water, some to the bees, some to the stores, some to textiles, some to preparation for trade." It was clear to all that this is what Udge had asked Cilia to say.

One family head, trembling with age, stood and said, "But Protector, many of us know nothing of these things. We have always managed. These are lowly things. You must arrange our city so the changes will not be too harsh."

"Of course, Geryana. We will consult with great care. Now, this meeting stands adjourned." The remaining guardsman thumped her long-sword, and all rose to leave.

 XI

AT U Bend events moved slowly but steadily. Under Nim's direction, the slaves did manage to kill one dog without drawing suspicion. But they came to see that there was little point in piecemeal harassments.

Syle noticed that one Nicfad was in the habit of mounting the guard tower by walking up a single notched log leaning against the river side. Everyone else either went around or went up on all fours, but the Nicfad was proud of his balance, which was good, and he ascended easily. The Peshtak contrived to mix mud and grease and coat a step near the top. That afternoon the guard trotted up the log, slipped, fell, and impaled himself on the palisade.

The dead man was unmarried, so the slaves buried him in the small interment patch outside the circles, then at great risk secretly dug him up again, the dogs whining in the distance, and carried him to a storage barn half filled with straw. This they set afire, and when called to fight it, went with a great rush of concern. Afterward, scratching in the rubble, they found a charred body and they lamented the loss of one of their own. The Nicfad were contemptuous and uncaring. Thinking the remains that of a slave, they ordered them buried in the north field for fertilizer.

This kept the slave count right and freed one of Nim's men, Muse, for living in the lengthening tunnel. Every night when two or three got out through the privy tunnel, glided down the river, and crawled ashore under the dock, the tunnel behind Muse was nearly choked with new loose dirt. The others waded it out into the river in baskets and bags, then quietly spilled it into the current.

Gamwyn, who was kept endlessly busy cooking, washing, moving straw, and waiting on the Nicfad, nonetheless helped by stealing food for Muse and teaching the others how to measure the tunnel's length by triangulation. The slaves were amazed at his mathematics, but he realized his knowledge of such things was little—what was necessary for an average worker in Threerivers.

They used a long string to measure the digging, with a knot in it for every arm. Every evening while on some errand, Gamwyn would pace the calculated distance by proportion inside the compound wall, drop something at the correct point, lean and pick it up, and continue. From a station by the corner of the smoking house Syle or a Siveri would note how far under the circle the tunnel had progressed.

One evening during smoke time, Gamwyn was late after running an errand for a Nicfad, who opened the door and threw him in. He wormed his way to Syle and whispered, "The river is coming up already. It's early. That may mean a real flood. I'm worried. We aren't far enough yet. It may be a long, slow rise, and a long crest. That would help us. It would soak the ground. But we may not make it."

"We have to."

"I hope. I hope and pray."

Two evenings later, Syle informed Gamwyn they were passing the tower underground. They were also having trouble breathing in the long tunnel. The solution—tunneling to the well Gamwyn had stoned and opening a passage into it to admit air—took delay, care, and tricky measuring.

The river continued to rise, with all the leisure of a gigantic, lethargic serpent, slipping slowly back into the trees on the west bank, swelling up the levees. Eventually it was well into the tunnel, and Gamwyn cursed himself for not starting it higher up the bank.

In the tunnel Muse dug uphill, but the water followed him. Finally he had to come out, breathing from the last handbreadth of air under the roof. A hurried decision under the dock called for his escape at that point, and he slipped downstream in the dark.

Gamwyn finally convinced them to close the tunnel at the privy, but the outside entrance was already in the water, and too muddy to seal tightly. They packed it with stone and bags of sand.

Coming back from the fields two days later, they were met by a party of Nicfad and dogs. They had captured Muse, and led him, stumbling and beaten, back to U Bend. The slaves all watched in silence as he was led toward the compound. Torture, perhaps a confession, would follow.

Once the slaves were back in the compound, grim Nicfad lined them up in rows near the main guardhouse. They could hear Muse screaming inside.

A Nicfadleader mounted the guard tower and looked down at them. "So," he said. "You thought to escape. To cooperate." His jaw rippled. "You will soon see results of such folly. We will learn it all, slackers, dead fish, swamp rats. We will crush all involved." His tone changed. "You had part with us in building of this society, but you rejected it. You given place on work force on which we stand, but you have scorned it. I treating you all as guilty, from oldest on down. You will do well to tell us what you know. Otherwise, we will start with one of you and work through all until we learn what has happened. All." He laughed. "But I know it will not take that. We will root out this evil early enough. No evil tolerated. We will crush it. Now. No food tonight. Get to smoking house. No talking. We will post guards inside. Think it over. Either we cut out this evil easily, or we crush pack of you!" The Nicfad waved his fist in the air.

As he turned to leave, another Nicfad appeared with him on the platform and began an animated discussion. Gamwyn could see they were arguing. Finally the Nicfadleader threw up his hands and turned to cry out, "Halt, all of you. Return."

The guards turned the slaves and brought them back into line. The Nicfadleader leaned on the railing and shouted, "There is seep into inner field. We will need all to work on levee. Now. Do not think I have forgotten what I said. After this emergency, we will proceed. Now, guards, march them out in squads!"

As it grew darker, torches were brought, and the whole slave population was put to bailing the inner field, which covered the neck of the river bend, bringing stone from far beyond the circles, piling stones and dirt sacks against the softened wall of earth. Gamwyn was startled to see how quickly the river had risen, now high on the levee. Soon workmen from the circles were brought to help protect the low, broad field, which had been prepared for cotton planting. Already much of the levee had been stoned, but the work proceeded slowly, and the river did not gain. The Nicfad seemed more surly than ever. At one point, a guard knocked down one of Nim's men, and the frustrated Siveri stood up and swung his water-laden bucket.

Immediately five guards converged on him with staffs, beating him, but the Siveri nearby rushed them and bore them down. Nicfad horns blew, and guards rushed to the spot in a black crowd. The Siveri, nervous from the loss of their evening smoke, scattered or fought back. The Nicfad had to hand the torches to slaves, threatening them, but the slaves ran and flung them out into the river. More Nicfad could be seen running from the city, while, up on the levee, a frantic group of slaves began trenching across the earthwork. Soon Nicfad arrows flashed into them, but then a strange rumble started and grew, and as some turned and looked, the dim white tower on the hill tilted slightly, held on an angle, then fell in a grinding rush. The swollen river cut a rapid gap through the center of the circles, widening from the point where the rise of earth had previously turned it westward.

For a moment everyone seemed balanced on a pinnacle of awe and horror. Then the Siveri set up a cheer and swarmed toward the Nicfad, who began retreating up the levee. A squad of Nicfad running across the inner field also sprinted for the levee as the freed mass of water spread to submerge the flat land. They were caught and rolled under.

Gamwyn was yelling. "To the palisades. Tear down the palisades." They had planned to make instant rafts of them, but in the confusion many had forgotten. Now they turned and ran for the compound, where the levee still held. Some Nicfad followed, sending arrows ahead of them, but most realized that all of worth in the fields was swept away and ran along the levee toward the crumbling circles on the hill, yelling for their families.

"Before they organize!" Nim yelled. "And get Muse!" His men marshaled the Siveri into groups, chanting and rocking the log walls, throwing them down in sections and climbing fearfully on, as others pushed them into the river. Muse, though limp, was rushed onto one of the first.

Gamwyn was among the last to go. He felt a hand grasp his arm in the dark. It was Syle, who embraced him, saying in his ear, "You'd make a good Peshtak, boy. Good boy. And good-bye. I'm going to take a log and cross. I hope you get your shell. Be careful."

Gamwyn embraced him in return, and pushed him out into the dark rush of the river, watching the Peshtak paddle away with a board. Then the Siveri were calling him, and he waded out to the last raft and spun out into the stream, feeling its giant, casual power whirl them into blackness and freedom. Looking back, he could see the last torches burning in the stockade. The site of the Tusco city itself was wholly dark.

 XII

THAT night Gamwyn slept fitfully as the Siveri linked up all the rafts into a flotilla, calling to each other and

singing endlessly to celebrate their escape. Gamwyn's feelings stirred in his stomach like uncooked batter. He was
jubilant, but he had also watched the Tusco city vanish
into the river, with many of its people, including, no doubt,
the girl Daw, who had saved his life. While the destruction
of Jaiyan's ramshackle structure had been an accident, this
had not. He had engineered it. Gamwyn felt horror creep
through him like the night chill.

But with dawn, and the evident joy of the Siveri, he felt
relief. Nim stayed close to Muse, who was severely hurt
but laughed as he described repeatedly the Siveris' bursting
into the guard tower and impaling three startled Nicfad
when they threatened him.

Morning saw the flotilla draw back into the flooded trees
on the east bank, where the slaves prepared to set out for
home overland. They were more nervous than ever from
their lack of smoke, but Nim and his men kept urging
them on. The Siveri wanted Gamwyn to accompany them,
but he would not. He was eager to continue downstream,
passing the last Tusco settlement on the river while it was
in flood.

"That's called High Tower," one old Siveri said. "It's
on the west bank. It ain't so large as U Bend, but it's got
plenty of Nicfad. You'd best be careful. Sneak by at night.
Stay in the trees on the east bank."

Soon the Siveri, standing in the mud on the shore,
cheered a good-bye to Gamwyn, as he poled a narrow raft,
four logs wide, back out into the current. His heart beat
hard with fear, but he never questioned his resolve. He even
wondered about that. He turned once and saw that the
crowd of Siveri had already turned away from the river
and was headed east through the green-powdered trees and
white spring blossoms.

Gamwyn poled and paddled easily, fishing as he went,
catching nothing until he worked back into the shallows at
dusk. Then he landed a large catfish, which he skinned and
cleaned with the knife Sagan had given him. The Tusco
had never taken it away, thinking it a harmless neck orna-
ment.

Gamwyn beached his raft and went back a full half-ayas
from the river to cook his fish, to hide the fire. He ate as
much as he could hold, and dried the rest with slow cooking. Then he groped his way back through the dark woods
to the river. He knew he was a long way from High Tower,

so he poled back out into the current, letting the raft drift, feeling lost and miserable.

After a time he thought he heard something—then someone, a woman, calling. It was a sound of misery. Gamwyn lay down on his raft and kept silent. Perhaps one of the Siveri had become lost. No. He recognized the slow, slurred Tusco dialect. He paddled quietly, drawing closer.

In the dim moonlight broken by passing clouds, he saw two figures on a raft of debris, one sitting and calling out, one lying down. Eventually he drew close enough to hear the one lying down groan weakly. The seated shape leaned over and murmured something. Gamwyn silently stroked closer, lying full length on his raft, his heart beating hard.

"No, Mother, no food. I not know how to fish. We'll get to High Tower. Not worry. We'll make it."

It was Daw. Gamwyn was sure of it. He thought at first to slip by in the night. But he owed her his life. His breath came fast in his fear, but eventually he called quietly across the water, "Daw."

She uttered a light cry, standing, almost losing her balance, then sitting back down.

"Who? Who you? In name of Roara, Spirit of Spirits, help us."

"Gamwyn. It's the Pelbar. The one you saved at the well."

Daw's hands came up to her head as Gamwyn sat up and paddled closer. "No. What you going to do to us? No. Get away."

"Do? Nothing. Don't worry. I have some dry fish."

"Fish?"

"Not a whole lot. Enough for you and your mother to eat some. We'll catch some more."

She said nothing as his narrow raft bumped and grated against hers, which proved to be a piece of the white tower. Some bones were still fastened to one edge of it.

Gamwyn took a cord and fastened the two rafts together lightly. "Are we friends?" he asked.

"Friends?"

"You aren't going to harm me, are you?"

"Harm? Oh, no. Where this fish?"

Gamwyn fed the two, then worked the double craft to the east-bank shallows. Daw's mother lay scarcely moving. Gamwyn set out his two fish lines, searched Daw for weapons, though she scolded and writhed as he chucklingly patted her. He searched the older woman as well. They had nothing. Clearly they had somehow been swept up as the river broke through, and in the dark scramble had come up with their raft.

The two young people regarded each other in the dark. "I will see that you get to High Tower, but you must not enslave me again."

"I promise you nothing. It proper that you serve."

"Daw," the woman groaned. "Not now. Let him help us."

"I see. So you can trick me later," Gamwyn said. "That's the Central Committee's idea of truth. Well, in any case I will help you because I owe Daw that. But I must go on."

"On? Where?"

Gamwyn told them the whole story of the shell. Daw's mother sighed. "You crazy. It only chance that brought you this far."

"Chance? Maybe. Somehow in my mind I see Craydor knowing that I would be on this journey. I know that's foolish. But it's as if she thought it out—the getting of the shell. Someone would do something. I happened to be the someone."

"That religious fanaticism, boy. It enslaved you and it probably will again."

"Fanaticism? Is it worse than the social fanaticism you have so much regard for? To enslave and brutalize all in the name of a stupid system you have so much confidence in? Then to build your city where the river was sure to take it?"

The old woman groaned again.

"At least we have some values, some ethics," Gamwyn added.

"Shut up, won't you?" Daw said.

Startled, Gamwyn looked at her in the dark, seeing only the cock of her shoulders held up in exasperation. He leaned over and put his cheek to hers, holding her so she couldn't draw back. "I'm sorry," he said. "Let's just rest. In the morning we can make a bed for your mother and get some better food."

That proved harder than Gamwyn had imagined because of the flood and the soggy flatlands. He managed to add a log to the raft, roped on with a grapevine. He built a frame for the injured woman, wading back into the woods several times to get enough old leaves to pad it. All the ankleroot was deep under water, and though he managed to find a few mushrooms back from the river, and several stalks of wild asparagus, they had to eat mostly fish. Gamwyn washed the woman and splinted her arm, which was clearly broken. She lay passively, uncaring, her eyes glazed and distant, her mouth set in a line. Daw was of little help.

Gamwyn could see that the older woman was more deeply shocked than dangerously injured. He knew her whole world had been wrenched away, and there was no easy cure for that. "I will sing you a hymn," he said.

"Keep your filthy hymn," the old woman replied without conviction.

"I'll sing it for myself, then," Gamwyn said, and quietly sang all four stanzas of the "Hymn for Spring, Sign of Renewing." It gave him only slight comfort. The others said nothing. Then Gamwyn, too, fell silent. He looked out at the river, which lay broad and empty, save for the trees and logs riding the flood.

"We ought to go," he murmured. Poling out, he kept to the east bank. All day they saw nothing, nor did Gamwyn's lines pick up any fish. When they camped at evening, though, he soon came up with a large carp, which he roasted back from the river again, using drilling sticks to start his fire.

When he brought it back to the raft, something seemed wrong. Daw sat like a tableau. Her mother stared upward, blinking slowly. "What is . . ." Gamwyn began, but from behind him a rope snaked out and took him around the neck. He turned and saw a Nicfad, who jerked it tight, but not enough to pull him down.

"Careful of that fish, slave," the Nicfad said, grinning. Gamwyn cried out and dropped it into the murky water. The man, enraged, yanked him off his feet and dragged him through the mud and water, finally lifting him, choking, by the rope. "No more of that," he growled. "You have debt to pay at High Tower." He loosened the rope, and Gamwyn gasped and panted for breath. The Nicfad dragged him to the raft and threw him on.

"What about our supper?" Daw asked. "He bringing our supper." The Nicfad said nothing, but pushed the raft out into the darkening river. "What about eating. We have to eat," Daw said.

"Lie down, Committeewoman," the man said. "I don't

know how many of this murderer's friends around. If we paddle all night we should get to High Tower early tomorrow. Then you safe. Plenty of food there. And justice for this murderer."

"Murderer? Gamwyn? He helped us."

"He one of them. Murderer. You will see. What does other Committeewoman say?"

"Tie him up, Daw," her mother said. "Nicfad right."

Daw tied Gamwyn, though not brutally. She leaned over close while fixing the last knots. He could feel her warm breath and her young breast against his shoulder. "There," she said. "He tied enough." She moved away from him. Gamwyn knew she sympathized with him, but he felt a sudden revulsion for her as well as the others. It was all so dismal.

In the middle of the night it began to rain, fitfully, with much wind and some lightning. The Nicfad said nothing but continued to paddle. Daw lay down. She touched Gamwyn with her foot, letting it lie against his leg. He said nothing all night. What did the Nicfad mean? How would he pay what debt at High Tower?

Morning dawned gray and raw. The light had not fully grown to day when they rounded a bend, and the Nicfad said, "Committeewoman, here High Tower. They take care of you. And girl. And this murdering slave."

As they neared the landing, they were met by a squad of black-leather-clad Nicfad. Gamwyn was jerked and shoved out toward the slave quarters, which lay near the river. Looking up, he saw the tower, white with bones like the one at U Bend, but much taller. It stood on higher ground somewhat back from the river. Again the listless Siveri stared up from their work as Gamwyn was cuffed and buffeted by Nicfad to the room at the base of one of the guard towers. He was kicked inside and the door locked behind him. He lay, exhausted and hungry, in the dirty straw. Around high sun, a Nicfadleader jerked the door open and stared in at him, then slammed it again. Wind and rain returned, then some sun.

Gamwyn tried to pray, at first vainly because of his hunger, thirst, and fear, but then he calmed himself with Pelbar hymns. He was still angry with himself for having been fool enough to try to help Daw and her mother. But he still felt he had owed it to them.

After it grew dark again, Gamwyn heard sounds outside,

and the door grated and opened. He looked up and saw a squad of Nicfad. He was jerked upright and led out toward the river. Looking around in wild fear, he noted that the whole community seemed to be present, standing in the wind, arranged in rows.

He was led to a platform near the river. Looking around, he saw lines of slaves. Behind them stood a row of Nicfad, legs spread, staffs in their hands. Beyond the Nicfad the workmen stood. Looking behind them as he was jerked along, Gamwyn could see the whole tower was crowded with faces, all looking down at him. Sudden fear drained him. What did they have in mind? Behind the tower the sky rolled and boiled with heavy clouds in a strange, yellow light. Some of the clouds seemed to hang like heavy dark grapes. The wind picked up, and a spurt of rain passed.

Gamwyn was prodded and kicked up onto the platform. A rough table stood there, with a log at the west end. Suddenly Gamwyn realized that they intended to cut off his foot as punishment for escaping. He fought and twisted, but the Nicfad simply tightened the rope around his neck. He was wrestled up onto the table and held down by eight grim Nicfad, his ankle over the round of the log.

A Committeeman from the tower spoke out through a great megaphone, and each of his phrases was repeated by a Nicfadleader with a megaphone standing on a platform just behind the Siveri slaves.

"People of High Tower," the Committeeman began. "You see here worst kind of social wretch. Taking advantage of disaster at U Bend, he did not stay to help but took opportunity to escape. He responsible for much misery, then. It proper that he severely punished. But true to our practices of mercy, we intend to inflict only just punishment for escape—removal of one foot. Then slave given chance to redeem self through hard work.

The man continued, but Gamwyn had ceased to listen. He struggled grimly, but it was no use. His mind seemed to burst open. All this was unreal. He seemed to see a shell forming in the sky. No, it was not the right one. It was columnar, like some land snails, like the whorls of water that pierce the river on each side of a paddle stroke.

"It's not the right one," he screamed out. The Nicfad stared at him, teeth gritted. The Committeeman droned on, the Nicfad chanting his phrases after him as the wind picked up.

Suddenly Gamwyn's mind returned, and he watched with horror as the shell became a tornado, which neared and darkened, dipping and twisting. It approached from behind them in the west and south, and since all watched him, no one saw it. Its speed seemed to increase. Finally, Gamwyn heard the Committeeman say, "Has prisoner any word of apology and contrition before we execute punishment?" The Nicfad's repetition was almost drowned by the wind.

Gamwyn struggled in the arms of the Nicfad and screamed out, "I call all the gods of the sky down on you in wrath and without mercy, for you know neither pity nor justice!"

The wind rose higher, and within it another distinct sound grew, a coherent roar overwhelming all speech. As one Nicfad reached for his axe, another happened to look west. He let go of Gamwyn's leg and screamed, then the others turned, as the tornado raced the last fifty arms toward the tower. The onlookers turned and yelled, and Gamwyn stood, free for a moment, as the black funnel arced its base into the tower, exploding it. Wood, bones, and people flew, cutting down through the line of workmen, lifting as the sloping land pulled down from it toward the river.

Gamwyn never looked. He had shucked the rope from his neck and jumped from the platform as the twister struck the tower. He raced for the river as he felt the tornado pass over him, knocking him into the mud, where he was pelted by debris, then roar out over the spinning and churning water. A Nicfad grabbed for him. Gamwyn twisted. He heard a strange gurgle and turned to find the man impaled by a long splinter. He wrenched free and then stumbled down the bank and out into the river, swimming for one of the boats bobbing and plunging at a mooring in the water. Only once he had rolled over the gunwhale into it did he turn. Through the heavy rain he could see the tower was gone, the slope covered with people, lying, crawling, running. Gamwyn dug an oar in and headed downriver.

A Nicfad arrow stuck into the boat, but as Gamwyn turned again, he saw a Siveri swing a post and fell the archer. He heard a nearby shriek and saw two small figures swimming desperately toward him. One was a girl. He paused. Was it Daw? No. Both wore rough Tusco slave clothes. A boy reached the boat first, and Gamwyn hauled him over the side. The boy immediately scrambled for the oars, and as Gamwyn grabbed the girl's wrists, the stranger began to dig in long strokes. The girl was surprisingly wiry, and came over the side in a surge, with Gamwyn's help. She lunged for an oar, and the boy moved over, leaving Gamwyn merely a passenger as they stroked together, driving out into the current and downstream through the storm.

Gamwyn looked back. No one was following. He slumped down almost faint in the bottom of the boat, dimly watching the two stroke, silently and evenly, their young faces grim and desperate. Gamwyn raised up and looked back again as they reached the first bend. The rain had slowed, but blown rain and mist obscured all behind them. The two rowers rested on their oars, allowing the boat to drift, their chests heaving. For a time, no one said anything. The two looked at Gamwyn apprehensively, but he simply lay back in intense relief, enjoying the feel of the rain on his face as it washed over him.

 # XIII

DEEP by the stone-lined wells at the base of Three-rivers, Warret and Bival drew down on the rope together, lifting the bucket up the shaft to the first way tank. Bival was sore, her face strained.

"Rest, Bi. I can lift alone awhile. I just won't fill the bucket quite so full."

"No. If you can do it, I can. I just wish those old ladies wouldn't take quite so many baths."

Warret chuckled. "We've all said that often enough. There seems no limit to their cleanliness. Anyway, this is better than the cell, isn't it?"

"On one account. I'm with you again. I hadn't known . . . I have so much to make up for."

"No. We both needed to rethink things. I needn't have

been so proud. Anyway, it doesn't matter. That's all behind us."

"But what's ahead? Six more women left last night to join their men."

"They'll have a long trip. I just heard most of the men have gone far beyond Northwall, to start a community way up in the area of the Sentani winter hunt."

"Who told you?"

"A guardsman. He took the message from the aviary to the Protector."

"She will never announce that."

"No."

"Do you think we will survive?"

"It depends. On the Peshtak and on Pelharigan."

"On the Peshtak? Even if there were only four or five of us here, they could never get in."

"I don't know. I don't know. Bi, do you want to leave? I'll go if you want to."

"No. We started it. We need to see it to the end, whatever that is."

"I wish I understood about Brudoer. He seems to have vanished. I'm convinced that the guardsmen didn't kill him. The refugees said they didn't take him. He refused to come."

"I don't know. I just don't know."

Meanwhile, Brudoer was still exploring the inner structure of Threerivers. It was not easy. He found that while Craydor had arranged for small cracks of light to enter the passages from the inside, those had long ago been plastered over in most places. Only in the high arcing walls of the Judgment Room, or on the tall stairs, and in some odd corners, was light available to the inner spaces. Many places in the inner structure one could only crawl. At others an occasional small room lay cupped under the heavy inner arches of the city.

Brudoer had found seven other wedge stones, each with an iron handle on its back, all allowing egress into the city itself. In each case the stone was locked in from the back.

He also found a passage into Craydor's tomb, long sealed off. His arrival at the tomb surprised him. He had seen etchings of the interior, with its high, arched windows leading nowhere, supposedly for air, but when he came to one from the other direction, it took him a few moments to orient himself in the flickering light of his lamp.

The tomb occupied a small room, up at the high tip of the pyramid that had been an early external structure of the city. Brudoer was fascinated to see how the geometric shape had been planned, so the city fit around it, hooking into it ingeniously, wedging all securely.

Worming through the small arch, he dropped into the room. In the center stood the block of the tomb itself, of rough limestone like the rest of the city. On it was the neat inscription, "CRAYDOR, FOUNDER OF THREERIVERS. I know that what I have done here is for a time only, as I was, but I have tried to channel the underlying principles of harmonizing of parts and interests into it, to make it last. When it is time to rebuild, those principles will be present, as vital as they ever were."

Brudoer recognized the passage. It was from her last essay, the "Unfinished." Brudoer wondered who was to read it, shut up here, then realized that it was for him as much as anyone, or for anyone present at the unbuilding, the starting over, whenever that might be, if it would be. He ran his fingers over the stone. At the foot he found another inscription. It simply said, TAKE HEART. He walked around to the head and found there inscribed, TAKE THOUGHT. Otherwise the room was bare.

Brudoer also found ways of renewing his provisions of food and lamp oil. The lowest reaches of the passages descended to well level, so he was supplied with water. A small bathing stone was also cupped into the rock, and a drain. Clearly the inner structure was built for a fugitive.

One day he found a long passageway leading east, he thought, though orientation was extremely difficult in the passages. Following it, he eventually came to what he knew to be the living rock of the bluffs back from the river. They were hollowed out into rooms. Evidently he had found the original quarry from which the rock of the city had come.

While hostile peoples passed and repassed outside, and the city mysteriously grew during their absences, these chambers must have teemed with workers cutting rock and trimming everything to fit. Brudoer found living quarters, the remains of an ancient mushroom farm, fish holding tanks, even a slaughterhouse with an icehouse adjacent to it.

One room contained the remains of a large stock of Sentani weapons and some dried clothing of Sentani type. Brudoer puzzled on this a long time, finally realizing that the early city had fed itself in part by having its hunters masquerade as a Sentani band. It seemed hardly possible. Yet he could see no other ready explanation, unless some Sentani had allied themselves secretly to the Pelbar.

He remained interested in the current life of the city, now so changed, but his insights into it were extremely fragmentary. He could see they were struggling, with such a large female population, many too old to work, or unwilling because of their social standing. He longed to help, to make contact. But it seemed somehow the wrong time. He had been beaten enough.

At this time Udge fretted and planned in the Broad Tower, but the rhythm of the city she had grown up in seemed to have slipped away. She relied on the quadrant counsels almost entirely. The mood of the city had been slowly turning. She could feel it. Perhaps some accommodation should have been made. Perhaps it was severe to beat the boy. Perhaps a reconciliation should have been tried. The wind in the high stones of the city seemed to whisper it. Udge reacted, though, by becoming even more adamant.

Cilia brought a petition from the family heads of her quadrant. "Could not Pelbarigan be asked for help?" she read. "Food production, water, honey, trade products are all down. We are in need of men for heavy work, fish-cleaning, carpentry, rock-cutting. Could we not even install one of the far-speaking communication systems the dome people had brought to Pelbarigan?"

Udge sighed. "Do you not see, my child? These are only signs of weakness, of drifting from Craydor's ideal, of accommodation? The design of our city is sound. The city will renew itself. It has simply purged itself of the unworthy. If there is less food production, there are fewer mouths to feed as well. If stoneworkers are needed, then the men will simply have to work a little harder."

"But there are only thirty-four men left here, and some are old, Protector."

"New ones will come. Was not one born only two weeks ago?"

"He is already gone, with his mother, Protector."

"Were they not pursued?"

"By whom, Protector? The guardsmen are all doing double duty now."

"The answer to your petition, in any case, is not negative, Cilia. We will take it under advisement. We will see how things go this summer."

Cilia sighed and murmured, "Yes, Protector."

"May we have a date, Protector?" Lamber asked. "For the decision, I mean?"

Udge raised her eyebrows. "A date? Is that necessary. It will all come in good time."

"Yes, Protector. Still, it might help us deal with the people if we had a date. It gives them the feeling that everything is being dealt with in proper order and with efficiency."

"And you think it is not?"

"That is not the question, Protector. Is it not time we gave some thought to the people and their feelings? While some of them are still in the city?"

Udge rose. "Gind," she said to the guardsman, "please remove the Eastcounsel so she may think about decorum for a time."

The guardsman moved toward Lamber, who waved him away. "No need, Gind. I am going." Udge stared after her, her lip trembling.

West of the junction of the Heart and the Oh, a Peshtak sentinel jerked a cord, which, running from tree to tree, lifted a small flag some distance away. Immediately a detachment of the small force loped out toward the watch post. When they arrived, silently, the sentinel said, "It's all right. Sorry. It's Steelet."

The scout and two of his men were ushered into the river-bottom brake where Annon awaited them. "Well?" the Peshtak leader said, behind his bland mask.

"It's Threerivers, Command Annon. Something has gone wrong there. We think it's grown weak. They may be our chance."

Annon laughed bitterly. "After our probe force was wiped out last winter? By the Pelbar? With their new weapon? Think, fool. You advise us to take Threerivers?"

"We've seen no bloody evidence that the weapon is at Threerivers. But people keep leaving the fishsucking place. There seem hardly any men left. They coop themselves up inside."

"And if we take it, what then? The Pelbar will come from the north with the weapon and take it back."

"We may treat with them. They may compromise."

"Treat with us or wipe us out. Why we sent such a swine-scratcher as you I don't bloody know." Annon mused, pressing his fingers against his face mask. "Suppose the men are gone. Could we get in?"

"With surprise, yes. Once we are in, we could take the place."

Annon laughed again. His face was itching unmercifully beneath the mask. "Remember Northwall. Remember what the fishsucking Pelbar did to the Tantal. We well know those hogsniffers are no pushovers."

"All right, Command Annon. I'll go back. I am merely reporting as you requested."

Annon stood, offended by Steelet's tone. His hand went to his short-sword. Then he relaxed. "All right, Steel. Go back. First get some provisions. We have to do something this snoutrooting summer. Word has it the Innaniganis have sent a new probe into the mountains. The Kitats captured one. 'To wipe out the plague,' he said under torture. We are the plague. Well, if we are, somebody else is going to feel it."

"Yes, Command," Steelet muttered. He wondered still if the plague would appear on him. He and his men turned and sauntered through the brake. Annon slumped back down in his chair, drumming his fingers. If only his face would stop itching.

Far to the north, at Pelbarigan, Ahroe, the guardchief, bowed at the door of the Protector's chambers and was admitted. Sagan waved her to a chair. Ahroe sat.

"Have you made contingency plans for the aid of Three-rivers? Yes, I know you have. Review them with me."

"We can move in to reconstitute the government if the city finally revolts against Udge, Protector. We can also accommodate the whole remaining society if it abandons the city. We can even see them safely north to join the refugees. We have made some plans to defend the city in case of Peshtak attack. We are also stocking winter stores if they run short. We can run those downriver, protected, at any time but full ice. I am concerned about our plan if we have to supply them in dead winter. That is, only because of the Peshtak. We have no signs of them lately, but the Tall Grass Sentani have had two more raids." Ahroe pushed several broad sheets of paper toward the Protector. "Here. I have summarized the contingencies for you."

"You have not mentioned taking the city."

Ahroe wearily shook her head. "I don't see how we could, except by surprise. Craydor really designed the city flawlessly. A handful could defend it. I can't see losing any Pelbar lives to dictate to Pelbar."

"Have you had any success in planting a radio there? So they could summon us for aid?"

"No. None. The likely candidates have all left. We have seen they are well supplied with message birds. But that means delay."

Sagan fell silent. "One other thing, Protector," Ahroe said.

"Yes?"

"I think we are making progress with the Peshtak prisoners, finally. It's their fear of the disease. Each one has asked me privately if he is the one who has it."

"Have you told them?"

"No, Protector. I have done what you said. We will let them know if they cooperate. We are careful to treat them all as if they have it."

"And Royal? Has he made progress with it?"

"Yes, Protector. Much. He thinks he can cure it. Though it was generated in ancient times to plague an enemy, it has evolved somewhat, he thinks. He also feels it is less virulent than it used to be and only very mildly contagious—except that he feels that some other animal is acting as a host."

"Whatever that means. What animal?"

"Royal has questioned them without revealing his reasons, but they say little. He thinks it is pigs. They use pigs when they swear all the time."

Sagan smiled wryly. Then she laughed outright. "You mean it is transferred by eating?"

"Probably. And handling the animals. He thinks the cycle could be broken unless the disease changes again."

"Can he cure it once it is established?"

"He is working on an old formula of his own called panimmune. But he lacks the materials. He thinks that would arrest it. He feels also that the character of the individual has something to do with receptivity to the plague."

"The character?"

"Yes. I didn't understand his explanation. Something about the changes of secretions in someone with a tendency to anger."

"Then the one who has it is the one we call Red. The tallest one."

Ahroe raised her eyebrows. "Yes. That one."

The Protector stood, and before Ahroe could stand, leaned over and kissed her forehead. "How's the little one?"

"Fine. Stel is spoiling her, I think, but she is fine."

"Don't feed her any pigs."

"No."

"Let's work on these Pcshtak then, to see what we can learn. You would think they could be civil if we can help them."

"I don't know, Protector. There seems no limit to their viciousness."

"There always is a limit, Ahroe. There has to be. They are humans."

"Humans. But what humans are capable of!"

"Both ways, Ahroe, both ways."

☐ XIV

AFTER a brief rest, the two young Tusco slaves resumed their rowing, in long, slow strokes. Watching them, Gamwyn saw they must be brother and sister, and not much older than he. He could see them looking at him, but they didn't seem unfriendly, only desperate.

Finally, he said, "My name is Gamwyn. I am a Pelbar from the city of Threerivers. I am going to the South Ocean to find a shell."

"Threerivers?" said the boy.

"Yes. Do you know it?"

"Heard of it." Gamwyn felt he drawled out his speech, slurring across the consonants.

"I am Artess," the girl said. "This is Reo. My brother. We are twins."

"Where are you from?" Gamwyn saw their hesitation. "I'm sorry. I shouldn't ask. You don't sound like Siveri."

"We had been living at Murkal, with the Alats, until we escaped. But then we were captured by the Hightower Tusco. We've been there a full half year. This is the Alat boat we escaped in."

"Ah. I see you handle it well."

"A lot easier goin' downriver."

"Murkal. Can we get by it? I, I mean is it like the Tusco?"

Artess sighed, resting on her oars. "In some ways it's better, in some worse."

"No. Not worse."

"Maybe. Trickier. Yeah. We can get by it. We'd already decided ta go downriver if we ever got the chance. You goin' all the way ta the South Ocean? We'll go along together, huh, Reo?"

"Yeah. But we have to get by Murkal. That's got me worried."

"Do they enslave like the Tusco?" Gamwyn asked.

"Not exactly. They might as well. They just keep yah in debt."

"In debt? What do you mean?"

"Yah work yur wazzooobee off, and it still costs yah more ta live than yah get out of it. The investors. They get it all."

Gamwyn was silent. Another problem society. "Do they have a Nicfad?"

"No. Only a military. I'm pretty sure we could slip by there at night," said Artess. "We'll pick a dark one and slide by down the west shore all tangled in with some brush."

"How far off are they?"

"A good ways. Not much to worry about now but the Nicfad."

"I think they've got problems of their own," said Gamwyn. "Give somebody a really big problem and they tend to ignore small ones like us."

Reo chuckled. "I'm gettin' hungry," he said. "You fish?"

Gamwyn looked startled. They looked at him, expectantly. All at once he felt a great relief. They needed help. His help. They wouldn't betray him while he was of use.

"Yes," he said. "We've got no line right now. Let's find a good brushy island, and I'll make some traps."

During the next days, as the leaves filled out on the trees, Gamwyn and his two new friends drifted south into warmer country, at last seeing strange, gray beards hanging from the trees and larger flocks of egrets, some reddish tinged, winging around the river.

He fished and taught the others, using traps and weirs, and dug ankleroot when the floodwaters subsided. He would have loved to strip, as Reo did, completely unconscious of his sister's presence, but he did tear off his Tusco slave clothes and spent most of his time in a small length of it, pinned like a diaper.

One evening, as they sat by their fire eating catfish, Artess said "Gamwyn. Yah know what we are?"

"No. You don't have to tell me."

"Tantal. We're Tantal."

Gamwyn sat up. "What?"

"Yah know where we were born?"

"No."

"Threerivers. Where you were."

Gamwyn stood and backed up. He was confused.

"Sit down, Gamwyn. We were from the survivors of the invasion. After we lost at Northwall, we were sent downriver. Mama was heavy with us, and she stopped at Threerivers where we were born. That's what she told us."

"What? How did you get down here?"

"We were sent on. Our ship seemed too big for the Tusco to attack, and they let us go on—they wouldn't have if they'd known how undermanned it was. The Alats were friendly. They took us all in, 'for a rest.' But then we all went into debt, and those that are still alive are still there. Working."

"Your mother?"

"She died. Then we stole this boat and left. But the Tusco caught us."

"We were trying to get back to Threerivers," said Reo. "We were born there, so we thought they might take us in."

"They would have. But you wouldn't have had it easy, Reo. You're a boy. Boys have it tough, and men."

"Doesn't anybody know how to make things good for everybody?"

"It doesn't look that way."

As they continued downriver, Gamwyn was troubled by a recurring dream in which the whirling tornado smashed through the Tusco tower again and again, sending people and pieces of the structure flying. Sometimes the tornado became the shell in his mind, then a river eddy, a twist of rope, a spiral of climbing vine, the curl of a fern fiddlehead, the three-tiered loops of the Protector's hair, the curve of the main staircase at Threerivers, all whirling, shifting, and mixing, all smashing through the tower, spraying it out on the gale-wild air.

He would awaken sweating and groaning and have to bathe his face in river water to calm himself. What had happened to Daw? To her mother? To the rest? Was it worth it, this trip? Was it his fault? Would they and the people of High Tower have taken shelter if they hadn't been so intent on chopping off his foot? And what of the curse he called down on them? He had done it to scare them, as in the old story of Conn, but he shouted out the words fiercely, hoping they were true. No. Aven would never answer a curse. Aven blessed men but did not curse them. Still, people had been hurt—and killed. He was sure of it, though he had seen none but the Nicfad who chased him.

Finally, as he woke, he found Artess holding his shoulders. He struggled briefly, but she leaned down to him and put her cheek by his, whispering, "It's all right, Gamwyn. Don' worry. It's the tornado, isn' it. Let it go. Yah didn' cause it. It just came." She kissed his forehead. He could see her in the moonlight as a glowing circlet of hair around a dark head. He never replied, but she sat holding his hand for a long time in the dark.

In the morning, she looked at him. "Yah all right?" she asked.

"Yes. Thank you."

"We're gettin' near Murkal now, yah know. We'll have ta go slow. They have fast boats and slow. This is a slow one. We want to wait for the moon to grow old."

Gamwyn had sensed that they were nearing the city because of Reo, who found continual reasons for hiding out on islands, holing up, striking westward, resting, or fishing. But the moon was waning, and the dark nights were coming. They had to be in position to glide by at night. Soon they took to traveling at night only, and eventually passed what Artess called the "upriver docks" one night late.

They found a brushy island and waited out the next day, seeing two boats of fishermen checking set nets as they hid. That evening the weather turned rainy, and they knew their chance to make the last few ayas past Murkal had come.

They neared the city late. Through the misty rain, Gamwyn could see it looming dark on the east bank. "There. See?" Artess whispered. "In front is the parade ground. The main gate is flanked by guard bastions. See that thing sticking up?"

"With the three levels?"

"Yeah. That's the Godswagon house that the priests guard."

"Godswagon?"

"Yeah. They think they're favored, and when God comes back, he'll ride in some ancient thing they have up there."

"Quiet," said Reo.

"It's all right. We're almost by it now." She paused, then added, "Look. The fishing dock is out in the stream. Let's stop and see if there's a knife or two."

"No, Art. Please. No." Reo's voice trembled. But she expertly steered the boat to the float. The three reached out to it silently. A man lay on it, snoring slightly. Artess stepped lightly onto the float and crawled across it like a spider. The man stirred and smacked his lips, then settled back to sleep.

Artess came back and whispered, "Here. Two knives. There's some rope, too."

Reo whimpered, but she had turned away. The man yawned and sat up. Reo let go of the float and let the boat glide downstream. Gamwyn was furious, but when he took hold of the boy's shoulders, he felt him trembling violently. He had to slip into the rower's seat and turn the boat upstream, all without making noise. But as he did, he heard a slight hiss, and Artess came gliding along in a long, slim craft, a larger version of the Pelbar arrowboat, it seemed.

"It's all right. He's drunk. Sleeping in the rain," she whispered. "Come on. Let's trade boats. We'll really run away in this one."

"What about the other?"

"Let it drift. They won't recognize it for a long enough time if it hangs up and they get it. They all look alike."

They drifted together a good half ayas, then transferred all their gear to the new craft. One paddle lay in it. They also took the two long oars, and all three began to dig into the river in deep strokes, paddling silently and steadily for the rest of the night. They never looked back, and no one followed.

Finally, near dawn, Reo said, "Who was that?"

"The fisherguildsman. Drunk as a slug."

Reo laughed nervously. "We goin' ta hide today?"

"No," said Gamwyn. "Let's just keep going. One person with the paddle. Taking turns. Any more people down here?"

"None to the Atherers, near the South Ocean. They won't hurt us."

"Who would have believed that a river could be this long, even the Heart?" said Gamwyn.

"As I gather, there's plenty of it left," said Artess. They looked ahead, as the dawn flared into day, and the broad river seemed to flow on forever.

 XV

FROM where he stood, safe outside on the back of the city of Threerivers, where the wall was highest, Brudoer saw that heavy cloud cover had darkened the night. He breathed the drifting summer night and looked into the darkness. He leaned back against the solid side of the Broad Tower, where the guardsmen passed normally only twice a night quarter because it was so inaccessible. But with the guard force nearly depleted, guardsmen seldom passed there, and if one were to come, Brudoer had only to roll down under the curve of the tower to be completely hidden.

He had been leaning back and musing on his strange situation for some time when he heard a faint sound far below. He leaned out and looked down. He could see nothing in the blackness, but he could hear noises, soft but

numerous. Then he caught a low voice. Something grated
lightly on the wall. Something else touched. A force was
trying to scale the wall. Brudoer looked a moment longer,
then ran for the stairs.

Warret and Bival lay in each other's arms, completely
drained from water-lifting, when Brudoer blundered into
their room in the dark. He put his hand on something. A
leg. Bival started. Hands frantically worked up her body
and shook her shoulders. "Warret, Warret," a voice whispered frantically.

Warret stirred, then heaved upright, rolling Bival aside
and grappling outward. Brudoer came in to him and held
against him. "Warret, it's Brudoer. Come. Alarm the
guardsmen. People are trying to scale the rear wall. Behind
the Broad Tower."

"What? Brudoer? What?"

"It's true. Wake up. Do something. I've got to get out of
here." Brudoer gave him one more shake, then wrenched
free as Warret stood. Brudoer blundered his way to the
door and disappeared outside.

"What in Aven's—"

"Go, Warret. He might be right." Bival swung out of
bed, groped across the room, and blew up the punk, light-
ing a candle. Warret was struggling into a tunic. He raced
out the door and up the wide stairs, yelling, "Guardsmen,
guardsmen!"

A torch appeared before he reached the terrace levels,
and a guardsman, short-sword drawn, awaited him. "To
the rear wall, quick," Warret yelled, racing by. The guardsman sheathed and followed, torch streaming. As Warret
came toward the wall, he saw an arm reach over it. He
grabbed it, twisted, and threw. The arm came back and
clung, but the guardsman, right behind him, leaned over
and thrust at the man's face with the torch. With a scream,
the man let go as the guardsman took an arrow through
the neck and fell backward.

Yelling for help, Warret snatched the short-sword from
her dead hand, and raced to hack another arm as it appeared over the wall farther down. He dodged back quickly
and several arrows whisked by from below. More torches
approached from inside, though, as the entire duty force
arrived. If they showed themselves as they hurried to their
posts, arrows flashed up at them almost instantly. Finally
a guardsman brought an archer's wall—a wooden barrier

with one willow-leaf hole in it—and guardsmen flung oil-soaked torches over the wall while the guardcaptain leaned the archer's wall over the edge to look. He could see men below scurrying to put out the flames already spreading on the grass. With the arrival of two more archer's walls, guardsmen began putting arrows into the attackers.

"Peshtak," the guardcaptain yelled. "At least three hundred. Thank Aven you were awake, Warret. How did you ever find them? Who would have thought that they would try the highest side. Look at that scaffolding."

"I . . . uh," said Warret.

"Sometimes we get too tired to sleep and come out to look at the night," Bival answered from behind him. Warret whirled and looked at her.

Just then an arrow from below whacked into the very edge of the guardcaptain's peephole, and she jerked back, trembling. "Whew," she muttered. "They can shoot."

Three more archer's walls came up, and arrows also began to flick from the row of narrow loopholes on the whorled tower to the north. A horn blew below, and the Peshtak began to draw back.

"Kill them as far as you can shoot them," the guardcaptain shouted.

"That is not the Pelbar way," a voice said behind her, and she spun to see Udge standing in her night robe, puffy-eyed, back from the wall.

"Pardon, Protector. We need to sting them. There are more of them out there than we have here. But for Warret and Bival, they would be killing you in your bed right now. Should we send a message bird to Pelbarigan?"

"Did you not repulse them?" Just then she looked down and saw the dead guardsman with the arrow through her throat. She let out a little screech and turned away. "Any others hurt?" she asked, looking upward.

"Two over here, Protector. Only wounded," a guardsman called.

"Very well. Secure the walls." She turned away and returned to her chambers.

On the far side of Threerivers, a Peshtak threw his grappling hook up to the small garden niche that faced west, just below the level of the second terrace. He pulled down, testing the hold, then started up the rope. Five men waited below, one holding the rope end. The man had scaled most of the wall when a small bell rang and he felt a grating above him. Suddenly the wall rock pivoted about its middle, and with a slight cry, the man fell, spinning, landing with a thud below. Above, the wall rock pivoted back into place. The Peshtak below felt their comrade's wrist but found no pulse. They looked up but could make out only an old man. He held something in his hand.

Another Peshtak screamed and clutched his side where an arrow stuck out from it. Three arrows flashed up toward the high battlement, but the old man was gone. Then a longbow shaft thudded into another attacker. The rest looked, saw nothing, then ran, dragging the wounded man. Another Peshtak went down as they ran. They left him behind on the ground.

In the morning, the only Peshtak the Threerivers Pelbar could see were the dead—a total of fourteen. "Not many out of that force," the guardcaptain said.

"I wish the Protector would let us send a message bird to Pelbarigan," a guardsman said.

Another nudged her, nodding toward the guardcaptain. "She already did," she whispered. "At dawn."

"Sssst," the guardcaptain said, glaring.

They all smiled, saying no more.

That afternoon Bival and Warret set out on separate but related missions. Bival stopped into the guardcaptain's room where the woman's husband was rubbing her shoulders with soybean oil. "Something you should know."

"Umm?"

"I know you won't tell. I saw the message bird go."

The guardcaptain looked at her through narrowed eyes. "Umm," she said again.

"It was Brudoer that saved us. Brudoer came from somewhere and woke us in bed. He told us somebody was on the east wall, then run off. This is the truth."

"Brudoer? You're sure?"

"Yes, guardcaptain. He saved us all. We will need to remember that."

"Umm," the guardcaptain said. "Good to know."

Bival turned and left. "Think that's true, love?" the man asked, rubbing in the oil. He was a small man, but his arms rippled with strength.

"That's good. Ah, right by the neck. But softer." The guardcaptain sighed. "Who knows? She may be easing her conscience. But if he turns up, we will treat him as if it's true."

"And the Protector?"

"Stick the Protector."

"Where, my love?"

"Anywhere you'd like. Figuratively, of course."

"All right, love. Anywhere in her figuratively."

Warret had stopped in to see Pion a moment and told him of his encounter with Brudoer. He found the boy's father noncommital. It dawned on him that Pion already knew Brudoer was all right. Of course. The boy would have communicated.

"Where is he? How does he hide?" Warret asked.

"Who knows?"

"Please. Bival knows her mistake. We need to work together now. If we can help Brudoer in any way, we will."

Pion looked at him. "Who can help anyway so long as the city is run the way it is?"

"Well, we have to keep it running. Something will develop."

"Or collapse. When have I ever done anything but keep the city running?"

"You aren't alone, Pion. I, too. It's not so bad. That's what people do."

"Some of them." Pion turned away. Warret stared at him a moment, then left.

Back from the river, Annon stood in a circle of Peshtak. He spat. "We almost had it. They are undermanned, clear. How many did we lose?"

"Fifteen, Command Annon, including the one who died this morning."

Annon spat again. "And got nowhere. Well, we'll move south again and await the probe below the Oh, down where Misque is. We'll let these cool down. They may call the others. At least we know these only have arrows. We'll think of something. Not bad, Steelet. We almost had it. We did it well enough. It was only a chance. Next time maybe it'll be our chance."

Two weeks later, Jaiyan's Station was burning. Dead Siveri old ones littered the yard. Misque knelt, crying, grappling the knees of Rute, the Subcommand. "No," she said. "No, don't kill them. No more. They'll do no harm.

This is all there is here. The big young one is simple-minded. The other one is a good man. Please? No."

Rute jerked his knee into her cheek and she fell back, crying. He looked down at her in disgust. "When have any of them showed pity on us? Any?"

"These would. Please?" She fell at his feet, moaning and crying.

He looked at the other men, nonplussed. One said, "Just don't hurt her, Subcommand. She's my sister-in-law. I'll take it hard."

Rute spun away. "All right, Atchun, you take care of her. When she's recovered, tell her I want a full report on what she knows here and south. Tell her we'll keep the rest safe. We'll have to drag them along."

"For now?"

"If I give my word to a Peshtak, Atchun, I keep it. Generally. But Annon will not be bound."

Misque sat up, her hands covering her face. Alongside her, Atchun hissed, "Stop it. Stop it. You've shamed us all. What's got into you."

She looked up at her brother-in-law's face, and saw the sores at the base of his nose. She gasped. "Oh, Atchun. No. What will we do? Oh, no, no."

"Stop it. Others have borne it. I will bear it, too." She stood and put her arms around him.

Far to the north, in the Pelbarigan ice caves, the Peshtak called Red by the guardsmen also felt the root of his nose. It had been sore a long time. So he was the one diseased. He heard voices outside the cell coming through the caves.

A guardsman appeared and remarked, "Well, Red, here's Royal to see you. Be good. Promise?"

Red said nothing.

"All right, then." The guardsman deftly pulled the two chains that drew the Peshtak's manacled arms back against the wall. The Peshtak grimaced, watching the dark old man come slowly into the cell, carrying a box, which he put down and opened. The Peshtak saw something glimmer inside.

"It's me, then. It's me. Bull dung. I know it is."

Royal looked at the Peshtak. "I'm afraid it is. But here is something we'll try. I think it may help—at least arrest things for a time. You'll have to pardon the needle. It's a little crude. It may hurt." Royal washed the Peshtak's shoulder. The guardsman held a sharp short-sword against that side of the Peshtak's throat so he couldn't lunge at the old physician as he had before. Red glared at him, then felt the sharp needle glide into him, hold, and draw back.

Royal sat down across the cell. "Now, my son. May I ask you—do you eat pigs at home?"

"Pigs? Are you crazy?"

"A simple yes or no would help us find a cure for you."

Red trembled in a sweat. "Yeah. Of course we do. What fishgutted difference has that to do with anything?"

"And the other two men? Do they?"

"Of course they—" He paused. "I don't know. There's nothing to the pig theory. We thought of that. Plenty of people eat pigs and never get it."

"Perhaps they eat pigs that are clean? Or maybe they do something to the meat that kills the microorganisms. Or maybe they don't handle the uncooked meat or live pigs."

Red surged against his chains, flailing and struggling. "How long are you going to keep me like this?"

"We have no wish to. You are a mad dog. You'd hurt somebody."

The Peshtak glared at Royal and the guardsman. "We'll let you go home if we find a cure to this Peshtak plague. We think you won't be so murderous if you aren't so desperate."

Red sank down on his bunk, his arms still held up by the chains. The guardsman gave him some slack. As they turned to go, he said, "One thing." They turned. "Tell the others it isn't them. Tell them."

"We did."

Red lay back on the bunk and stared at the rock ceiling of his cell.

 XVI

BRUDOER continued his exploration of the tunnels and caves, seeking to gain a thorough knowledge of them so he could move freely and give the oppressed Threerivers people safety if some insurmountable crisis rolled over them.

The caves seemed the most impregnable area, if there were a way out of them. As he searched, he found another box of old manuscripts. Since he had seen Craydor's hand, he recognized its distinctive flourish. Brudoer knew the manuscripts to be unpublished material since all children at Threerivers read Craydor extensively. Perusing one, he was increasingly astonished for he found the old sage questioning all her own accomplishments, and even the Pelbar system of woman's dominance. "While it may seem natural for males, since they tend to be physically stronger, to do the heavier work while the women handle administrative matters, still unfairness develops. Reward does not always come to those who genuinely contribute. Others are promoted because of gender, and from their positions of prominence do mediocre work. The ideal society would appear to be one not oriented by gender. But in our present primitive state, that seems impossible."

Another essay, in a shaky hand, questioned the concept of Threerivers. Slowly picking his way through the difficult script, Brudoer made out, "There will be a time when Threerivers is no more. That has always been the way with human things. However, I hope deeply that my unlocking system is never activated, but, rather, that the city is taken down stone by stone to use for other things or new building, or else that other structures will have grown up around it and out from it so that when it is time to take down the old, it will not be missed." What did she mean? What unlocking system did she hope was never activated? Brudoer couldn't fathom it.

Far down the river, Camwyn and his two companions paddled deeper and deeper into the flat country of the lower Heart. They passed two empty spaces along the river, where weeds and grasses barely grew. As they journeyed, the river seemed to flatten and slow down, spreading and meandering. Great, moss-draped trees hung over the banks, and the three were surprised one afternoon to see a long, scaled animal with a knurled back and a great long mouth slide off the bank into the water and vanish. Reo shuddered, knotting his forehead.

Flocks of white water birds seemed to be everywhere, rising from the shallows, flying overhead in delicate, translucent brilliance, yellow bills stretched forward, black legs thrust out behind.

The three took their time, fishing and floating. Using his folding knife, Gamwyn made a bow and managed to trim a few straight arrows and even to fletch them, though he had had little practice in that.

Though the river maintained a channel, it was increasingly braided by muddy islands and swamps, seeming to frazzle out into a maze of confusing side passages and dead ends. More than once they had to turn and seek the main river again. Eventually, all solidity seemed lost. They were moving through a labyrinth of water, trees, vines, hummocks, and occasional stretches of grassy swampland. Snakes glided in the water and hung on vines and trees. Mosquitoes whined and stung constantly, and the three grew irritable and frightened. Reo wished he had never left Murkal.

One day, seeking the main channel again, they heard a shout. Looking behind, they saw three slim boats, far up another channel. A man waved a paddle. The three dug in and surged out toward a nearby bend, hoping to lose themselves in the swamp beyond. One boat began to follow, gaining rapidly. They could faintly hear someone calling. It sounded like, "Come back. Come back. Don't go that way."

They reached the flooded trees and moved their boat through them, twisting and crouching, until they finally felt safe. Gamwyn guided the boat up against a projecting root, panting and sweating. But as he gently set the paddle down, the boat that had been following glided slowly out across his bow. Five men were in it, dark-skinned, with bushes of tightly curled black hair and broad noses. One was standing, holding a fish spear at ease.

He grinned. "Well, children," he said. "Where you goin'?" He held up his hand as Gamwyn reached for his bow. "No. None of that. You're in Southocean country. Ours. That don't matter, really. There's plenty of it. We just wanted to catch you before you ended up in the dead flats."

"The dead flats?" Artess asked.

"All poisoned. Nothing there. No good to go there. The river goes through it. At least one part. Where you goin'?"

"To the South Ocean," Gamwyn said. "To find a shell."

"What kind of shell?"

Gamwyn described it at length. The men frowned. "I don't know no kind of shell like that," one said.

"You'd best go east to Sagol," another said. "A lot of shells there."

"Sagol?" another said. "How'd they ever get there?"

"How far is it?" Gamwyn asked.

"About a hundred fifty kiloms, a lot of it open sea. But you could follow the curve of the islands outside the empty bay. You could do it."

"So long as there ain't no big storms," one man said.

"Too early. Won't be none yet. Too early," another remarked.

"You got a sail?"

"No," said Gamwyn. "Just paddles."

"You'd best come with us," the standing man said. "My name is Samme." He held out his hand, and the three clasped it in turn. The slim boat turned, then, and led the way through the maze of passages out into the open again, then north to where they first had encountered the dark men.

They found a settlement with sixteen of the slim boats and forty-two people, all living in families in houses built upon stilts, some using living trees as a part of their support.

The three soon found themselves the center of a conference that seemed more like an amorphous argument than anything else, but out of it came several rapid decisions. Gamwyn would leave the boat with them. He, Reo, Artess, and seven others would traverse the swamps—portaging when necessary—eastward to the open sea in two boats and take them to Sagol in payment for the boat. They would also take a quantity of reed baskets with them for trade.

Though it was afternoon, they set out immediately, through narrow, watery aisles. The Southocean men called themselves Atherers, and Gamwyn gathered that they belonged to a loose alliance of several groups, all mostly self-governed. The Atherers seemed to know exactly where they were going in the maze of swamps and channels.

That night they camped on a small knoll, surrounded by swamp. The men built a fire and occasionally spread it over with damp tree moss for smoke to drive away the insects.

"Not long now," Samme remarked. "We'll see the ocean by midmorning."

As they settled down, the three slept together in spite of the heat, with Reo in the middle. But Gamwyn felt Artess's hand come across her brother's head to touch his shoulder and reassure herself he was there. Somehow they felt safe with the Atherers, but the great strangeness made them uneasy.

Just as Samme had promised, in the morning they emerged into an area of swampy sand islands, an ill-defined shoreline. In spite of what he had heard and imagined, Gamwyn was not prepared for his first sight of the ocean, which stretched to the horizon, bright and greenish blue. It was restless in the calm summer air; so vast, with such a sense of incipient power and indifference, that the great river he had grown up with seemed small and tame by contrast. The ocean seemed an active, understandable, animate presence. Here was an eyeless and careless immensity. It seemed to reach to the rim of nothingness.

But the Atherers didn't hesitate to launch out onto it, shaking out their gray sails and pointing their small, slender boats directly at the empty horizon to the northeast. Gamwyn looked at Reo and saw the boy was visibly frightened. But Artess seemed comfortable enough.

She reached over and touched her brother's hand. "It's better than hoeing cotton and beans," she said. That afternoon the party saw two low islands to the south, and as evening neared, another, much longer than the others, appeared. They steered for it, beaching the boats near sunset, drawing them far up the sandy beach. As the group sat at ease, cooking and eating, Samme questioned Gamwyn, Artess, and Reo about their background, and Gamwyn filled him in on everything he could. He felt an openness and honesty in the Atherers that he hadn't since leaving home. The Atherers laughed a great deal, and they sang beautifully. They seemed family-oriented. But Gamwyn couldn't understand how they functioned so well without apparent authority. No one was obviously in charge.

After sunset the Atherers knelt and sang a hymn to the Lone One. Later, Gamwyn asked them if that was the name they gave to God.

"No," one said. "God is God. We know that name and share it with others. The Lost One is God and he ain't. He brought God to the ancients. That is, the sense of God.

Somehow, everything known about him vanished in the turmoil of the terrible time after the great burning. We've never learned nothing about him since. You. What do you know about him. Anything?"

Gamwyn sighed and said no. He told them about Pelbar religion, and one man shook his head. "Another religion created after the burning," he said. "By somebody who didn't like men."

"Not that bad," another said. "You can see the outlines of the Lost One in it."

"You ought to come to Pelbarigan and talk about it," Gamwyn said. "They're gathering people there from all over—as far west as beyond the great mountains. Somebody might remember something. Even the Tusco had some scraps of paper from the ancient times." Gamwyn recited it to them. They looked at him silently, and had him repeat it until they all knew it by heart. A hush fell over them.

"It's the faint voice of the Lost One again," Samme said. "It is. It surely is." He sighed. "With knowing that, I don't see how the ancients managed to burn everything. But they did."

The whole group fell silent, watching the fire die. Then they unrolled their light cotton bed bags and slid in for the night. Gamwyn lay awake for much of the night listening to the light curl of surf slapping soothingly on the beach. Then he shut his eyes a moment and woke in daylight, with the gray-backed gulls crying overhead, wheeling and touching at the air with their wingtips. The Atherers had cooked more fish and were nearly ready to go. They laughed at his sleepiness, but they looked at him differently since he had recited the Tusco scripture.

Samme put an arm around him and said, "Are these the uttermost parts of the sea? Maybe to somebody from the uttermost parts of the river. But they're home, you know."

Toward evening of the third day, they saw the coast at Sagol ahead, and soon were hailed from the beach near a small stream entering the sea. A crowd gathered, and the three travelers were surrounded and engulfed, the whole group surging toward a large, low building back from the beach. Beyond it, Gamwyn could see a number of open, conical houses, thatched with leaves and fronds, arranged in arcs.

Sagol was an Atherer summer town, he was told. In winter, they moved back from the shore a bit to a place called Adant, where they prepared a spring crop before returning. That night a communal supper was held to celebrate the coming of the strangers, and afterward, Gamwyn was asked again to tell his story. While the vernacular of the Atherers tended toward what seemed to Gamwyn a slightly blurred drawl, it was closer to Pelbar speech then was that of Artess and Reo, and they understood him clearly enough. He gathered that they had a written language, and that proved to be the case. Their library, he was told, was at Adant, but books were around the summer town, some traded from the eastern cities. Gamwyn was disappointed to learn that none came from ancient times. He also learned that children were schooled four days of every ten the year round.

Gamwyn was told that the Southocean people were united in what they called a federation all of whose members lived along the north sea rim of the South Ocean, in peace with each other, meeting annually for a long governmental conference. "Most are dark-skinned, like us," one old man told him, "but some are lighter, and a few even light-haired, like you and your friend." He pointed to Artess, who smiled faintly.

"Tomorrow," the old man added, "is a school day. You will begin school with the others under the canopy."

"But my shell," Gamwyn said. "I've got to find my shell and get back."

The old man shook his head. "We all talked about it. There ain't no shell like that here, though the hermit may have one. He has a good many." He called to a boy and had him run up to a conical house nearby. Soon the boy returned with a blue-gray, ridgy shell, which he held out.

"Thank you, Welle," the old man said, smoothing the sand off it. "This is the nearest thing we have to it. But it ain't separated inside, and yours had no ridges. These are common enough."

Gamwyn took the shell and examined it. It was thin and fragile, a beautiful spiral, much like Bival's, but it lacked the exquisite flaring shape. Suddenly he felt a wave of despair, set the shell down, and sobbed, hiding his face in his hands. Artess's hand came to him, went around him, but seemed not to help. He didn't understand. Everybody had said the shell came from the South Ocean.

He cleared his eyes, finally, and saw the old man pa-

tiently regarding him. "You'd better go see the hermit. No
school for you just now. But you two—you go to school."
Artess made a face, and the old man laughed, showing an
expanse of toothless gum.

The next morning, Gamwyn set out for the hermit's with
the old man, who was thin and stooped, but surprisingly
wiry. They walked eastward along the beach for about two
ayas, then turned inland, mounting a slight rise. On the
way, the old man, whose name was Aylor, scarcely said
anything, except to explain that the hermit lived alone at
the edge of a ruined area, collecting things from the ancients, cleaning them up, and explaining them. "He ain't an
Atherer," Aylor explained. "He came from Innanigan
when I was young, and he's been here ever since, building
his junk pile." Aylor chuckled, fell silent, then chuckled
again. Then he added, "You'll like him. He's alone so
much, you'd think he'd lose the power of speech, but he's
just sharpened it." Then the old man chuckled again.

Soon they mounted another rise, toward a grove of
scraggly trees, in which Gamwyn could see a ramshackle
building. Soon they could hear someone humming and
found the hermit seated at an old plank table scrubbing at
a chunk of old iron with a piece of sandstone. He looked
up at them, at first vaguely, his eyes swimming.

"You. Aylor," he said. "I'd better get a dog. He who
sneaks like a snake must be minded like one."

"Nobody's sneakin', you old gator face. I brought somebody to see you. Gamwyn, this is Darew the hermit.
Darew, this is Gamwyn, come all the way down the Heart
River and here to find a shell. We tell him there ain't none
like it here. Thought you might have one."

"A man who envies the possessions of others ignores the
great goodness he has, boy. Gamwyn, huh? From the
Heart, huh. He who has a heart already has more than he
who has a shell. You would trade the better for the worse.
Would you trade your skin for cotton pants? You have the
essence and you expend it on trifles."

"Stuff it, Darew, and listen to him. He's come well over
a thousand kiloms."

Darew looked at him. "A thousand kiloms. Never escaped yourself in all that distance, did you."

Aylor sighed. "Gamwyn, you tell him."

Gamwyn sat down across from the hermit on a section
of old log and described the shell, stressing why he needed

it so badly. Darew pulled at the thin gray hair on his crown as the boy talked. Then he stood abruptly, saying, "I have one of those. Found it in the ruin. You may find one there, too. I will keep mine. He who keeps what he has will never need to seek what he has not."

Beckoning, Darew walked back into the grove, where Gamwyn saw, arranged in neat rows, stacks of curious and baffling rusty objects, then rows of other objects—stones, pine cones, types of wood, mostly broken ceramics, and finally shells. Darew picked one up, tossed it up in the air, caught it, and handed it to Gamwyn. It was the shell, the very type Ravell had brought to Bival. The boy found his hands trembling.

"You—you have no other one?" he asked.

"No. Only one. They don't come like that around here. The ancients brought it from someplace. See the hole they drilled in it?"

"Can I earn it from you?"

"No. Spoil the collection. It's the best one. That's how I knew it right off. He who sells the ham must be content with snout meat and pig's feet."

Aylor spat in disgust. "Might have known. He's always sure have some stupid aphorism to shroud his selfishness in."

"He who can't gain his end by worth, tries to gain it by words," the hermit replied.

"Where'd you find it? May I look there?" Gamwyn asked.

"Found it at the finding place. And—"

"Yeah, yeah," Aylor said. "He who looks with the hawk's eye, finds what the hawk would find. He who looks with the eye of a clam, finds what a clam would find."

"Eye of a clam? My old friend, I believe you've had too much sun. Anyone—"

"Yeah. He who gets too much sun, gets from light darkness."

"That's good. That's very good. I'll have to remember that."

"And he who always has a saying never has to have a doing."

"Jeez I cry, Aylor, look how busy I am. Someday this will all make sense. All is in order if we can find the order."

"Order is awful the way you see it."

"No, my friend. Ordure is offal."

Grumbling but amused, the old Atherer left Gamwyn with the hermit and took his way back to Sagol. Darew promised to take the boy to the place where he found the shell when he finished brushing away the loose rust from the latest object he had unearthed. While he worked at it, Gamwyn moved through the aisles of his collection, frustrated and a little angry. Soon, quite naturally, he came back to the shells, and noticed for the first time the richness and variety of the collection. They were arranged in the open on rough planks, all in groups resembling each other. As he moved through them, Gamwyn was startled to see what was obviously the exact image of the rear tower of Threerivers. He took it up. Yes. It certainly was the right one, with its broad and spreading spiral, its large, hooded opening.

He ran to Darew with it. The old man paid no attention at first, then looked up quizzically. "That one? You can find bags and baskets of that one down on the beach." He snorted. "That's no rarity."

"Nothing is rare where it is in plenty, but where I'm from, it's not only rare but unknown. It's the main guard tower, in miniature, even to those mottled colorings."

"Nothing is rare where it is in plenty, eh. Very good. Smart boy. I'll have to remember that. Rare is not plenty. Clever. Why didn't I think of that. I've been neglecting my philosophy." He laughed raucously. Gamwyn felt chagrined. Darew scrutinized him, then put down his sandstone abrader. "Tell me what the other towers are like. Shells?"

"The water tower is a tall spiral quite like some of our local snails, but different. Longer. It's as though you took a coil of wet clay and spun it up to a point in your hands."

"I have those over there," the hermit said, pointing a long, crooked finger. "Many kinds. What about the others?"

"Oh. The other main one is curious. It's really used for produce storage. It isn't like the others at all. It's large, humped, with openings on the ends. It curves over like a roof." Gamwyn gestured with his hands. "Inside you walk down a center aisle. The sides curve in and around toward you, forming shallow bins for compost. Above them are shelves and racks."

"A money shell."

"What?"

The hermit sighed and stood up, dusting himself. Finding

two old sacks by a tree, he handed one to Gamwyn, then started for the beach without a word. Once there, they turned east away from Sagol, and sauntered on the sand, Gamwyn looking quizzically at the old man, who absently splashed in the light surf like a child, watching the sea birds, sand, waving grass, and the sky with an unabashed delight. Gamwyn walked along beside him wondering what they were doing. After they had walked about three and a half ayas, they came to an area rich in shells. The old man stooped over, moving slowly, putting shells in his bag, humming lightly.

Gamwyn followed suit, soon becoming completely enraptured by the varied shapes, colors, sizes, and textures of the shells. Some curved broad and flat, like the small river clams at home, but ridged in many ways, patterned, colored, toothed, or bent. Rifts of small spirals of various kinds lay in miniature handfuls. Large, heavy, knobbed shells lay half filled with sand, and worn and broken ones revealed inner structures of bizarre design.

Finally Gamwyn found the miniature of the storage tower, then found a slightly larger model. Darew suddenly appeared at his shoulder and put a tight spiral in his hand. It was not quite the water tower, but almost. In a quarter sun's looking, Gamwyn had nearly a dozen varieties like it, including what seemed to his memory to be the exact model. Walking up beyond the reach of the waves, he laid them all out in rows, fascinated by the shapes. But there was nothing like the shell he had come for.

Darew's shadow crossed the shells. "See? No shell like the one you want. But he who can modify his wants to suit the possibilities can live happily. He who desires the impossible cries because he cannot soar like the birds—who cannot think or read."

Gamwyn sifted dry sand through his hands. "Somehow I'll find one," he said. "There have to be some. Craydor had one. Ravell brought one. You have one, too. There must be others."

"In the ruin. They must have been brought here. I found mine in the ruin. Out of the old may often come the new. You may dig with me. Eventually we may find one."

"But I don't have all my life. Who knows what they are doing to my brother while I scratch around in your ruins."

"Patience is often an attitude that simply makes comfortable the inevitable."

Gamwyn looked out over the water and felt inside the broad emptiness he saw there. Maybe the old man was right. Well, he would continue to look. He would dig if he had to. He would never give up.

But that evening, when he had left the hermit and returned to Sagol, things looked much more bleak. Aylor put his arm around the boy and patted his shoulder, but said nothing. Aylor's family, a large one, with three married sons and their children, all seemed very solicitous. But Aylor also said, "School tomorrow. For you, too, Gamwyn. You'll have time."

"School?"

"You won't mind, Gam," Artess said. "It isn't like Murkal. Today we went fishing."

"Fishing?"

"How else can you learn tides, weather, currents, navigation, fish, and work?" Aylor asked.

Gamwyn felt relieved. "Jeez I cry," he said.

"Picked that up from the old man already, eh?"

"What does it mean?"

"Don't know. Now, time to pray to the Lost One and then to bed. We shake out sail before sunup tomorrow."

The next three weeks saw Gamwyn fishing far off shore, drying fish with the children, measuring, cutting, and splitting wood for dwellings, weaving rush mats, and grinding shell to burn for mortar—all in school. When the others had free days, which they often spent in singing, working, or swimming, Gamwyn worked with the old hermit at the ruin site.

It had evidently been a town in ancient times. Back from the beach, it was still choked with sand where it wasn't buried. Darew had shoveled away great quantities of sand, exposing broken streets and shattered buildings. He was interested in small artifacts, which he continued to collect and speculate about. Some of his conclusions Gamwyn found very shrewd, but others seemed strange. However, the old hermit didn't like disagreement, so Gamwyn always kept silent or agreed with him. The old man talked incessantly, peppering his talk with endless aphorisms, some of them amusing and incisive. Sometimes others came to dig or talk, always bringing Darew something to eat or some small present. The hermit was grateful for the company, though he never admitted it, preferring to seem aloof.

As time advanced, Gamwyn grew more despairing. Day

seemed to flow into day without hope of solving his dilemma. The Atherers lived a rich life of leisure and work, replete with social enjoyments and the gentle religion of the Lost One that all of Sagol embraced. But Gamwyn seemed no closer to his shell than he had been when he left Pelbarigan. Artess and Reo seemed settled, and Reo was seldom separated from Aylor's granddaughter, Daun, who took care of him like a mother.

One morning, as summer was well advanced, Gamwyn arose to find a number of men on the beach, staring southward with shaded eyes. Gamwyn noticed a mass of clouds, but it seemed to him little different from those he had seen in the past.

"What do you think?" one man asked.

"I think it'll be a big one. I think we ought to begin to move now."

"We may waste a lot of time if it isn't."

"We may lose everything if it is."

"Call Oin."

A boy ran off to get her. Oin came down from her stilted house slowly and painfully, carrying a stick. She advanced toward the beach in a slow shuffle, chewing something with toothless gums. At last she arrived among the men and squinted southward, still chewing. She stood for a long time, but finally said, "Start moving now." Then she turned and started back.

One of the men sighed. "Begin with the boats," he said. Someone blew a large seashell, which produced a mournful bellow, and people began to tumble from their houses. Soon Gamwyn was caught up in the mass move back from the beach. The smaller boats were slid along the sand, then in a trough that led inland. The three larger boats were lifted by a crowd of men onto large sledges that accommodated their keels, and dragged back over the rolling flat land on the main road inland. The whole village dragged and carried, even the small children. Gamwyn helped haul a small boat with a rope, wondering why the Atherers traveled so far, for they went over scrubby hills almost two ayas, finally sliding the boat up a long, high hill. Behind it he saw the houses of the winter town, Adant, and fields, now weedy. He knew a storm was coming, but surely nothing could demand such work.

The men trotted all the way back. Gamwyn arrived tired, but he was given little chance to rest. The clouds to the south, now a dark, swirling mass, had moved closer. The surf had risen, too, and now lifted, rolled, and slammed into the beach in hollow roarings.

After the boats had been moved, the crowds began to lift the shelters using long poles that slid under the raised flooring, carrying each structure entire. Soon the long communal building had been taken down, its planks and logs tied into bundles for dragging. The wind picked up as the cloud piles reached in over Sagol, blowing from the west along the beach. Weel, one of Aylor's sons, looked up at it as he worked. "God help us," he shouted. "This one's coming straight on in."

By the time Gamwyn had made three trips back from the beach, he was exhausted. But much of the summer settlement still remained to be moved. He sank down a moment. Someone grabbed him roughly by the arm. "Not now. Later." The man was furious, and as he wearily stood up to work, Gamwyn realized dimly that was the first time since arriving at Sagol he had seen anyone angry.

He took hold of a pole and helped walk another of the conical houses along the road inland. Soon the wind began to tug, then tear at the thatch. The Atherers he was working with stopped to lash the structure to the poles, but as they finished, the wind rose, heaved the structure upward, and ripped it from their hands, tilting it and rolling it into a mass of heavy oaks. The men ran back to help by the beach, but their effort was of no use, for the rising wind had torn away the remaining houses, and the whole body of people began to flee inland.

Gamwyn felt a tug on his arm. It was Aylor, who leaned close to his ear and shouted, "Have you seen the hermit?"

"No," the boy shouted back.

"I'm afraid for him. The sea will reach his place."

"How could it?"

"Trust me. I've lived here. It will. Come on."

"I'll go get him," Gamwyn shouted, his words whipped away in the wind and pelting rain.

Aylor grabbed his arm. "No. Too late. He'll have to get along himself. He should know better than to stay. Maybe he's gone. Come."

Gamwyn looked at the old man's lined face streaming with water, his eyes nearly shut against it. Aylor took his arm and led him inland. As they moved, sideways to the wind, Gamwyn could scarcely believe what he saw, for the

whole landscape seemed to bend and pitch in the screaming gale. Leaves and branches blew by. The force of the
wind threw him to his knees several times, but others lifted
him. They moved in a tight mass, supporting each other.

At last they came over the long hill. At its summit,
Gamwyn turned around and glimpsed a surge of the sea as
it rose and toppled far inland among the scrubby trees.
Aylor moved him on. In a short while, they stumbled into
a heavy, stone-walled house, and suddenly everything was
still and muted.

In the dim light, Gamwyn could make out many huddled
bodies, as the Atherers relaxed and waited out the hurricane. At first they were still, but eventually one of them
started a slow hymn to the undying love of the Lost One.
Others took it up. The mellow voices had a calming effect,
and eventually Gamwyn nodded off to sleep, waking only
when people moved over him to go outside. He himself
eventually stood up and stooped out the door, finding the
wind very light and most of the people climbing on the
summer houses, refastening their bindings after tying them
together tighter in a single mass.

Gamwyn climbed up the hill and looked seaward, but
the deep gray sky and blowing water kept him from seeing
far. He heard a voice and turned to find Artess calling and
beckoning. He stumbled down the hill. When he reached
her, she took his arm, saying, "It's not over yet, they say.
This is just the middle of it. Come on now. The wind's
picking up again."

It was. Gamwyn felt the storm come quite suddenly,
from the east this time, and he crouched into the door of
the stone house as the sky began to howl again. Inside,
candles were lit, and some of the people were playing a
game with pebbles, chuckling and joking. But when the
singing began again, all joined in.

Gamwyn didn't know how long the storm continued,
since he drowsed off again, his exhausted body lying limp.
His whole interior self seemed to rise out of it, leaving the
empty shell below, as he rose unblown high into the air to
look for the old hermit. He felt as if he stayed there, distant
and still, untouched by the anger of the wind, seeing nothing
but gray sky, dark rain, and blowing debris.

When he finally jerked awake, it was almost evening.
The wind had died down, and the stone house was nearly
empty. Outside, he found the Atherers working on their

summer houses, separating them, tightening lashings, re-fastening thatch. He walked to the top of the hill again, but he couldn't see the road southward. Suddenly a thought settled on him like a vulture. He had done it again. Every time he joined a society, it experienced some disaster. Was it a curse? What would he do next? He turned and saw Artess walking up the hill toward him, disheveled by the storm.

"Come and eat," she said. "A big fish chowder. You look awful. What's the matter?"

"Oh, nothing." He suddenly realized how hungry he was. Artess slipped her hand into his as they went down the hill. He looked at her.

She smiled. "I was scared," she said. "But they don't seem too worried about it. All the valuable things are in these stone houses. Look. They are used to such storms—even though this was a bad one."

As he finished his chowder, Gamwyn became aware of Aylor standing over him. "In the morning, you go look for Darew, Gam. The storm's about over now. A lot of work left. But we have the time. We're all safe. Ever see anything like that?"

"No, sir. Only a tornado or two."

"We have a lot of rebuilding to do. Lost some crops. But nothing so bad. We'll have to see how the beach is. Something like this will change it all around. Had enough food?"

"Oh. Yes." As Gamwyn said this, Aylor turned away. Gamwyn could see that the old man was tired, too, dragging his feet toward the long stone house again.

☐ XVII

IN the evening, Pion appeared in the door to Bival's room with a tight roll of paper, which he handed to War-ret. "This is from Brudoer. He says to read it. He says the original is in Craydor's hand and that he found it."

"Pion," Bival said, rising and running out into the hall after him. Pion stopped. "Pion, where is he? I don't understand."

"I don't know where he is," Pion replied tonelessly.

Bival took his shoulders and faced him. Then, like a cup filled to overflowing, she began to sob, putting her head against his shoulder. Pion looked past her at Warret until, finally, Bival stopped. "May I read the roll?"

"I think Brudoer meant that, though his note said Warret."

"We are on the same side. Don't you see?"

"Yes. I see. That is a fact, but my emotions haven't agreed yet."

"All that other seems like something in another world."

"It was. Another world but not a forgotten one. It's all right, Bival. Don't worry. We know if we are going to survive, we'll have to do it. We'll get nothing from the Protector."

They regarded each other silently for a moment. Then Pion smiled slightly and turned away.

Near the South Ocean, the morning after the hurricane dawned clear and bright, with a few scudding clouds. As Gamwyn walked toward the beach with most of the Atherers, he could hear the long rollers still pounding the shore. As they walked they cleared debris from the road, but still it remained gullied and clogged with sanddrifts. Gamwyn could hardly believe that a storm could have such massive force. As they neared the site of the summer village, it seemed wholly strange. All had been swept away. The shore itself revealed jutting rocks where none had been seen before.

The Atherers seemed undiscouraged, and immediately set about measuring out the village again. After a short while, Aylor took Gamwyn aside and said, "You'd best go see about Darew. He's been through these before, but maybe none this bad. He ain't so careful as we are, and he might worry about all his junk. Look sharp for him. Take your time. Bring him here if he needs help."

Gamwyn set out immediately, but the shoreline seemed so much altered he had trouble telling where to turn away from the beach. Searching where he thought the hermit's camp had been revealed nothing. Eventually, though, he recognized a tree. Yes, that was on the south end of the old man's collection. Where was the rest? Nothing was visible. A bit of shell here, or a stick there, might have belonged to Darew, but nothing was obvious.

Gamwyn turned east toward the ruins, hoping to find the hermit there. He was astonished to see the sand all washed away, and the ruined streets and buildings gleaming in the sun. He walked through the ancient streets calling. Some cellar holes were scooped out, and Gamwyn looked down into the rusty remains of clotted and shattered ancient artifacts.

He began to pick up whole bottles, many clear, with milky rainbows in the glass. Eventually he took off his tunic and filled it with bottles, carrying them back to the beach and on to Sagol.

He set them out for Aylor's inspection and they were immediately taken for use by any who saw them. Soon a small party set out for the ruin to gather more.

Aylor frowned at Gamwyn's claim that Darew's whole camp had been carried away, but the old man was too busy to see into it at the time. In fact, three days passed and all the remaining houses were moved back to the beach with the boats before Aylor set out to see for himself. Gamwyn and Artess accompanied him. All was as Gamwyn had said, and Aylor stood sadly among the torn shrubs of the camp area regarding the one tree the Pelbar boy had identified. Looking up into it, he said, "What's that?"

Gamwyn shaded his eyes. "Looks like a bag up there." He ran up the trunk, caught a branch, and swung up into the tree, climbing to the old bag, which was fastened to a branch with cord wrapping Untying it, he dropped the sack to Aylor, who opened it and pulled out a shell. Gamwyn's jaw fell, for Aylor was holding the very shell he had wanted, unscathed, packed in rags. He silently held it up. Gamwyn dropped into the sand by him and looked at it. Aylor felt around deeper in the bag, finding a large shaving. Scratched in its surface, in a crude hand, was the sentence, "The shell is for Gamwyn. May it bless you. And for Aylor this: Jeez I cry is the name of the Lost One. Darew."

Aylor looked puzzled. "He always said, 'Jeez I cry.' He just said it. What has that to do with the Lost One?"

Gamwyn shrugged. "I don't know."

At that point, Artess, who had wandered off, shrieked and came running. "A hand! A hand!" she gasped.

Aylor said, "Stay here, both of you," and, following her tracks, pushed through the bushes. He was gone several sunwidths before returning. When he did he simply announced, "We'll go home now," then walked grimly toward the shore.

They returned along the shore in silence, Aylor walking so fast that the other two had to trot at times to keep up. When they reached Sagol, Aylor's son, Weel, greeted him. The old man said, "We found Darew—his hand, sticking out of the sand. I covered it up."

"You covered it? Why didn't you bring him back to bury him right?"

"His hand. It was black."

"So is yours."

Aylor flashed a look of anger at him, but saw his son's earnest look and simply said, "Mine is supposed to be. And Darew thinks the name of the Lost One is Jeez I cry. Darew left a note on a stick. It said, 'And for Aylor this: Jeez I cry is the name of the Lost One.'" He looked up at his son again and found him open-mouthed. "What?" Aylor asked.

"Yesterday Gelis found a sign in stone in the ancient ruin. It said, 'Jesus Saves.' He told me. They used it with a lot of other rock to fill a low place in the road."

All those who heard fell silent. Finally somebody said, "I never thought of the Lost One as a person. I don't know. Is this right? Is it a person?"

"Who knows? What if it is? What does it mean?"

"It can't be a person. No person can do much saving."

"Maybe the Lost One is some other being called Jesus by the ancients."

"I still wish I could see how something that saves could get lost."

"Maybe," Aylor said, "he was really lost to the considerations of the ancients. Before the great burning. Maybe they just forgot him and that caused the great burning."

"Maybe this is wrong. Maybe Jeez I cry isn't the Lost One at all."

"Well, we don't know, do we. We know something was lost. There has to have been. We see the threads still unwinding from ancient times."

A young boy joined the group. "Ansy wants to know if you'll help him move his boat," he said. They all stood and followed him down the beach.

That evening, Aylor found Gamwyn and said, "It's been decided. You have your shell. You'll be going back. We're going to send twenty people with you. If they know anything about the Lost One at Pelbarigan, we want to know it. Besides, you may not make it by yourself. You had trouble enough getting here."

"I'm going, too," Artess said. "Back to where I was born."

Gamwyn looked at her, slim and earnest, a spattering of freckles on her face, her hair over her shoulder in a single braid. He was startled to find she was beautiful in the firelight. He looked again. She smiled at him, her smile radiating implications.

"You?" he asked. "What about Reo?"

"He's staying right here," Daun said. "Right, Ree?" She turned to him.

Gamwyn could see Reo struggling within himself. Finally he said, "I've never been happy before this, Daun. I don't want any more than this. Artess, are you really going?" She embraced him tightly and held him a long time. "I guess that means yes," he finally said. "Maybe someday I'll come."

Two mornings later, five of the slim boats launched through the surf and unfurled their sails, with the whole town on the shore. Artess bit her lip hard as she waved one last time to Reo, but then she spun her head away and wouldn't look back. Eventually, when she did, she could see only water.

Again they portaged across the maze of swampy land to the river, visiting Samme and his small village on stilts. They all had to see Gamwyn's shell, laughing, tossing it to one another across the water. Gamwyn was uneasy, but they never dropped it.

As they talked about the storm, and Darew, Gamwyn said, "I've been thinking about him. I may be wrong, but I think he was sent there by the eastern cities to keep track of you."

Samme laughed. "That old crazy? Why do you say that?"

"He asked me too much. He wanted to know about you here. He wanted to know about us."

"He was just curious."

"Maybe, but we've always been careful about what we've told other people, and we know right away when somebody's probing us for information."

Doon, Aylor's eldest son, said, "Father always thought that. What difference? We ain't doing nothing they'd be interested in. He always liked the old pelican."

"Even so, I don't like it," Samme said.

As it turned out, Samme was footloose enough to join the group, and two others joined with him.

To avoid the current, they began the long ascent of the river by sticking to the shore. They stroked all day, and when the wind was favorable, set their sails.

As they drew closer to Murkal, Gamwyn grew more and more apprehensive. The city had looked so ominous when they had slipped by it in the dark. They discussed the passage, thinking they might run by at night, but the Atherers were confident that a determined front and ready bows might convince the Alats that it would be wise to let them alone.

It was midmorning when Murkal came in sight. Gamwyn shaded his eyes and stared at the city as they drew abreast of it. They could see men running down to the river bank, armed with bows and spears.

"Those are the military," said Artess. "We have to worry if they get in those long boats. But I don't think they will. They only act on orders, and we'll probably be gone before they get any."

Gamwyn could see a strange building on top of the three-tiered pyramid. "Is that where they keep . . . what did you call it?"

"The Godswagon."

"What's that on top of it? A row of letters? P-A-C-K-A-R-D? What does that mean?"

"That's the name of the Godswagon. Nobody knows. They don't even know. They don't write the way you and the Atherers do."

"Stop talking and paddle," said one of the Atherers. They did, but Gamwyn couldn't resist a few more glances over his shoulder. The city still seemed mysterious.

"Don't worry," said Artess. "You wouldn't like it, Gam. You really wouldn't."

They paddled hard the rest of the day, then camped on an island, leaving almost all their gear in the boats and setting a double watch. As the night waned, they heard voices downstream, and the thump of paddles on thwarts. Instantly the Atherers were armed and ready, the fires quenched. From downstream, a voice called, "Hal-loooooooo. Halloooooo. Travelers."

"We'll wait and see what it's all about," said Samme.

The boats approached, and they heard a voice say, "Yah sure yah saw fires?"

"Yeah. I'm sure. Two of 'em."

"Yah think we missed 'em?"

"Don' know."

"What'll we do? Can' go back now. Tusco up ahead. Damn it all, yah fried snakeskin. Why'd I ever let yah talk me into this?"

"Better'n shoveling chicken pens all y'r life."

"Not Tusco slavery isn't.'

"Over here," Samme called, then, turning, said, "Light a torch."

Both sides struck torches, and Gamwyn's party saw two boats much like the rowboat Reo and Artess had stolen. They counted seven people. As they neared, Gamwyn could distinguish five young men and two women. In the boat were some crates with birds in them. The boats grounded and the Atherers pulled them up into the weeds.

"We wan' ta come," said one man. "We're chicken workers. Brought some chickens. Wherever y'r goin', we wan' ta come. Some people told us the Tusco have lef' High Tower. There's nothin' but thankless work at Murkal for the res' of our lives. The investors own it all."

"Chickens?" said Samme.

"Yeah. That's one thing we got. Give eggs and meat. Raise 'em."

"I don't know," said Samme.

"Let them come, Samme," said Gamwyn. "Isn't that all right, Artess?"

"Artess? Is that you? Where ya been?"

"Hello, Ture. Yeah. It's me. I been all over. Now I'm goin' with Gamwyn all the way to Threerivers to be a Pelbar."

"Can we come?" asked a freckled, thin man. "We're really sick of things at home."

"We'll have to search you," said Samme. "Come on, then." He sighed. "We'd better start out now in case your people follow."

"We fixed it. They won' even know til tomorrow. Probably toward evening. We're supposed to be on fertilizer duty tomorrow. But we think it's been changed."

Artess laughed. "Same old trick. Still workin'."

The chicken workers were searched and fed fish soup.

Then, after a rest, they started out again upriver, the curious fowl clucking and prodding their heads out through the bars of their cages. The Atherers were amused at them, but some were layers, and soon enough they were also enjoying eggs and getting seriously interested in chickens themselves.

It was over a week after leaving Murkal that they stroked by the site of High Tower. It was deserted, strewn with wreckage, and weed-grown. Gamwyn felt a sinking fatigue and realized that he'd been dreading it. But as they began the long voyage toward U Bend, he seemed slowly constricted by a growing fear of that place as well. Artess noticed it. So did some others. But Gamwyn set his jaw and stroked in time with the rest, as the Atherers chanted their slow, melodious boat songs.

One morning while Gamwyn's party paddled against the current in Tusco country, far upriver, at Threerivers the guardsman's horn blew to announce the arrival of a visitor. An adolescent girl, by her dress a Sentani, stood on the message stone. She was hailed by megaphone from the wall and a rope ladder was rolled down to her.

She was greeted by the guardcaptain when she finished the long upward climb and rolled over the terrace wall. She sat a moment, catching her breath, as a ring of guardsmen scrutinized her.

"My name is Misque," she finally said. "Sentani from the Tall Grass. I'm looking for a refuge. Can you take me in? We were wiped out by those cursed Peshtak. I was bathing and hid in the reeds."

"How many?"

"I don't know. I saw quite a few. I heard many voices. They killed a band of forty-nine. Except me."

"Forty-nine. Aven help us. Why didn't you go to Koorb. Or north?"

"I thought they were going that way. South. I don't know. I'm so frightened. May I stay?"

"The Protector will decide that. Meanwhile, come and eat. We'll tell you."

Gind brought the problem to Udge in the Broad Tower. She pushed out her lower lip in thought. "A Sentani girl? How old?"

"About fourteen. We didn't ask, Protector."

"I see no harm in a girl. Do you?"

"We know nothing of her, Protector. She could be a spy."

"We can surely use workers, especially young women. Keep the usual watch on her, Gind. Accept her. See how she works. Put her to routine things. That will test her."

"Yes, Protector."

Across the river, Steelet's scouting party watched all day. Misque didn't reappear. They slapped each other in elation. The main band was about eighteen ayas to the west, resting, awaiting word. This time they would succeed. Steelet was sure of it.

☐ XVIII

BIVAL sat hunched over her lamp, reading the manuscript Brudoer had copied in a careful hand. Again Craydor expressed unsureness:

> I tremble when I think of the tightness, the exclusiveness of the organization of this society. Is it all a mistake? Should I have ever initiated it? Knowing as well as I do the human tendency to freeze institutions, to glorify mere procedures into ultimate truths, have I, in my attempt to create a wholly defended society capable of growth, simply walled one in with irremovable barriers? I have suggested modes of change and growth, but they have not been taken up. My words about mundane matters have been regarded as final truths, while I have not felt these words to be revealed by Aven, or even to deal with ultimates—only with social organization in this time of hostility. I am in agony now in my last days. I only hope that future generations will include the independent as well as the faithful, and that Threerivers will evolve and change, preserving our ideal devotion to Aven. But what if that does not happen? I have reached the ends of reason and design. I now can only pray.

Bival sighed and looked up. Warret was fast asleep after a day of heavy work, but even now enough sand had run into the red bowl to tip the beam and ring the small alarm bell. It was time he stood his guard duty. She shook him gently. He didn't awaken. She shook a little harder. He groaned but didn't move. She then took his short-sword, buckled it on, and left the room to stand his watch. Warret continued to sleep.

As she walked the terraces, she never noticed Misque in the shadows. When Bival had finished Warret's tour and reentered the upper hall door, Misque dropped a note attached to a bit of white cloth, beyond the water tower. She heard a low click from below, so stole away, down the curving stairs to the room assigned her. Her hands were blistered from water-lifting and garden work. She rubbed them with bean oil and crawled back into bed.

By midmorning, Annon had her note, which he unrolled and read:

> In two weeks at the dark of the moon, I will roll two rope ladders off the front terrace just after high night. They are getting used to me slowly, but they watch me. This place is mostly women because many of the men have left. Many who stayed are old. Remember your promise not to kill them. They are quite gentle. I think you can capture the city easily. Then you can turn them out of it. Please remember. Please take care of Jaiyan and Jamin. Remember, you promised.
>
> Misque.

Annon snorted. "A pig-snouted bleeding heart. Well, at least she got in. At least she will get us in. We'll have to make some ladders. At least twenty, and those at least twenty-five arms long. I think we will get in this time." He rubbed his face mask to get at the itching below it. He then held out his palm, and Steelet slapped it with his. Both men laughed.

When Gamwyn's party at last came in sight of the U Bend settlement, the Pelbar boy couldn't believe so much change was possible. The whole river had established its course through the gap he and his friends had started. The former slave quarters was an island, and the former course of the river a silt-barred backwater, still and weedy.

Before they came within a half-ayas of it, the party

slowed, and one of the Atherers said, "Smoke. I smell smoke. A lot of it." Then Gamwyn smelled it. Soon they could see a black stain on the hillside behind the former place of the circles, on the high ground east of the river. Some smoke drifted up from it yet. Figures moved in the area, and as Gamwyn's expedition drew closer, staying close to the west bank, people came down to the bank and hailed them. Gamwyn's party slowed their boats. Soon three people in what Gamwyn recognized as craftsmen's clothing pushed a boat off and paddled toward them.

"I'm not sure we should wait," Gamwyn said. "I don't trust these people."

"Just three people in a boat? We can handle them for sure," Doon said.

As they drew closer, Gamwyn recognized Ahks, in whose home he had stayed while recovering from the cold of the well. The Tusco boat drew alongside. "Have you anything to eat?" one man called. "We have nothing now. They took it all."

"Who?"

"The Siveri. Two nights ago. They burned us out, killed all Nicfad. We have nothing."

"Why don't you fish?"

"We don't know how. We have no slaves, no Nicfad, almost no Committee. Rest of us builders and craftsmen."

"Where is Daw?" Gamwyn called.

"Who? Committee girl? Fat one? I don't know. Never came back from High Tower. Now. Can you feed us? We begging you."

Gamwyn's party conferred, then set up a camp on the west bank, fished, made dough cakes from rice flour. As Gamwyn learned, the U Bend Tusco had decided to make a new start. When enough Nicfad had gathered from the two settlements, they had set out on a slave raid into Siveri country. For the first time, they met organized resistance. Still, they managed to return with twenty-six slaves, but in less than two weeks the Siveri visited in force and burned the Tusco out, killing all the Nicfad and most of the Committee, sparing the artisans and some of the bureaucrats. The Tusco were having a poor time of it and only forty-two remained. That evening they begged Gamwyn's party to let them join it. After some reluctance, the travelers accepted.

Fortunately, the Tusco had enough boats from High

Tower to fit everybody. They consisted of twenty-two men, mostly builders, nine children, and eleven women, several quite old. Gamwyn remained wary of them, but Samme was amused. "Here we go to Threerivers," he laughed. "The Lost One is picking up all his children. Not to mention chickens."

They shoved off next morning, their progress slowed somewhat by the weariness and debilitation of the Tusco. Soon they divided the peoples among the boats so there were no slow ones. After some initial hours of suspicious silence, Gamwyn thought he saw signs of friendships springing up between the Atherers and the Tusco.

He also noticed that the farther north they went, the redder the bankside sumac became. Even the goldenrod was aging, and the asters powdered the woods' edges with blue. He was worried about the cooling of the weather. How would Threerivers feed all these people during the winter? Some would have to go on to Pelbarigan, and even that city might have a hard time of it.

After some days of paddling, and two rest days for fishing and hunting, they reached Jaiyan's Station. This, too, had been burned, but they landed and Gamwyn called repeatedly. Samme blew his shell horn. Eventually nine old Siveri ventured out of the woods. They greeted Gamwyn with pleasure and relief, and explained about the Peshtak raid. They had successfully hidden. Then they had returned and buried the others.

"We stayed," one old man said with a trembling voice. "Nothin' else to do. We just stayed around. They took Jaiyan and Jamin—and Misque."

"They took Misque?"

"She weren't around when we come back. We was in the river, hidin'."

"You're sure they didn't kill them?"

"Not here. We looked all around, but we didn't find nobody. Now. How about if we come with you? It's lonely around here, and winter's coming."

Samme again laughed. "Pile in. Plenty of room. Now, Gam, how many more settlements are we going to hit? We'll have an invasion."

"This is the last. Unless we meet some Sentani. Or unless . . ."

"Unless what?"

"We meet some Peshtak. That will be the end of it for us."

"Peshtak?" said one of the Tusco. "A large force?" He looked worried.

"It could be. Let's pray that doesn't happen."

But the Peshtak were at Threerivers. Misque had rolled down the ladders, as she promised. Two at a time, men had climbed them with additional rolled rope ladders on their backs, silently fastening and unrolling them from the terrace lip. Misque had pointed out the guardsmen, and Peshtak had silently moved off for the kill but the third guardsman approached was able to cry out, and the Protector's guard ran out of the Broad Tower, only to take an arrow in the stomach. He grunted and went down. The Protector opened the door behind him and screamed but managed to bar the door. Gind, holding the arrow shaft in his belly, could hear her shutting and barring the doors. He sucked in his breath and let out a long shout, which was nipped off by another arrow through his chest. He rolled back and lay still.

"You promised," Misque hissed as Annon came over the wall. He knocked her down with the back of his hand, then reached down and hauled her to her feet.

"Now. You'll tell us how to get into the heart of this place."

"You promised you wouldn't kill them."

Annon took her by the throat. "I'll kill you, too, in a wink, if you don't tell us." He dropped her and she fell in a heap.

Three guardsmen ran up the stairs and out onto the terrace, only to be cut down, and the Peshtak poured in through the door and down the stairs. It was dark. Somewhere a horn sounded, long and repeated. So the Pelbar were warned. There would be a fight. Four dark figures scuttled out of a side doorway. The Peshtak drew swords and hacked them down, screaming.

"All old women," one said. They plunged ahead. The horn sounded again, and as torches came from above, the Peshtak found the way barred by stone doors. They called for rams from the shore, hauled them up, and began battering at the stonework. Fanning out through the rooms they had already seized, they found them deserted.

Annon had Misque brought to him. "Now. How do we get beyond this?"

"I—I know nothing of this. I didn't know they could bar the stairs."

"Pah." Annon knocked her aside. His sweating face burned, but he couldn't get to it behind his mask. "We'll batter it down, then."

Suddenly a wall slid aside, and four Pelbar bowmen quickly placed arrows into the nearest group of Peshtak. With a yell, a large party of the invaders dashed through the gap, chasing the Pelbar down a winding staircase, which seemed to narrow rapidly. Finally the point man could go no farther. He was wedged in by those behind him. He grew frightened and shouted. The crowd heard a rumble, as the stone roof folded in on them. Those at the head of the stairs saw only fallen rock.

Annon screamed in rage. He had lost at least twenty men. The Pelbar would pay when he had finally taken the city. He would leave none alive.

But morning saw little progress. The Peshtak on the ram were frazzled. They had made a deep dent, but the stone still held. Annon put on another shift. He had now brought his entire band, over a thousand people, up over the wall, and they occupied the entire upper section of the city, except for the Broad Tower, where the Protector and Dardan had taken refuge.

Shortly before dawn, Gind, the Protector's guardsman, had dragged himself slowly and silently around the Broad Tower to the message-bird cages. Tearing off a corner of his duty roster, he printed it with thumb marks of his own blood, and carefully tied it to a bird's leg. Then he had released the bird, but in the darkness, it fluttered stupidly and sat on the roof of its cage, cooing softly in distress. Only at dawn, as some Peshtak approached, did it take off. They saw no significance in it, and only briefly glanced down at Gind's staring, dead eyes with contempt. One spat on him. He continued to stare, unmoved, as the pigeon circled twice and set out for Pelbarigan.

After another group of his men was caught in a wall trap, Annon went more slowly, building log cribbing over the heads of the rammers. Finally they breached the main-hall barrier, worming through the intertied cross wall, and advancing, gaining another level of rooms, only to have another roof peel loose on the heads of fourteen men, crushing them. Ahead, they found the hallway blocked again. They advanced the cribbing and set to work once more with a savage determination. When night fell little progress had been made. But Annon said, "We will get them out of here and kill every last hogsbutt of them. It's just going to take time."

He summoned Misque and tried to get more information from her, but she offered little he didn't know. Clearly she could explain the layout of the city but knew nothing of the trap system. Annon didn't trust her. He had her thrown into a storeroom and guarded. She lay on the floor weeping because she knew now Annon would kill Jaiyan and his son when it suited him.

Brudoer had been exploring the caves for some time, and was unaware of the invasion until, picking his way through the wall tunnels, he noticed that one of the wall traps had been activated. He heard faint pounding and knocking, so sought entrance to the city proper through a secret entrance to an unused room. In the dark, Misque heard a grating noise behind her. Suddenly a lamp appeared from the wall as Brudoer moved a portion of the wall aside. She crouched down, unsure of what was happening. The boy slid into the room and replaced the stone, then crawled across the floor.

The lamp flared slightly on his face. "Gamwyn," Misque gasped.

Brudoer flicked out a long knife. He moved to her. "Who are you?"

"Misque. You aren't Gamwyn. You must be his brother. He said he had a brother."

"What's going on here?"

"The Peshtak are in the city."

"The Peshtak! How did they get in?"

"I let them in," Misque whispered, sobbing.

"You what?"

A light flared. "Here. What's this," the Peshtak guard said. In an instant, he had arced his sword and Misque thrust herself in the way, taking on her forearm the cut meant for Brudoer but shrieking as it bit through her flesh. The Peshtak tossed her aside, only to receive Brudoer's thrust through his neck. He dropped with a gurgle.

The boy swung the door shut then stooped to the writhing girl, but footsteps neared in the corridor so he dragged first Misque then the dead Peshtak through the gap in the stone wall, went back, mopped away the spatters of blood, and slid through himself, again reinserting the stone and fastening it in place.

"Ahhhh, ahhhh," Misque moaned.

"Don't worry. I'll take care of you. I think your arm is broken. Can you walk?"

"Yes. Yes. A little."

"Gamwyn. How is Gamwyn?"

"I don't know. I haven't seen him since late last winter. My arm. My arm."

"Come on." Brudoer led her down through the wall passages, slowly and carefully. Finally she fainted, and he had to carry her down to the largest chamber below, where he bathed and bound the wound.

She murmured faintly, "Gamwyn? Don't leave me, Gamwyn. You'll never find your shell. You'll never make it through Tusco country. Stay with us. Stay with me."

Brudoer looked at her in the flickering lamp light. More misery, he thought.

The main body of Pelbar, gathered in the Judgment Room, was steeling itself for the end. "Listen," said Warret. "They're working on the last barrier between us. After that there are only two more we can retreat to. The first level has one, then the bottom levels. In any case, we are shut in already. We can kill a lot of them with the traps, but eventually they will get us."

"But what are we to do?" an old woman asked.

"We'll fight them, every arm of the way," Pion said. "Every arm."

"If they're going to win, then we ought to give up. Perhaps they will be merciful," the same old woman said. Several others agreed.

"You can give up if you want to," Bival said. "Some of us won't. You'll just die sooner. What we can do now is to let them know there's a price for what they do. We can set all the traps so they will continue to die even after they get all of us."

"This is the voice of cruelty," another family head said. "Aven would not do that."

They heard running on the stairs. Two guardsmen appeared. "We'll have to move," one shouted. "They're nearly through the barrier." They all rose and hurried out the south entrance. "Run," a guardsman said, wiping the sweat out of her eyes. "We'll harry them as they come through."

"You come," Warret said. The guardsman started back toward the stairs, but Ason took her arm and dragged her through the door, growling, "We want to lower the barrier. You'd be trapped."

"It's my duty," she rasped. Ason paid no attention, hauling her along, his jaw bunched tight. From behind them came the first yells of the Peshtak as they broke through.

Worming through the gap above, the invaders gathered a body of sixteen before they started down the stairs ahead of them, arrows nocked. Suddenly the floor tilted from under them, and they dropped into a pit. The floor swung back up. It had all happened so fast there was no outcry. The next group of men also fell, but others saw the trap and bridged the gap with poles. When they swung the stairtrap down and cast a light inside, they saw the men below all impaled. Annon, when told, beat his fist on the wall.

Just then a man came down the stairs and announced, "Command Annon, Misque has disappeared."

The Peshtak leader shrieked in his anger, swinging around. His face mask came loose, falling with a trivial clunk. He stooped to pick it up, as the men around him saw a raw-flesh-covered skull revealed. Hardened as they were, they froze in horror. Annon replaced the mask. This was followed by a small silence. "Just wait," Annon said. "You'll get to look like this. It goes with being Peshtak. Now. We're going to take every closet and every cabinet in this sinkhole, and kill every Pelbar, mouse, and roach in it. Get going, hogsnouts!"

The Peshtak moved with caution, knowing now that the city itself lay in wait for them with its interior traps. They were a full day breaching the next barriers, and even so found another in front of them.

"It seems to lead down to the lowest levels of the city, Command," one man told Annon. "I think we have them now."

From the wall above a long horn sounded. The Peshtak sentries had seen two large ships arrive from Pelbarigan, full of guardsmen. "Let them come," a squadleader said. "They won't get in here any easier than we did."

As they watched, a small boat left one ship, and three

men came ashore. One was a Peshtak, who came across the forefield to the wall and looked up. "Let me in," he called. "It's Osel. The Pelbar have an offer." They tossed him a rope ladder. and he slowly climbed it, panting heavily as he swung over the wall.

He sat puffing. "I've been in prison. Out of shape."

"What's this offer?"

"The Pelbar say they can cure our disease. And prevent it. They say they will trade that for the lives of the Threerivers people."

The squadleader spat. "We'll tell Annon." He snapped his fingers at a sentry, who set out trotting. "What makes you believe that rot?"

"I had it. The first signs. Right here. I don't now. It all went away. I think they can do it. It'd be worth it to us. We could come back later and take the city."

"Do you know what bullgutted trouble we've had?"

"I can imagine. It would still be worth it. You don't have the disease. I can see. You don't know what it's like."

When the sentry told Annon, the Command paused. He was at a loss. He sent for Osel and listened. Then he shook his head. "It's some kind of trick. We've come too far. We've lost too many men. And me. What of my face— people like me. Can they give me back my face? And all the others?"

The men around him were subdued, and Annon felt their disagreement.

"Shall I go back and tell them this, then?" Osel asked.

"You'll stay here with us."

"I promised to go back."

"Dried hogskin. Let them chew on it."

"They said if I didn't come back, they'd shoot anyone off the walls who showed himself."

"They can't."

Osel summarized the defeat of his band in the winter.

Finally, one man said, "Annon, it's worth it. It would be worth more than anything we could get—"

He stopped, holding his stomach, with Annon's shortsword in it. The rest drew back, as Annon, flanked by his two personal guards, drew out the sword and wiped it on the leg of the victim. "Now," he said, "we'll finish with the taking of this city."

* * *

As the sun set brick-red over the river, Ahroe leaned on the ship's rail and said, "So Red isn't coming back. I thought he would, really."

"Maybe they wouldn't let him."

"Maybe. We still hold the bottom level. See the signals?"

"And the foundation level underneath as well, guardcaptain."

"What is there?"

"Prison rooms, ice, a water pit, mushroom culture, storage."

"What trouble they've had here."

"And are having, guardcaptain. It's only a matter of time now until the Peshtak have all of Threerivers."

"So unnecessary." Ahroe pushed the hair out of her face, her eyes brimming. "We can still pray. Something may still happen."

Inside, the Peshtak finally breached the bottom-level barrier, leaving only the city foundation as a refuge for the Pelbar. As they gathered there for a last stand, they heard pounding behind them. They turned. "Are they there, too?" one woman asked.

"No. It comes from the cells." Warret trotted off and found Brudoer looking through the door bars of the fourth cell, beating on the planks with the hilt of his long knife.

Warret swung the heavy door open. "Bru. How did you get there?"

"No time. Quick. Get everybody here. We can get out this way into the tunnels."

"Tunnels?"

"No time. You'll see. Get them."

In a few moments the Pelbar were filing into the cell and crawling through the hole into the small room and the tunnels behind it. They were amazed, unbelieving.

Finally Brudoer shoved the square stone back into place and dogged it down. He turned to see Bival staring at him. With a small cry, she embraced him, saying, "I'm sorry. I'm sorry. What do we do now?"

Brudoer worked his way to the front and led them all to the small room in which he'd left Misque.

The Ursana immediately set to work on her arm. Others were furious, knowing now that Misque had betrayed them.

"Don't harm her," Brudoer said. "If she hadn't taken that cut, you'd all be inside now, awaiting your deaths."

"If she hadn't let them in, we'd all be safe in bed," one woman replied, drily.

"Enough," Brudoer said. "If you want to get out of here, I'll get you out. But not if she isn't taken care of. She knows Gamwyn. She helped him. That's enough for me."

"For me, too," Pion said. "Come on, son, we ought to move on before it gets light."

As Brudoer led the group through the tunnels, Osel slipped over the wall high above. Soon the Pelbar on the river heard the splash of his swimming, and he came up over the side. "They won't agree," he said, panting. "I think some would. But Annon won't. He's too angry. He's lost too many men in there. And he's too far gone in the disease."

"Then why did you come?"

"I agreed. And I'm afraid. That whole place has the feel of death."

Inside, Brudoer was whispering to his father, asking him to lead the Pelbar across the field to the river. He would follow last. It was important. He would need Ason with him.

Earlier, Brudoer had found a side shaft to the outside wall. He had studied it. Craydor's people had planned it well. Two large stones had to be slid out, leaving only the facing to be pushed away. They had even left two crowbars. With much effort, Brudoer and Ason slid the stones away. Then Ason punched the facing out with a bar. Pion crawled out. Looking up, he saw they were below the water tower.

The Peshtak could not get many archers around that side. He began lifting the family heads out through the hole. All were subdued and silent. Faintly, they could hear the Peshtak pounding on the last intertied barrier. The Pelbar gathered silently along the wall. Then Pion began leading them across the field. The Peshtak never saw them until over a hundred were well out toward the river. A sentry sounded his horn. A puff of fire gouted out of one of the ships and riddled the sentry with shot from a Pelbar cannon. As more Peshtak rushed to the walls, the Pelbar on the field broke into a run, and cannonfire from the ships began rolling and flashing.

Soon small boats were launched, filled with riflemen, and the Peshtak had to concede the walls and loopholes to their pecking fire. By the time the first Peshtak had slid through the last barrier, Annon knew it was too late, and that somehow the Pelbar had escaped. But at least he had taken the city.

Brudoer was the last out. "Now," he shouted to Ason. "Put the bar in there and pry that stone out."

Without thinking, the huge man did as the boy asked. The stone resisted. He threw his whole massive trunk into it, grunting. It slid, rotated, then groaned loose. For a long moment, nothing happened; then a sharp crack split the stone above. The wall gave a slight grinding sound, raining grit, as Brudoer and Ason ran across the field. Brudoer fell with an arrow through his leg. Ason scooped him up and stumbled on.

Behind them, the wall groaned again. More fragments spattered down. Then the diamond pattern in the wall shifted. In a row, the facing stones showered off like falling play squares. The whole wall collapsed in a rush and fell out with an enormous roar. The water tower tilted, turned, and fell through the upper terraces. In the first morning light, the high north wall of the city disintegrated, falling outward with a deep rumble. After that, the entire city fell inward in a continuing thunder, burying the entire Peshtak invasion force in tons of falling rock and rising dust.

As they arrived at the shore, Ason set Brudoer down. "Good suffering Aven, Brudoer. You've torn the entire city down. Everything. Now we've got nothing." He screamed in exasperation and disbelief.

"No Peshtak, either," Bival said by his shoulder. She laughed almost hysterically. "I can't believe this. I can't believe it."

Brudoer lay on the ground, his face contorted with the pain of the arrow. "Craydor built it that way," he gasped. "Craydor meant that it should come down if it had to."

"The Protector was right," Cilia shrilled. "You should have been whipped to death!" She made for Brudoer, but was blocked by a Pelbarigan rifle barrel. "Get away!" she screamed.

"Much more from you and we stow you in the hold with the potatoes," Ahroe said. "He just saved you all and you don't like it. Now, everybody, get in the boats. We'll think this out on the ships. There might be a few more of these rabid skunks around."

But as the dawn grew, the city lay still, a great pile of

broken rock, up through which thrust a steep pyramid, near the tip of which lay Craydor's tomb. And on the very end the Broad Tower rested, balancing. Bival leaned on the rail, musing. "Another of Craydor's jokes," she said to Pion. "She said the city would never fall until she left it. She has." Bival laughed ruefully.

"She didn't go far," Rotag said.

As they watched, the main door of the Broad Tower swung open. They could see a tiny figure in it. The door then shut, and as it did, the Broad Tower seemed to rock a little, then slid rumbling down the side of the pyramid to the rubble at its base.

"It's amazing it's still intact," Bival said. She could see the guardsmen trotting across the field toward the tower. "I imagine that if the tip hadn't been trimmed off the pyramid, it would still be up there."

By the time the guardsmen arrived at the Broad Tower, which was tilted but still unbroken, the door swung open again, and Dardan stood in it, shaken and bruised. The guardsmen lifted her down and stepped inside. Everything was jumbled, the furniture all piled at one end of the room. In the middle of it, Udge sat in her favorite chair, a broken cup in her hand. A guardsman slid down the floor and lifted a table off her lap."

"You all right?" he questioned.

"Are you addressing me?"

The guardsman looked around. "I don't see anybody else. Want help getting out?"

"Protector! Protector!" she screamed at him. "Are there no manners left in Pelbarigan?"

"Maybe not. But Pelbarigan is left. Want to get out? Or do you want to stay? We could hook some ropes on this thing and drag it down onto the field. Then you could be Protector of yourself."

"How can—how can you talk to me this way? It's completely unbelievable. Where are my guardsmen?"

"Your own? All dead. All dead, they say."

Udge struggled to her feet, and with the aid of the guardsmen walked, slipped, and crawled up the sloping floor to the doorway. She hadn't even looked out before. Now that she emerged into the sunlight, staring around her at the rubble that had been the incomparably beautiful structure of Threerivers, she screamed and beat on the stone door frame with her fist. The guardsmen stood by patiently.

Below, Dardan looked up at her. "It's no use, Udge. It's all gone now. Come on down. They have promised us some hot soup. If you give Brudoer back his bracelet."

 XIX

ON Ahroe's ship, the Peshtak, Red, also stared at the city ruins, unbelieving. He was fuming and cursing under his breath. "You killed them. You killed them all. You are the rottenest gang of sanctimonious sludge pits. Worse than the Innaniganis. You're the foul swill of a thousand fishgutting slaughterhouses. You grew from the ooze like snakes. You—" He cried out and buried his face in his fists.

"What should we have done?"

"All my cousins. My uncle."

"All their city. Most of their guardsmen."

"We'll pay you for this. Every drop of blood. Every shred of flesh."

"We've already paid a good deal. Now, Guardcaptain Ahroe wants to see you."

Red struggled and spat. Finally he had to be gagged and shoved into the guardcaptain's room, where Ahroe sat at a long table. Red was placed on a stool opposite her.

"Red," she began. "We're going to let you go—back to your people. Now will you talk? Can we take that gag off?"

The Peshtak stared at her. Then he went limp. The guardsmen took off the gag. "Go home?" he said. "Almost everybody I know is here, under your bullgutted rock pile."

"We regret that. As much for us as for you. We want you to tell your people we can cure the Peshtak plague, and if they come in peace, we will do it. We'll trade with you. We'll live at peace with you. But if you come raiding again—even one small raid on the Tall Grass Sentani— we'll gather all the people and wipe you out. Finish you. The Shumai have agreed. So have the Koorb Sentani. We'll talk to the Tall Grass people. You've seen our weapons. You know what they can do."

"You can do nothing, you dung heap. You fermenting maggot garden."

Ahroe laughed. "I'll have to tell Stel that one. Fermenting maggot garden. I wish you'd stop cursing and think."

Red did stop. He looked at the floor a long time. Then he said, "I'd never make it through the Sentani alone, anyway."

"If you can hide a thousand men, you can surely hide one. Besides, we'll give you a letter of safe-conduct. I think they'd honor it."

"A letter? Safe-conduct?" The Peshtak could hardly believe what Ahroe was saying. But after they talked for some time, he calmed and began to see the opportunities offered. His people could decide about the invasion afterward. If they really could be freed from the terrible disease, what else would matter? He finally agreed to carry the message.

"One more thing," Ahroe said. "Destroy all your hogs and wait at least a decade before you get any more. All of them."

"Destroy the hogs?"

"We think they are carrying the disease. Not alone. We think they are a strongly contributing cause. We don't really know. We think so."

Red pondered. "The hogs. We thought about that. It didn't seem reasonable."

At last Red was prepared to go. "What's your real name, Red?" Ahroe asked. "You've never told us."

"Osel."

"Osel. Well, good-bye, Osel. If I embrace you, will you harm me?"

"Not if he wants to live," the youngest guardsman said.

"Please, Garet," Ahroe said.

"I won't harm you," Osel muttered.

Ahroe put her arms around him and placed her cheek against his. "May Aven go with you, protect you, and bring success to your journey," she said. "May you always prosper, and if you return, may we be friends."

Osel pulled away and looked at her. "You see," she added, "it isn't we who are enemies. It's the concept of hostility. There is no reason why the invaders and the Threerivers people couldn't have been having a feast together right now—except for their concepts. It helps to separate the whole unsuccessful complex of Peshtak ideas from the people. I reject the Peshtak ideas, but not the people. Sometimes, unfortunately, we have to combat the people who push these absurd ideas." She remained wary and unsmiling, however.

"Good-bye, then, guardcaptain," Osel said, turning away. "We'll see what happens."

"You're welcome back here anytime—without an army."

"Yes." Osel looked back at her, a swirl of emotions welling up in him. Then he turned toward the shore.

Ahroe, too, had mixed feelings as she watched him being rowed ashore. "I hope this works out, Garet. I hope."

"There doesn't seem a better idea."

"Now," she said, sighing. "I supposed I'd better see Udge, the ex-Protector."

Udge was brought by the same boat that had taken Osel ashore. She puffed up the ladder and over the side with difficulty.

"Very inconvenient," she said. "Very inconvenient. I should think you could have greeted me ashore."

"You need to understand right now, Udge, that you are not in command of anything anymore. You have no constituency, unless the survivors of Threerivers are foolish enough to reelect you. You need to understand, too, that Pelbarigan will oppose it and will offer no further aid if they do choose you again."

Udge's mouth fell open. "I—I will see you reported. I will talk to Sagan."

"Sagan's last message from Threerivers was a blot of blood on a scrap of paper brought by a message bird. If you wish to talk with her, we can do it now with the radio. We even have a voice system now, though the dome people say they will be able to do much better with it."

"Face to face will be good enough," Udge said, turning her head.

"Provided Sagan sees fit to receive you. You ought to know that you will never be a family head in Pelbarigan. You have been tentatively assigned a place working in the laundry."

"In the laundry!" Udge shrieked.

"The laundryworkers objected, of course, but we prevailed on them."

"The laundryworkers objected!"

"We had to promise the men you would be giving them no orders. They—"

"You promised the men!" Udge took her hair in her hands and shook her head back and forth.

"We nearly had a mutiny. Some said they would rather go north to the new colony, but we told them that you would have to scrub in silence if you were allowed to come at all."

Udge opened her mouth, but nothing came out.

"You must understand that all of Pelbarigan really holds you responsible for destroying this beautiful city. It would still be here, full of life and happiness, if you weren't so rigid."

"Put me ashore. Right now. I don't have to listen to any of this."

"Very well. But no one seems in a mood to take care of you—perhaps a few old-fashioned women. But they are of little use to themselves. However, we will see what the people decide. What they decide will be honored, of course." Ahroe rose and urged Udge out onto the deck.

At that point a longhorn sounded from the lookout on the mast. "Boats, Guardcaptain Ahroe," he shouted down. "Quite a flock of them."

"Peshtak?"

"Can't tell. A strange group. Someone's waving." He squinted through his long glass. "What? How did Brudoer get down there? No. It isn't Brudoer."

Ahroe cried out and scrambled up the rope ladder. "It must be the twin, Gamwyn," she yelled. "Blow the horn again." As Ahroe looked through the glass, a guardsman blew the longhorn of greeting.

Ahroe saw a dark-skinned man pick up a white thing, and faintly they heard a hollow horn sound in return. "Good Aven," she said. "I'll be a snakeskin in the mud. It is Gamwyn. What a strange group. There must be over a hundred people." She leaned back and let out a long, quavering Shumai yell that startled everyone used to the modest and ordered guardcaptain. "They'll be hungry. What do we have to eat. Any game? We need a wild bull," she called down.

"We have one, guardcaptain."

"Roast it up, then. Radioman, tell Pelbarigan. Cooks, we'll have a feast on shore. Aven, look at that crowd."

When Gamwyn got within range of a megaphone, Ahroe

had a big guardsman boom out, "DID YOU GET THE SHELL?" They saw Gamwyn wave a cloth sack in the air. The guardsmen on the ship cheered.

Brudoer was helped, limping and pale, up on the deck to see his brother coming. "Bring Misque," he said. "Misque should see."

The reunion took place on shore. The twins held each other in a long, laughing embrace. Gamwyn was rangy and sunburnt, Brudoer pale from his months inside. Gamwyn was astonished to see the city in ruins, and when the whole group from the south sat around eating and listening, they all grew more and more silent with amazement as the story unfolded.

Gamwyn was worried about his brother, but Brudoer assured him that he would be all right soon enough. Misque was silent and preoccupied, just waking from a long sleep below decks.

"Not glad to see me, Misque?" Gamwyn asked.

"Oh. Yes. Amazed. Now there are two of you, when I—I thought there would be none. Now that I've recovered some, I'm worried, Gam. It's Jaiyan and Jamin. A few of us still have them. West of here. You have to save them."

Gamwyn instantly became serious. Misque explained everything to him. He spoke to Ahroe. She frowned and stared off at the sky, her mouth straight. She was suspicious of Misque still. But then she summoned some of the guardsmen, and Misque explained everything to one side of the gathering. As the sun went down, thirty-two well-armed guardsmen rowed across the river. Soon the boats returned without them.

That evening, a feast was held, and all heard the crackling greetings from Sagan on the radio, welcoming the strangers to Pelbar country. They finally settled down for the night with many questions open. What would they all do now? Could they settle here? Should they move on?

Brudoer and Gamwyn had much to tell each other. Artess stayed close to Gamwyn all the time, especially when Misque was present, but the Peshtak girl seemed not to notice. Her arm still pained her sharply. Her conscience lay in fragments she could not seem to piece together. Ahroe suggested she go to Pelbarigan long enough to mend because there was no shelter left at Threerivers. Brudoer, though, saw no need for her to go. "We can all live here in the caves," he said, "until we decide what to do."

"What caves?" Ahroe asked.

"Behind the city. In the rock. Craydor's people lived in them when they carved out the city. I'm sure we can move enough rock to get in there. I think I know just where to start."

As dawn slowly sifted its first light down on the prairie west of the Heart the next morning, one of the six Peshtak guarding the two Sentani sighed and rolled over. "How long we going to have to keep these two pigs alive?"

"Just until we are sure Misque kept her agreement."

"What's holding them. It's a long time now."

"We'll find out soon enough. Where's Aroth? Still on guard? Why didn't he wake me?" Both were instantly awake and on their feet, looking around.

"Drop the swords," a voice called, waking the other two off-watch Peshtak. One lay still on the ground, but the second started to crawl off.

"Stop right there," a voice called from another direction.

The Peshtak sat up to flick an arrow at the voice, but a longbow arrow pierced him instantly and he pitched forward, snapping the shaft.

"*Drop* your swords," the voice called again. "We have your two friends tied."

The three Peshtak looked at each other, then at their dead comrade, then lay down their swords.

An unarmed Pelbar guardsman came into view. "You understand that you will die as soon as he did if you move to pick up one of those swords."

One of the Peshtak spat.

"Stand over there," the guardsman said. Neither moved. "Do it now or we will kill you." They moved. Two more guardsmen appeared from the brush and picked up the Peshtak swords, thrusting them into their quivers.

"You," the guardsman said to the other Peshtak. "Stand up." The man rolled upright and rushed the guardsman, who jumped aside as another arrow thwacked into the man's leg. He went down, writhing. "All right," the guardsman said, "You'll be something for the others to carry."

"Loathsome pile of unwashed hide scrapings!" one of them said, spitting.

"Come on," the guardsman replied. "At least let me be washed hide scrapings. Now. We'll take our Sentani friends, and your weapons, and leave you with your dead man and your wounded. You're free to go home. You might as well know. Annon and all your men are dead. Misque alone is alive."

"Liar," one man shouted.

"Come and see. The whole city fell with them in it."

The Peshtak were bewildered. The rest of the guardsmen appeared now, with Jaiyan and Jamin freed. The two Sentani were worn and famished, and rubbed their wrists where their bonds had cut into them. The Peshtak stood around with no one paying obvious attention to them. They were not sure what to do.

"One other thing," the same guardsman said. "We can cure the Peshtak plague now. If you have it, you might want to come with us."

"Liiiiaaaar," one shouted again.

The guardsman laughed. "We cured Osel and sent him home. He's been a prisoner at Pelbarigan. Know him? We told him to tell your people that any more raids will bring their entire destruction. We'll all go together and do it. Are you hungry? We have some bull meat here. All cooked and dried."

The nonchalance of the Pelbar guardsmen unnerved the Peshtak, though they knew they were being watched. As the party set out for the river, the Peshtak came along, bringing the wounded man on a litter. Late in the day, when they came through the last brakes and woods, they saw the city of Threerivers now a pile of rubble, the pyramid thrusting up through it. The two ships and the crowd of small boats on the east bank bewildered them.

"You might as well come with us," the guardsman said to the Peshtak, as several boats pushed off from the east bank in answer to their horn. "We'll look after your wounded man."

The Peshtak were not genuinely sure that they were free to go, thinking the offer might be some trick to allow the Pelbar to kill them as escaping prisoners. They got into the boats with the others, one to a boat. On the east bank they were amazed to find a crowd of Pelbar, Tusco, and Atherers together.

Gamwyn greeted the two giant Sentani with a shout and led them to Misque, who lay under a tree with Brudoer. "We want to rebuild, Jaiyan. You can stay with us. You can build your organ. We can all use it. Really. You're just in time to hear our evening songs. You can imagine how the organ might help them."

"Gamwyn, I—" Jaiyan began. "I don't know what . . ." The big Sentani fell silent as a choir of guardsmen and Threerivers people sang a hymn to Aven, the restorer, the one true builder, their voices swelling in a harmony that brought a blank amazement to Jaiyan's face. Several songs later, he was wholly enraptured and decided to stay with the Pelbar.

After the singing, the travelers from the south all gathered around Bival, and Samme made an announcement. "We wish to make a presentation. Gamwyn is now ready to make restitution to you. It took him awhile, and like most boys, he did a lot of other things along the way, but—well, we will let him finish."

Grinning, Gamwyn presented Bival with a rough cloth bag—the same one the old hermit had tied in the tree during the hurricane. Inside, Bival found not only the shell of the Broad Tower but the shell models for the other towers that now lay in ruins nearby. She was overcome with emotion and sank to the ground crying, covering her face with her hands. Warret put his arms around her.

"For her, we thank you. We thank you all," he said. "She will thank you herself in a while."

The evening was chill and dry, with a slight breeze. There was much to organize, but somehow the entire array of people felt relaxed and relieved—even the old Threerivers women, to whom the loss of the city in which they had spent all their lives was a great wrench. The tumbled heap of the city lay south of the riverside field where they bedded down for the night, with a circle of fires around them and guardsmen from Pelbarigan on watch. On one of the ships, someone played a pellute, though it was barely audible on shore over the loud calls of the fall insects.

Morning brought a heavy river mist, shrouding the two ships save the mast tops. With the new day courses of action became clearer. The old Threerivers people would go to Pelbarigan, unless they wanted to stay and work to rebuild and refashion Threerivers' society. The Tusco artisans wanted to stay, as did most of the younger Threerivers people. The Atherers wanted to press on to Pelbarigan to learn what they could about the Lost One. Jaiyan and Jamin would also stay. Misque would not leave Brudoer and the two Sentani, and Artess had attached herself to

Gamwyn. For his part, Gamwyn knew already he never wanted to be very far away from her.

Surprisingly enough, the five remaining Peshtak who had been guarding Jaiyan and Jamin also decided to stay. That way, they said, if the disease appeared, cure could be near. They had been talking with Misque, and after their initial anger at her betrayals, as they saw them, they calmed. It was a long trip home, and trouble waited at the end of it. At least here was a possibility, a new society, just forming, a relaxation from danger.

Brudoer described the location of the tunnel leading to the caves, and with some effort, they dug to it behind the city ruins. The boy explained to Bival that all Craydor's plans lay there in a stone chest, dry and well preserved.

It was decided to leave the ruined city as it was, as a monument to the past and a grave for the Peshtak. They also feared the consequences of digging into it with so many infested dead in it. Initially, they would use only stone from the two walls that fell outward.

On the second afternoon, one of the ships from Pelbarigan got under way with many of those leaving. The next morning saw an opening made from the caves directly outside, something Craydor's people had never done. That evening, all those who were staying gathered in the field north of the old ruin to decide about a new government. Initially, they agreed to use the Pelbar representative system, with some changes. All the peoples there would have a part. Males would have an equal voice. The family representational system would be abandoned. The Protector would be elected by all. No decisions would be made except by the entire council. The Protector would have a regular term of office. Ownership would not be communal but individual. They would reconvene in the spring to forge more carefully a basic document of government.

Udge was present, but her vehement statements simply swung others more insistently toward a looser system of government. "Appalling. Utterly appalling. Disorderly and anarchical," she muttered repeatedly.

"Will you be quiet?" Dardan hissed. "Do you want to go to Pelbarigan and work in a laundry?"

"Unthinkable. Unthinkable."

When Bival was appointed to design the new settlement, she immediately asked if an open form, of individual houses, like the Shumai farm town west of Northwall, would be acceptable. No one objected. She pointed out that a central citadel could be built for safety if need be, but they didn't have to live in it all the time.

The old Ardena had been killed by the Peshtak, and Bival openly wished she had the advice of her former antagonist. "She knew that the design of anything begins with the life that is to be lived in it," Bival remarked. "Craydor knew that, too, but she was forced by her times into choices that would become outgrown. No doubt the choices we make here will eventually also be outgrown. We have to make them easy to alter."

When Samme and his Southocean friends floated downstream four weeks later, all wearing Pelbar winter coats, they could already see the rough outlines of a settlement beginning to take shape.

Samme found the chicken workers especially happy with the chance to direct and profit from their own employment. Freedom from the watchful eyes of the Nicfad and the Committee had left the Tusco artisans baffled at first, and they were only beginning to learn to direct their own choices.

The Peshtak had become the chief fishermen of the settlement, and they seemed to reconcile themselves to their unexpected lot fairly quickly. One of them, Ustral, was very young—scarcely older than Gamwyn and Brudoer. He was merged quickly into the household of Pion and Rotag. Jamin also spent most of his time there, under Misque's watchful eye, since his father had gone to Pelbarigan to build an organ there. No one could haul rock like the giant, simpleminded Sentani, and he was content to do that.

Udge had refused to leave the Broad Tower, and to humor her, since she had returned Brudoer's bracelet intact, they had dragged and rolled the great structure down onto the level ground, where she lived alone. She had already found that no one would care for her as a drone, so she had reverted to the occupation of her youth, becoming a potter to the settlement.

One day, when Dardan stopped in to tell Udge she was marrying one of the Tusco artisans, the old Protector, after initial shock, resumed wedging her wet clay in silence. "Well, I never would have thought it," she remarked, digging the heels of her hands into the plastic substance. "I never would have thought a lot of things. I wish . . . I wish a society could be shaped as perfectly as this. But there are lumps in it. And air bubbles. It'll never make a perfect bowl."

"And you'll never make a living pot," her old friend said. "By the way, one of the older Tusco might be just perfect for you. He isn't used to managing his own life. He—" Dardan stopped when she saw Udge's face, then simply said, "He wouldn't be a very good bowl, though."

"I imagine not," said Udge. Then she smiled. "I'd have to cover over the eyes and eliminate the nose. The ears would be enlarged for handles. He would have to be depilated."

"He nearly is."

"So much the worse. I suppose he is acquiring a rounded bowlish shape, though. In the middle."

"No. Angular. Must be some sticks in there. You know, Udge, I really think you're happy."

"Happy? How can I be with what has happened? With my shame? But you might stop over sometime and play some cross squares. I still have the old set here. You may bring your . . . your Tusco. Provided he bathes."

Dardan laughed. "I will if you promise not to inspect his nails. Of course he would think your hairstyle dowdy." Dardan left, and Udge, who started to put her hands to her head, remembered they were covered with clay. With a grunt, she went back to her shaping.

The evening after his arrival, Samme stopped in to see Gamwyn, who asked him if he had learned what he wanted to about the Lost One.

The Atherer sighed and raised his shoulders in a shrug. "It was worth coming. There was a man named Jesus. I think Darew's 'Jeez I cry' was once 'Jesus Christ.' What that means, though, I don't know. It is a statement here, a bit of writing there. His adherents seemed to argue among themselves about him. Maybe they spent so much time doing that they lost him. Then there are other names, too—Ishmael, Mohammed, Graham, Plato. A mess. How could they have lost the Lost One?

"I begin to think, though, that the history ain't as important as the essence of the thing—and yet the history is important. But it ain't entirely lost. It'll be found. Somewhere we'll find the full story. I feel sure of it. Meantime, we'll have to get along on what we have—the kindness, generosity, love, goodwill. I'm sure there's much beyond that. But not every society has that. You sure saw that. When I come to you Pelbar, and find the same considerations I knew at home, I feel the presence of the Lost One. It ain't like the Tusco. Or these Peshtak. But you see them take to it like birds to air. There's something in them that'll respond.

"Look at Misque. We all know she was sent to Jaiyan's Station to spy. But they took her in. Look what it did to her.

"You know what, Gam? Maybe the Lost One is going to win in the long voyage after all. Maybe not. What could be worse than the great burning time? Something rose up to kill everything. Something was very afraid. But here we all are. It's very strange, after all."

They sat and watched the wood fire crumble for a while. Then Samme stood up and dusted himself. "Well, Gam, I ain't used to this cold. We're goin' in the morning. Two of us want to stay—Athe and Arit. They say with all the other people here, some Southocean people ought to be here, too."

"They'll be our hermits, our spies."

Samme laughed. "We'll keep track of each other. I hear your Jestak says we're all one people. Maybe he's right. We'll come back. The whole river is open now from the Bitter Sea to the South Ocean. We might as well use it all."

"Might as well."

In the morning a happy crowd watched Samme's party leave. Udge surprised everybody by giving him one of her first fired bowls, a deep red with bands of white. "Thank you," he said. "I'll keep it safe. We'll take it all the way home—beyond the end of the river. Who knows? Someday it may go to the uttermost parts of the sea." He looked at Gamwyn, and his broad mouth flashed white in a laugh as he dug his paddle into the mud and pushed out onto the misty river to begin his long trip home.

☐ Glossary

Adant: the Atherer winter town near Sagol.

Ahks: a Tusco workleader. Eventually, he and his wife settle at Threerivers, where he builds the community flour mill, powered by a windmill.

Ahroe: guardcaptain of Pelbarigan, wife of Stel, mother of Garet. A central figure in *The Ends of the Circle* and *The Dome in the Forest*.

Alats: a group occupying the lower Heart River Valley south of the Tusco. While their principal city is Murkal, they also operate five other settlements away from the Heart River.

Annon: chief officer of the Peshtak invasion force. Dies at Threerivers.

Ansy: an Atherer fisherman who eventually discovers the ruins of Galveston, Texas.

Ardena, Unset the: the head of the Arden family at Threerivers. She opposes Udge's severities with all the vigor of a mother of seven girls. Killed by the Peshtak.

Arit: an Atherer who settles at Threerivers and becomes a schoolteacher. He writes a book of children's detection stories, *Water in the Cave*, which becomes famous throughout the Heart River country. Never marries.

Arlin: a guardsman, nephew of the Ardena. Killed by the Peshtak.

Aroth: a Peshtak captured by the Pelbar west of the Heart while guarding hostages. Later a fisherman, and, still later, after suffering frostbitten feet, the chief librarian at Threerivers.

Artess: a Tantal girl born at Threerivers who grows up at Murkal, who eventually settles at Threerivers. Twin sister of Reo.

Ason: young Threerivers water-lifter, muscular but gentle.

Later opens and operates a stone quarry, augmenting his supply from the former walls of the city.

Atchun: a Peshtak, brother-in-law of Misque. Dies in a floortrap at Threerivers.

Athe: an Atherer who settles at Threerivers and eventually becomes a commission merchant when Samme opens his river trade.

Atou: the Sentani name for God.

Aven: the Pelbar name for God.

Aylor: an old Atherer fisherman-philosopher who befriends Gamwyn. Shortly after Gamwyn leaves, he sets out to fish in the South Ocean and never returns.

Bival: Southcounsel of Threerivers until replaced. Wife of Warret. A designer of considerable capacity, but quick-tempered until events grind off her edges.

Blu: a Shumai axeman who took over Tor's running band in *The Dome in the Forest*, then married Ruthan Tromtrager of the dome and settled with her at Pelbarigan. Serves the Pelbarigan guardsmen as a scout and tracker. Fond of roast woodchuck and popcorn.

Broad Tower: at Threerivers the largest of the four towers, shaped like a Nautilus shell on its side. The home of the Protector. Built extremely sturdily, it is really a separate structure in itself.

Brudoer: the more intense and penetrating of the identical twins whose plight and adventures constitute the main action of this story.

Celeste: a young woman from the dome (see *The Dome in the Forest*) who settles at Pelbarigan.

Central Committee: the ruling body of each city of the Tusco.

Cilia: Westcounsel of Threerivers, a generally agreeable person distinguished by pliability.

Conn: a man in an ancient Pelbar legend who travels through time after being hit on the head with a crowbar.

Craydor: designer and builder of Threerivers, a woman with an extraordinary range of talents who believed that design should be applied to all aspects of life, in relation and agreement.

Dardan: close friend of Udge, who replaces Bival as Southcounsel of Threerivers during this story. Short, fat, fond of honey candy, she adjusts easily. Later she marries a Peshtak, whom she obeys in every slight particular. Her first child, however, was fathered by Gind shortly before he was killed.

Darew: an Innanigani convict offered his freedom if he would emigrate to the country of the Atherers and spy on them for the Innanigani authorities. Settling near Sagol, for over fifty years he fed the Innangani traders with a steady stream of meticulously conceived misinformation while enjoying life as an eccentric hermit.

Daun: an Atherer, Aylor's granddaughter, who eventually marries Reo and bears him eleven children. Later tries to run away by sea to Innanigan but is wrecked on a Caribbean island, formerly Dominica. After suffering many hardships she is rescued by Reo. She is reconciled to him when he promises they will have no more babies.

Daw: a Tusco girl who befriends Gamwyn. She is the only daughter of the Central Committee chairman at U Bend. Dies at High Tower.

Doon: Aylor's eldest son, a somewhat shiftless Atherer fisherman always in demand for social gatherings because he is a gifted storyteller.

Durc: a Peshtak scout. Dies at Threerivers.

Finge: an old Threerivers woman who dies in the council meeting after having had tea the previous night with Prope.

Gamwyn: the more innocent and guileless of the identical twins whose plight and adventures constitute the main action of this story.

Garet: son of Ahroe and Stel of Pelbarigan. See also *The Ends of the Circle.*

Gelio: an Atherer and a delegate to the Southocean Federation.

Geryana: a conservative old Threerivers woman. Killed by the Peshtak.

Gind: a member of Udge's personal guard at Threerivers. He conducts Gamwyn south from Pelbarigan. Killed by the Peshtak. Just over eights months later Dardan bears his child, also called Gind.

Gnau: a Peshtak scout. Dies at Threerivers.

Grogan: a supposed Peshtak beast-god made up on the spot by Gamwyn to convince the Tusco that his folding knife is an amulet.

Haframa, the: before the arrival of Royal, she was the

chief physician of Pelbarigan. See also *The Dome in the Forest*.

Heart River: formerly known by Americans as the Mississippi, renamed by Amanda Pell in one of her rare moments of whimsy.

High Tower: a Tusco city providentially destroyed in the moments before its inhabitants intend to cut off Gamwyn's foot in a ceremony of punishment.

Innanigan: the largest of the eastern cities, lying south of the former American city of New York.

Isso River: once known as the Missouri, this river flows into the Heart somewhat south of its former course.

Jaiyan: a large Sentani trader who occupies the east bank of the Heart at the northern border of Tusco country. Fascinated by an organ he has dug from the ruins of an ancient church, he reconstructs it and devotes all his energies to it. Eventually he becomes the organist of Pelbarigan.

Jamin: the retarded son of the Sentani Jaiyan, a gentle, gigantic adolescent. Later an employee in Ason's stone quarry.

Jestak: a Pelbar of Northwall who was instrumental in uniting the Pelbar with the Shumai and Sentani. See *The Breaking of Northwall* and *The Dome in the Forest*.

Kitat: a Peshtak town referred to by Gamwyn in lying to the Tusco. Located in what were once the Pocono Mountains.

Knou: a U Bend Tusco bureaucratic servant. Surviving the fall of U Bend, he is taken by the Siveri in their counterraid and becomes a worker on a Siveri dairy farm, where he discovers that he is allergic to milk.

Koorb: the central settlement of the Sentani, hidden in the hills of what Americans knew as Tennessee.

Lamber: the Eastcounsel of Threerivers. Later an assistant to Bival and the inventor of the tripartite arch.

Lost One, the: the object of the religious searchings of the Atherers, who sought to clarify the finest of the values of the ancients.

Maatha: a kindly Tusco woman, wife of workleader Ahks. Later, she becomes famous at Threerivers for her catfish chowder.

Mall: an old servant to Prope who pours a bitter cup of tea, matching his feelings. He flees north as a refugee but stops at Northwall, where he marries an old Shumai widow and dies on his wedding night.

Misque (pronounced *misk*): a Peshtak spy who becomes emotionally entangled with her quarry. Later wholly devoted to Brudoer.

Murkal: the largest Alat city. On the Heart River.

Muse: a Siveri captured by the Tusco. He helps in the great escape, during which he is severely hurt. Nonetheless he goes home, marries, and fathers nine children, all girls.

Newall: a minister of Aven at Threerivers whose tendencies are compassionate and reconciling. Later the first Pelbar missionary to the Peshtak.

Nicfad: the military and police arm of the Tusco, a hereditary position.

Nim: a Siveri captured by the Tusco. Not only does he help engineer their mass escape, and lead the Siveri home, but once there, he manages to centralize their defenses and even raise an army against their tormentors.

Northwall: the northernmost of the three Pelbar cities, and at the time of this story the most open to the Shumai and Sentani, who have surrounded it with farms and industries.

Odsem: an old Siveri, once a farmer, next a Tusco slave, then later, as an old man, an inhabitant of Jaiyan's Station. Killed by the Peshtak.

Oh River: known formerly by Americans as the Ohio.

Oin: an old Atherer weather-reader, also famous for shrimp cakes.

Olla: a former member of the Tusco Central Committee at U Dend, his skull adorns the judgment desk in the white tower, and, later, the bottom of the river.

Onem: a Tusco town west of the Heart, near the edge of the old Shumai winter territory. Raided by Nim to recover Siveri captives, it is never able to rebuild, lacking slaves. Its Nicfad abandon it, going to Ultu, but find that also in ruins.

Osel: a Peshtak. After Royal cures his disease during his incarceration at Pelbarigan, he is freed and carries the Pelbar offer of peace and cure back to Peshtak country. There, he is killed as a traitor, but some believe him and seek to make contact with the Pelbar.

Ossi: an old Threerivers woman. After the Peshtak incursion she becomes an herb gardener.

Ount: a Siveri musician, taken by the Nicfad. He dies at U Bend shortly before the arrival of Gamwyn.

Oyt: an Alat fisherman devoted to the fisherguild and the game of padball.

Pelbar: the Heart River people living in three cities— Northwall, Pelbarigan, and Threerivers.

Pelbarigan: the largest and oldest of the three Pelbar cities, founded by Amanda Pell (or Pel), a former metallurgist from Peoria, Illinois, before the time of the fire.

Pell, Amanda (sometimes spelled Pel): founder of the Pelbar after the time of fire. Ms. Pell was spelunking in the Ozarks at the time of the holocaust. Not only a feminist, but also a disliker of men, she imprinted her views on the society she eventually founded on the east bank of the Heart River. An extremely able administrator, she not only founded a society, made its laws, and gathered its basic scriptures, but she also projected a future direction for its people all in the nine years between the time of fire and her death of radiation sickness.

Peshtak: a violent and often vicious group living in what Americans knew as Pennsylvania, especially in the mountains. Because of pressures from the east, they are beginning to migrate westward into the Heart River country.

Pigeon Island: an island in the Heart about thirty-four ayas south of the former site of St. Louis.

Pion: father of Gamwyn and Brudoer. Husband of Rotag.

Prope: an old Threerivers woman who invites Ossi and Finge to tea, and dies that night of the poison her servant, Mall, put in it.

Ravell: a footloose old Sentani trader who plies the Heart River, generally alone. Known to Bival and others at Threerivers. Held captive for a time by the Tusco.

Rawl: guardian appointed by Udge to replace Wim. Killed by the Peshtak.

Reo: twin brother of Artess, a Tantal born at Threerivers who spends his early years at Murkal. Later fathers eleven children among the Atherers and becomes well known as a deep-sea fisherman.

Ret: a member of Udge's guard at Threerivers, she helps

conduct Gamwyn south from Pelbarigan. Killed by the Peshtak.

Roara: one of six spirits prominent in Tusco superstition. This one is always depicted carrying his head under his left arm.

Rotag: mother of Gamwyn and Brudoer. Wife of Pion.

Royal: an elderly physician at Pelbarigan, whose story is told in *The Dome in the Forest.* In curing Osel of the Peshtak plague, by an absurdly simple injection, after a great deal of fiddling with instruments, he inadvertently rediscovers the ancient art of homeopathy.

Rute: a Peshtak subcommand who escapes death at Threerivers by having been assigned to guard hostages. He settles at Threerivers, marries a Tusco immigrant, and starts a farm, but his wife proves an unmerciful scold, and he eventually runs away to Black Bull Island.

Sagan: Protector of Pelbarigan and mother of Stel. Ahroe's mother-in-law.

Sagol: an Atherer settlement on the shore of the South Ocean, east of the Heart, and of the great empty place that was once Biloxi, Mississippi.

Samme (pronounced Sam-may): an Atherer from the mouth of the Heart River. Struck with the possibilities for trade after his trip to Pelbarigan, he begins the water-borne trade between the Pelbar and the eastern cities.

Sandra: a U Bend Tusco Central Committee member and legal counsel. She dies in the fall of the white tower.

Sentani: one of the three central tribal groups of the Heart River country. They are further divided into three groups: the Long Lake Sentani, the Tall Grass Sentani, and the Sentani of Koorb. The last group formerly ran its winter hunts through Pelbar country and now has integrated most markedly with the Pelbar. All Sentani are descended from a group of Explorer Scouts led by a Memphis watchmaker named Antonio Sentani. At the time of fire they were on an outing in a coal mine in Tennessee.

Sepp: a Threerivers beekeeper who goes north with the refugees and sets up his honey operation at Iver in what was once known as Wisconsin.

Shumai: a group occupying most of the old American Great Plains, but rapidly changing from hunters to farmers along the Isso and Heart, especially around Northwall. Originally, all the Shumai were descendants of the children of Aaron Schumaker, a farmer who lived in southwestern Minnesota. After the time of fire they became running hunters, having lost all their former technology.

Siveri: a group living in the central Appalachians around what was western Virginia and North Carolina. Frequently enslaved by the Tusco until they find means to resist.

Southcounsel: During this period, both Bival and Dardan occupy the position. It is elective, and, like the other quadrant counsels, goes to a woman chosen by the family heads of the quadrant.

Steelet: a Peshtak scout, squadleader of a small band assigned to study Threerivers. Dies at Threerivers.

Stel: husband of Ahroe, the guardcaptain of Pelbarigan. His story is extensively told in *The Ends of the Circle* and *The Dome in the Forest*.

Suth: the given name of the Ursana.

Suwor: Northcounsel of Threerivers. After the Peshtak incursion she visits Koorb and is converted to the worship of Atou.

Syle: a Peshtak scout captured and enslaved by the Tusco and befriended by Gamwyn. Later dies at Threerivers.

Tall Grass Sentani: the middle branch of the Sentani who occupy what was once central Illinois and western Indiana. All this land has gone back to the prairie it once was before European disruptions.

Tantal: a group that lives on the south shore of the Bitter Sea near the former American city of Cleveland. About fifteen years before the disruptions at Threerivers a large force of Tantal invaded the Heart River country and was defeated at Northwall. (See *The Breaking of Northwall*.)

Threerivers: the southernmost Pelbar city, located near what Americans knew as Grand Tower, Illinois. It is also the youngest of the three Pelbar cities, built by Craydor, an extraordinary genius of design and organization.

Tor: a remarkable Shumai axeman, a central figure in *The Dome in the Forest*.

Tusco: a group of slaveholding agriculturists inhabiting a

portion of the lower Heart River Valley. After the great escape at U Bend, they quickly cease to exist as a viable culture.

U Bend: a large Tusco settlement located on a river bend. This group temporarily enslaves Ravell, then Gamwyn.

Udge: an archconservative Protector of Threerivers until the Peshtak incursion.

Unset: the given name of the Ardena.

Ursana, the: head of the Ursan family and the chief physician of Threerivers at the time Gamwyn is injured. After further training by Royal, she travels north to join the new settlement at Iver.

Urstadge: Many years before the building of Northwall, a Shumai hunter was asked by his eight-year-old son, after a long train of other questions, what was the name of the place they lived in. The reply was "Shumai country." Naturally the boy wanted to know where Shumai country was. The hunter rose, threw a stick in the fire and said, out of the blue, "Urstadge. The name of it all is Urstadge, and beyond that is only the sea. Nothing is beyond the sea." Somehow the name stuck and spread, after his friends stopped laughing. The known world, and the unknown beyond it, became Urstadge. Even the Innaniganis and the Baliganis picked it up. In fact, after long discussion, they decided that they had originated the term and invented an etymology for it.

Ustral: a young Peshtak adopted by Pion and Rotag after the invasion. Even at sixteen he could beat Udge at cross squares every time, almost convincing her to abandon her favorite game, which she was used to winning. However, Ustral's visits were accompanied by small gifts, generally of blackberry preserves, which she relished so much that she came to consider the losses a price worth paying.

Warret: the husband of Bival at Threerivers.

Weel: a son of Aylor, the Atherer, very tall, cadaverously thin, though with an enormous appetite. Eventually he brings the Peibar windmill and Alat booze to Sagol.

Welle: an Atherer boy and would-be cartographer until, mapping the old Virgin Island of St. Croix, he decides never to leave. He then becomes the island's only archaeologist, and, during portions of each year, its only inhabitant.

Wim: a guardsman, temporarily appointed guardchief by Udge until her conscience will not let her obey Udge's vengeful commands. She eventually becomes guardchief at Iver, the refugee settlement west of the Bitter Sea.

About the Author

A native of New Jersey, Paul O. Williams holds a Ph.D. in English from the University of Pennsylvania. Following three years of teaching at Duke University, he settled at the tiny Mississippi River town of Elsah, Illinois, where he is currently a Professor of English at Principia College, teaching American literature and creative writing. He and his wife, Nancy, have two children.

His response to his small community has been varied, including helping to found Historic Elsah Foundation and direct its small museum, and serving as the president of the local volunteer firefighters. His poems, essays, reviews, and articles on literary subjects and Midwestern history have been widely published. While he has written largely on nineteenth-century America, and served as a president of the Thoreau Society, he has also developed a deep interest in science fiction and fantasy.

The Breaking of Northwall, The Ends of the Circle, and *The Dome in the Forest,* his first three novels, are set against the same background as *The Fall of the Shell.*